Lottery

≈

Patricia Wood

BERKLEY BOOKS, NEW YORK

THE BERKLEY PUBLISHING GROUP
Published by the Penguin Group
Penguin Group (USA) Inc.
375 Hudson Street, New York, New York 10014, USA
Penguin Group (Canada), 90 Eglinton Avenue East, Suite 700, Toronto, Ontario M4P 2Y3, Canada
(a division of Pearson Penguin Canada Inc.)
Penguin Books Ltd., 80 Strand, London WC2R 0RL, England
Penguin Group Ireland, 25 St. Stephen's Green, Dublin 2, Ireland (a division of Penguin Books Ltd.)
Penguin Group (Australia), 250 Camberwell Road, Camberwell, Victoria 3124, Australia
(a division of Pearson Australia Group Pty. Ltd.)
Penguin Books India Pvt. Ltd., 11 Community Centre, Panchsheel Park, New Delhi—110 017, India
Penguin Group (NZ), 67 Apollo Drive, Rosedale, North Shore 0632, New Zealand
(a division of Pearson New Zealand Ltd.)
Penguin Books (South Africa) (Pty.) Ltd., 24 Sturdee Avenue, Rosebank, Johannesburg 2196,
South Africa

Penguin Books Ltd., Registered Offices: 80 Strand, London WC2R 0RL, England

PRINTING HISTORY
G. P. Putnam's Sons hardcover edition / August 2007
Berkley trade paperback edition / June 2008

Berkley trade paperback ISBN: 978-0-425-22220-1

The Library of Congress has cataloged the G. P. Putnam's Sons hardcover edition as follows:

Wood, Patricia, date.
   Lottery/Patricia Wood.
   p. cm.
   ISBN 978-0-399-15449-2
   1. People with mental disabilities—Fiction.   2. Lottery winners—Fiction.   3. Self-realization—
Fiction.   4. Washington (State)—Fiction.   I. Title.
   PS3623.O638L68   2007   2007014130
813'.6—dc22

PRINTED IN THE UNITED STATES OF AMERICA

10   9   8   7   6   5   4   3   2   1

Praise for *Lottery*

"This wonderful first novel is about a guy who starts off with all the chips stacked against him and still comes out a winner. It's an underdog novel, and the underdog is a most satisfying hero, for more than any other protagonist, the underdog is the one we love to love. Perry L. Crandall, the underdog of *Lottery*, is profoundly lovable. Patricia Wood's portrait of Perry is so vivid and funny and poignant and joyful that it avoids the disappointing flatness of the predictable. Perry may be slow, but his motives are absolutely good. He has the wisdom of Solomon and the heart of a lion, and his decision about what to do with his winnings, while it may not surprise readers, still feels satisfying. Perry L. Crandall is the thinking man's guide to a happy life."   —*The Washington Post*

"Patricia Wood asks readers to experience life in an unexpected, sometimes uncomfortable, often humorous way. The consistent voice and emotional logic of the first-person narration anchors readers securely in Perry's world, gently prodding them to reexamine intelligence, capability, and at what point money affects society's perceptions. *Lottery* simply reads like a real story about real people in the best possible way, leaving readers with a memorable character whose voice and world linger in one's imagination."   —*The Miami Herald*

"*Lottery* is a compassionate look at the triumphs and tragedies in Per's life. It has an engrossing story to tell."   —*The Sunday Oregonian*

"In *Lottery*, Patricia Wood has created an altogether endearing character swept up in the most extreme of situations. A testament to the transcendence of friendship and the redemptive power of love, this startling novel is at once funny and poignant. Fans of Mark Haddon's *The Curious Incident of the Dog in the Night-Time* and Daniel Keyes's *Flowers for Algernon* would do well to pick up this captivating debut. I loved it!"   —Martha O'Connor

continued . . .

"When he wins the lottery, Perry suddenly faces a new set of challenges: What to do? Whom to trust? As Perry sets about living the life of a winner, he creates his family of choice, drawing around him a circle of loving friends. Wood makes us wonder if this will be enough to protect him from his unsavory relatives, but this is a tale of luck—and love. 'One word at a time,' his Gram tells him, and *Lottery* is a reminder of the power of that—the power of the perfect, simple word."

—*The Times-Picayune*

"*Lottery*'s winning narrator [is] wise beyond expectations. But there's more going on here than just giving readers some inside scoops on the world of lottery winners and the mentally challenged. *Lottery*, thanks to the stylistic constraints Wood puts on herself throughout the novel, also serves as a reminder that simple declarative sentences can do the trick in evoking a highly unusual view of the world—Perry's view."

—*The Seattle Times*

"Patricia Wood's vivid portrayal of Perry captures the reality of a life lived with cognitive disabilities. Perry is constantly belittled by those who think he's incapable of doing almost anything. At the same time he is supported by those who believe in him, what he can do, and who he can be. *Lottery* does a great job of showing how natural supports, such as friendships and love, make a difference in the lives of those with cognitive disabilities—just as they do in all our lives."

—Steven E. Brown Ph.D., assistant professor, University of Hawaii, Center on Disability Studies; cofounder, Institute on Disability Culture; and author of *Movie Stars and Sensuous Scars: Essays on the Journey from Disability Shame to Disability Pride*

"Wood keeps the reader guessing as to how the story will end, and the resolution is satisfying. She meets her goal of portraying a mentally challenged person as a fully realized, functioning human being. Perry's worldview is so charming and fair that by the end, you might think he's the smartest character in the whole book."   —*Library Journal*

"In her debut novel, Patricia Wood defines poignancy in words of one syllable. *Lottery* is solid gold."   —Jacquelyn Mitchard

"Wood's light humor and likable narrator should have mass appeal."

—*Publishers Weekly*

"[An] irresistible debut novel about what makes people good or bad, smart or stupid."   —*Good Housekeeping*

"Fear not: This novel about a mildly retarded man who wins the Washington State Lottery is no Forrest Gump retread—we much prefer this (admittedly folksy) narrator to Tom Hanks as a mentally challenged Zelig. Patricia Wood's mentor, Paul Theroux, lent his literary wisdom to a book that manages to be heartfelt and totally not corny."   —*New York*

"*Lottery* is a compelling and beautifully written story that will show you how it's possible to have a low score on an intelligence test and still be a genius at understanding other people's feelings and motivations. And you'll learn that having above-average intelligence may mean less than finding happiness with yourself, and the people around you. *Lottery* is a novel, but it reads like it really happened, right next door to you."

—John Elder Robison, author of *Look Me in the Eye: My Life with Asperger's*

"A sweetly satisfying story."   —*The Sacramento Bee*

"Wood's debut is a poignant page-turner . . . a sweet read about money, relationships, and life."   —*OK!*

"Sometimes, we all need a little hope. That's exactly what Patricia Wood offers in her debut novel, *Lottery*."   —*Asbury Park Press*

"[Patricia Wood's] debut novel is a warm tribute to the power of simple wisdom and honest-to-goodness goodness."   —*Honolulu Weekly*

This novel is dedicated to my father and mother,
Ragnar J. Dahl and Bernice J. Dahl,
and
Airborne the Wonder Horse,
without whom I would never have met my friends and mentors
Paul Theroux and Sheila Donnelly Theroux.

Ordinary riches can be stolen:
real riches cannot.

Oscar Wilde

Prologue

My name is Perry L. Crandall and I am not retarded.

Gram always told me the L stood for Lucky.

"Mister Perry Lucky Crandall, quit your bellyaching!" she would scold. "You got two good eyes, two good legs, and you're honest as the day is long." She always called me lucky and honest.

Being honest means you don't know any better.

My cousin-brother John called me lucky too, but he always snickered hard after he said it.

"You sure are a lucky bastard. No high-pressure job, no mortgage, and no worries. Yeah, you're lucky all right." Then he would look at his wife and laugh harder. He is a lawyer.

John said lawyers get people out of trouble. Gram said lawyers get people into trouble. She ought to know. It was a lawyer who gave her the crappy advice on what to do after Gramp died.

I am thirty-two years old and I am not retarded. You have to have an IQ number less than 75 to be retarded. I read that in *Reader's Digest*. I am not. Mine is 76.

"You have two good ears, Perry. Two! Count 'em!" Gram would hold my chin and cheeks between her fingers so tight that my lips would feel like a fish. She stopped doing that because of evil arthritis. Arthritis is when you have to eat Aleve or Bayer and rub Bengay.

"You're lucky," she said. "No evil arthritis for you. You're a lucky, lucky boy."

I am lucky. I know this because I am not retarded.

I know this because I have two good arms.

And I know this because I won twelve million dollars in the Washington State Lottery.

1

~~

write things down so I do not forget.

"Writing helps you remember. It helps you think, Perry, and that's a good thing," Gram said.

"You're only slow." That's what my old teacher Miss Elk said. "Just a little slow, Perry."

The other kids had different names for me.

Moron. Idiot. Retard.

Miss Elk told them to be nice. She said I was not any of those things.

"Don't you pay any attention to them, Perry," Gram told me when I cried. "Those other kids are just too goddamned fast. If you want to remember, you write it down in your notebook. See . . . I'm not slow. I'm old. I have to write things down," she said. "People treat you the same when you're old as when you're slow."

Slow means you get to a place later than fast people.

Gram had me do a word a day in the dictionary since I was little.

"One word, Perry. That's the goddamned key. One word at a time."

Goddamned is an adjective, like "I'll be goddamned!" Gram will be reading something in the newspaper and it will just come out all by itself. Out of the blue. "Goddamn." Or sometimes "Goddamned." Or even "Goddamn it."

At nine, I was on page eight of our dictionary.

"*Active.* Change, taking part." Reading is hard. Like riding my bike up a hill. I have to push to keep going.

"Sound it out, Perry." Gram chews the inside of her lip when she concentrates.

"Squiggle vooollll . . . caaaa . . . nooo . . ." It takes me a long time to figure out that word.

"That squiggle thing means 'related to.' Remember Mount Saint Helens?" Gram has a good memory for an old person and knows everything. On May 18, 1980, Mount Saint Helens blew up. Three days after my birthday.

"Ashes from breakfast to Sunday!" Gram hollered. "Breakfast to Sunday!"

The ashes were gray sand that got in my mouth when I went outside, just like the stuff Doctor Reddy used when he cleaned my teeth.

"What's breakfast to Sunday?" I asked.

"Don't be smart." Gram always cautioned me about being smart.

At ten, I was still in the A's. Gram and I sat down and added it up. Our dictionary has 75,000 words and 852 pages. If I did one word a day, it would take me 205 years to finish. At three words, it would take 51 years. If I did five words, it would take 12 years and 6 months to get through the whole book. I wrote this all down. It is true because calculators do not lie and we used a calculator. Gram said we needed to rethink.

"Does that mean we made a mistake?" I asked.

"No, it's not a mistake to rethink. Rethink means you get to change your mind. You're never wrong if you just change your mind." Gram clapped her hands together to get my attention and make sure I was listening. "Pick up the pace, Perry," she said. "We have to pick up the pace."

That is when we got our subscription to *Reader's Digest*. We bought it from a girl who needed money for her school band to go to Florida.

"This is better than chocolate bars!" Gram was excited when the first one came. "Word Power! Here you go, Perry!"

It was the February issue and had hearts on the cover. We saved every copy that came in the mail. I remember I was on the word *auditor*. An auditor is a listener. It says so in the dictionary and in *Reader's Digest* Word Power. Answer D. A listener. I decided right then to be an auditor. Answer D. I remember this.

We picked up the pace and by the time I turned thirty-one, I was on page 337. Gram was right. That day my words were *herd, herder, herdsman, here, hereabouts,* and *hereafter*. Hereafter means future.

"You have to think of your future!" Gram warns about the future each time I deposit my check in the bank. Half in checking and half in savings. For my future.

"It is very important to think of your future, Perry," she tells me, "because at some point it becomes your past. You remember that!"

My best friend, Keith, agrees with everything Gram says.

"That L. It sure does stand for Lucky, Per." Keith drinks beer wrapped in a brown paper sack and calls me Per for short. He works with Manuel, Gary, and me at Holsted's Marine Supply. I have worked for Gary Holsted since I was sixteen years old.

Keith is older and bigger than me. I do not call him fat because that would not be nice. He cannot help being older. I can always tell how old people are by the songs they like. For example, Gary and

Keith like the Beatles, so they are both older than me. Gram likes songs you never hear anymore, like "Hungry for Love" by Patsy Cline and "Always" by somebody else who is dead. If the songs you like are all by dead people, then you are really old.

I like every kind of music. Keith does not. He goes crazy when Manuel messes with the radio at work.

"Who put this rap crap on? Too much static! The reception is shit! Keep it on *oldies but goodies.*" Keith has to change it back with foil and a screwdriver because of the reception. Static is when somebody else plays music you do not like and you change it because of reception.

Before Holsted's, I learned reading, writing, and math from Gram and boat stuff from Gramp. After he died, I had to get a job for money. I remember everything Gramp showed me about boats and sailing. Our family used to own the boatyard next to Holsted's.

"It's a complicated situation." Whenever Gram says this, her eyes get all hard and dark like two black olives, or like when you try to look through that tiny hole in the door at night. That is not a smart thing to do because it is dark at night and you cannot see very well.

Just before he died, Gramp took out a loan for a hoist for the yard.

A loan is when someone gives you money then takes collateral and advantage. After that, you drop dead of a stroke by the hand of God.

A hoist lifts boats up in the air and costs as much as a boatyard. That is what the bank said.

2

≈

Gram says I have to be careful. "You're suggestible, Perry."

"What's suggestible?" I ask.

"It means you do whatever people ask you to do."

"But I'm supposed to." I always get in trouble if I do not do what Gram says.

"No. There are people you listen to, and others you don't. You have to be able to tell the difference." Gram slaps the kitchen table hard with her hand and makes me jump.

"Like who?" I ask.

We make a list.

"For example, a policeman." Gram draws numbers on the paper. "He's number one on the list."

"I always have to do what Ray the cop says." I already know this. That is the law. Officer Ray Mallory has a crew cut and wears sunglasses even when it rains.

"Don't ever call Ray a cop. He's a policeman." When Gram

scolds, her eyebrows get all bushy and her hair comes out of its bun like it is mad too.

"Keith calls him a cop," I say.

Then I remember when Kenny Brandt called him a cop, Ray chased him all the way down the street and Kenny had to hide behind Mrs. Callahan's bushes until way after dinnertime. I do not want to be chased by the police and go to jail.

"Okay, a policeman," I agree.

Gram is number two on our list. I do everything she says. I do not ever do what Chuck at church says because he is a jerk. A jerk is someone you cannot trust, so Chuck is not on our list. Gary Holsted is number three, because he is my boss. I do not do what Manuel says.

"Manuel's a jackass, Per! A jackass is an animal, and you don't do what animals say." Keith helps us with the list.

"Keith, you should be on the list." I say this at least two or three times a week. I want to make him number four.

"I don't need to be on any list, Per," he says. Per sounds like pear, but I am not a fruit. Keith is not on the list because he is my friend. I never have to do what he says. A friend is someone who calls you something for short like Per for Perry. You never have to do what friends say, but you want to, because you are friends.

We add and subtract people from our list all the time. Sister Mary Margaret used to be number five on the list, but Gram took her off because she tried to collect money from us.

"That goddamned church has enough money! It doesn't need ours!" Gram was mad and used a big pink eraser to rub out Sister Mary Margaret's name. When Sister is nice to us at bingo, we put her back on the list. She goes on and off so much the paper beneath her name is almost worn through.

On rainy days, I take the bus to work. On nice days, I ride my bike down the hill to Holsted's. It rains a lot here, so mostly I take the bus. It takes ten minutes and stops right in front of our house in Everett, Washington. Not in the middle of Everett, on the edge.

"Hanging on the goddamned edge of Everett." Gram squeezes her fingers tight like killing a bug when she says this. Blue veins stick out on her hand.

Everett stinks. When I ask why, everybody says something different.

"It's because all of us fart at the same time." Keith laughs, then lifts one cheek and lets one go.

"Don't be smart! It's because of the paper mills." Gram smacks Keith in the head with her paper for farting.

"What stink?" Gary asks. "I don't smell a thing." He has allergies and sniffs a squeeze bottle. That is gross.

"I think it depends on your nose," I tell them. "Some noses are fast and smell all the stinks. Some are slow and they don't. I have a very fast nose. I smell lots of stink."

"You sure do, Per! You sure do. You got a great nose." Keith farts again. I know because I smell it.

I am lucky to live with Gram. I have been with Gram since I was a baby. I am the youngest. There is John, my oldest cousin-brother. He has never lived with Gram. He looks just like me except he is taller, has jagged teeth, a gray-brown mustache, and gets married a lot. David is next oldest and looks just like John except he is shorter, thinner, and has blue eyes. He is married to Elaine. Gram calls her different names like *That Woman* and *HER*. David has never lived with Gram either. He is an MBA.

"MBA! It means *Must Be Arrogant*, Perry. You remember that! Marrying *The Ice Queen* is his comeuppance." Gram cackles like a witch on Halloween when she says this and rubs her hands together like she is trying to start a fire. She is good at witch laughs.

Gram says comeuppance means you get what you deserve.

John is a lawyer. David's wife, Elaine, is a lawyer. My mother, Louise, married my father who was a lawyer, but I think he is dead. I am named after a very famous TV lawyer.

"Perry Mason. The only lawyer worth a goddamn!" Gram said.

I only got the Perry part. That's okay.

"Money runs through your mother's hands like water. You remember that, Perry. Marrying a lawyer is as bad as being one! You remember that too!" Gram warns. "Not one of them goes on our list!"

I call my mother Louise. It is a pretty name and she likes it better than Mother. Sometimes I cannot tell who she is because I do not see her very often and her hair is always different. It gets longer or shorter and changes colors. That is scary. I hope my hair stays just like it is.

I do not live with any of them. I live with Gram.

"Everybody in our family is either a lawyer or married to one," I tell Gram, "except for you and me."

"That's a good thing, Perry," she says. "It's a goddamned good thing."

Gram can blow smoke out the side of her mouth and through her nose. She limits herself. "Only two menthol cigarettes a day. Count 'em. One. Two."

She will hold them up in front of me.

Sometimes, Gram loses count.

3

~~

Monday, I work all day at Holsted's Marine Supply. I unload big trucks, put away orders, and carry packages out to cars, trucks, and SUVs. I mop the floor, wipe off the counter where the register sits, clean the two front windows, and empty all the trash cans, even the metal ones outside on the sidewalk. I also file papers in the back office because you just need to know the alphabet for that. I am very good at the alphabet. Keith and Manuel do the cash register, and when Gary goes home, Keith lets me ring up customers.

It takes me longer to learn something, but when I do, I learn it good. This year I learned how to use the air machine. It is called a compressor and makes a *rumble rumble* noise. It blows up inner tubes and fenders. Those are squishy things on boats that need to be blown up. I am very good at blowing up fenders with the compressor.

"Yeah, Per, you're a good worker. A real good worker." Keith tells me this all the time.

I watch the store so he can take a nap. He needs naps at least two or four times a day. I don't take naps at all. Keith can sleep standing up. That is so cool. Sometimes he snores. He has a hairy face that has lots of gray and two scars. One is above his eye from when we had to change the towel dispenser in the bathroom. The crowbar I was holding slipped and the dispenser came off the wall too fast. It hit Keith in the forehead. The other scar is from a bar fight. I did not see the bar fight, I only heard about it.

"What's a bar fight?" I asked him.

"See, Per, um . . . a bar fight is when . . . uh, it's when a guy says fuck you, and then you say fuck you, and then you fight." Keith knows all about bar fights. I do not say the F-word. Gram does not let me.

"Only morons and jackasses talk dirty, Perry! Morons, jackasses, and Keith." Gram likes Keith even though he talks dirty.

On Tuesday, I have my special sandwich at Gilly's next to the marina. They have pretend crab, which I like.

"What do you eat that crab shit for? It's not real. It's made of fish guts!" Keith says. It is definitely not nice to say pretend crab is made out of fish guts.

After I buy my sandwich, I go to the Marina Handy Mart down the street. I buy a Coke Slurpee, five Lotto tickets, one PayDay candy bar, a bag of Hershey's Kisses, and the *National Enquirer*. The paper is for Gram.

"I only get it for the crossword puzzle." She shows me the front page. "See this, Perry? It's full of gossip! Look at this! Part human and part bat! That's impossible. How'd they make that picture? Look at this, Perry! Here's another one of them alien baby stories." She pulls her sweater tight over her shoulders. Gram is always cold.

"I can throw it away and just tear the puzzle out if you want." I try to be helpful.

"No! No. Don't waste your time. I'll toss it later." But she stacks them up in the back room. She really likes it when she notices they use the same picture twice.

"Ha! All they did was reverse the photo! Look here, Perry!"

I like talking to Cherry who works at the counter at Marina Handy Mart. She is pretty, funny, and her name rhymes with mine. That is what Gram says.

"Cherry and Perry! Get it? You're both *errys!*" Gram likes it when things rhyme.

"Only Lotto?" Cherry likes MegaBucks because you can win more money, but Gram and I are stick-in-the-muds. That's what Gram says.

"Stick-in-the-muds. We do the same thing. No sense changing. Lotto's good enough for us." Gram likes the fact that Lotto comes out like a cash register receipt and you get more numbers for your money. We always bought lottery tickets, right from the beginning. From the very first. It was cool then because you got shiny green tickets, but you only got one set of numbers. The very first person who won was a nurse. A million dollars. Gram said it was the Lord rewarding a selfless profession.

"A nurse, Perry, they're dedicated. It's a sign from God." She was very disappointed to read in the paper, years later, that the nurse lost all that money.

"How do you lose a million dollars?" Gram shakes her head. "What if we won? Just think of it. We could do anything we want! Hawaii! We could go to Hawaii, where it's not so goddamned cold!" Gram's eyes close. Like she is praying.

"We can do anything we want right now," I say.

That is true. If we save our money and decide, we can do whatever we want.

"Don't be smart." Gram frowns at me, but I laugh.

It is fun thinking about winning the lottery.

Gram and I have dinner once a week at Kentucky Fried. Gram

complains about the prices for someone on Social Security. She frets about the tiny little ears of corn and getting too many wings.

"Goddamn it, Perry! You'd think they raised chickens with nothing but six flappers and an ass, the way they pack those boxes." She only says this at home because she does not want to hurt the counter girl Loretta's feelings at KFC.

At seven o'clock Tuesday nights, we go to bingo at St. Augustine's Catholic Church. We are not Catholic, but we like the nuns and bingo. We like Sister Mary Joan because she is nice all the time. We only like Sister Mary Margaret when she is on our list. I think all nuns are called Mary something. They wear glasses and regular clothes, except for their feet. Their shoes are all shiny black with long laces. Gram said they used to look like penguins. I do not see how. But she said they did.

"How are you doing, Perry?" They are friendly and do not treat me like I am retarded. I am not retarded, but some people treat me like I am. The nuns are always very interested in how I am doing and ask if I will come to church on Sunday. I can't come to church because I have to work Sundays.

"Will we see you at morning mass, Perry?" Sister Mary Joan spits when she talks.

"Tell them you have to work!" Gram whispers this into my ear to remind me, so I do not forget to tell the nuns. If I say I have to work, neither of us has to go to church. Church is boring except for the music, but we do not tell the nuns this. It would hurt their feelings. Sister Mary Margaret has blue eyes and hair on her chin. I wonder if nuns are allowed to shave. God must not let them because Sister Mary Joan has hair too, only it is on her upper lip. Gram does not approve of gambling, but bingo and lottery are not gambling.

"Gambling's something people do that loses money, Perry. You remember that!" Gram lectures.

"What's your numbers, sonny?" Chuck the bingo helper says

this each time he walks behind me. I play one single card and Gram plays ten. She is an expert and won two hundred and fifty-two dollars once. Chuck shoves my chair, jabs me in the back, and smells like Listerine. He likes to let me know he is there watching over my shoulder. My markers slide off the numbers on my card whenever he pushes me. He also scratches my head and makes my hair stick up.

"Time for a haircut, sonny!" My name is not Sonny.

"Leave him alone!" Gram has eyes in the back of her head. That is what Chuck says. "Woman, you got eyes in the back of your head," he says.

I laugh. Her eyes are right where they are supposed to be.

Chuck is the only one at bingo who treats me like I am retarded. He is taller than me. There is always a person who is taller than you unless you are Michael Jordan or someone like that. Chuck is a jerk.

"Ignore him, Perry! He's a jerk! There are jerks all over. Everybody has jerks in their lives," Gram says. One of her jerks is the woman on the front desk at Social Security. Gram had a hard time getting Gramp's Social Security death benefit. I thought it was cool you got a prize for dying, but it was very hard to collect.

"And then there's the guy that answers the phone at Medicare." Gram has a lot of jerks, at least as many as me.

"We need another list for jerks," I say.

Thursday mornings are my favorite time. That is when I go with Keith and do extra jobs at Carroll's Boatyard next to the store. I have to wear my oldest blue jeans when I work there. Gram would not be caught dead in jeans.

"Those blue jeans, Perry! Women get all kinds of diseases from them. It's better to wear a good cotton dress from Kmart. Airs out my privates!" she says. "It's okay for you. You can wear jeans. Men don't need to air out their privates."

Privates are personal parts that you do not show people.

Gram and I get hamburgers at McDonald's on Friday after work and go to an early movie. The 5:45 show costs only two dollars. We buy the small bag of popcorn and sneak in our bag of Hershey's Kisses from Marina Handy Mart. The movie guys do not like it when we bring in our own food. I think we should be able to take our food anywhere we want. It is our food.

Saturday is the busiest day at Holsted's. Everybody needs lots of boat stuff on weekends, like rope, metal parts, and beer. They have to buy the beer from Marina Handy Mart. Holsted's does not sell beer. Our floor is gray tile and gets very dirty from wet and muddy feet. The parking lot is gravel and has puddles. Most people do not clean their shoes off on the mat before they walk into the store. That is so rude.

I have to work until six-thirty on Saturday. Gary and Manuel leave early. Keith and I close up together. He gives me a ride home and then stays for spaghetti night. We have our weekly cribbage contest. Gram makes the tomato sauce in the big pan. It has to simmer for two hours. It is the only thing she cooks now. Keith and Gram play first, while I boil the noodles. The loser sets the table while I play the winner.

Keith thinks he has to coach me.

"Throw two away. Come on, Per! Sometime today!" he complains, but I take my time. When I play cards with Keith, he gets antsy. Antsy is when you think everybody else is too slow. Most people are antsy. I always win at cribbage. You only have to know numbers like what makes fifteen and how to add up to thirty-one. The rest is luck. And I am lucky.

On Sunday morning before I go into work, Gram and I eat cinnamon rolls, read the paper, and check our Lotto numbers. This is my very favorite time because we pretend to win the lottery. I love pretending.

"Come on! Come on!" I cheer.

"This is it! I can feel it in my bones." Gram can feel a lot in her bones.

"Oh-two. Oh-five. One-four. Two-four. Three-two. Four-four." I read them off to Gram. She says *nope* after each number that is wrong and *yep* for each right number. We check all ten numbers twice. That is like getting more chances to win. It is as if we bought more than just five tickets. That is so cool.

We have another game we play. It is lottery list. The *What would be the first thing you'd buy if you won the lottery?* game. We play with Keith.

"A new TV!" That would be me.

"Hawaii!" That would be Gram.

"Cable!" That would be me too. I really like Animal Planet.

"A dishwasher." That would be Gram. I do not understand this because I am the one who washes all the dishes.

"Fix up *Diamond Girl*." That would be Keith. *Diamond Girl* is his sailboat.

"A year's supply of tequila." That would be Keith again. I am surprised he does not say beer too, or maybe Mexican babes. He talks about Mexican babes all the time. They are close to Texas in Mexico. That is a country.

"Fix Yo's heater." That is Gram. She is always cold. Yo is Keith's truck.

"Go to Hershey's chocolate factory and see how Kisses are made." That is me.

The end of the game is when one person can't think of anything else they would buy. It is always Gram. She says she is fortunate.

"I'm fortunate I own my own house, damned fortunate I have you to help with expenses, and goddamned fortunate your grandpa worked his ass off then had the courtesy to drop dead without lingering." *Lingering* is a word that means costing a lot of money to die. She says she hopes she does not linger. She is damned fortunate and I am lucky.

Gram says we make a good pair.

4

~~~

Fall is my favorite time of year, *Reader's Digest* is my favorite book, and my favorite candies are Hershey's Kisses. I like to wear flannel jackets, I bounce when I'm happy, and my bike is blue with red spray paint.

"Hey, Gram!" I yelled when I found it lying in our side yard all splattered. It looked like it was bleeding. "What happened to my bike?"

"Some asshole decided to be a moron, that's what," Gram said. After that, she made me lock it up in our garage every night.

I like to ride my bike to work so I can pretend I am flying or sailing. Keith and I earn extra cash by working on other people's boats. Boats are my favorite thing besides riding my bike. Sailboats run on water and wind.

"Sailing and riding a bike are like flying because of air and physics," Gramp told me. He taught me how to sail boats, and Keith teaches me how to fix them.

"Smoother, Perry, you missed a spot." Keith has to inspect my work. We are sanding teak on a boat that is supported on jacks high in the air. It is hauled out at the boatyard. They call it being on the hard. I think that is funny. *On the hard.* Keith makes dirty jokes whenever we help put boats back into the water. Keith and I work up on the boat. The foreman carries a clipboard and tells us to hurry.

"We don't have all day!" he yells. I think that is funny because we do. We do have all day.

Keith likes to joke. "Time to get her off, Per. Time to get her off the hard, man. Time to get the jacks off, Per. Get it? Jacks off? Jack off? Time to jack off, Per!"

I have to make sure anyone does not hear us talk this way. Gram would be mad to hear Keith say J-off. I laugh, but my face still turns red. I do not say J-off. We are supposed to help the workers on the ground put the slings in the correct place for the hoist. The wide bands have to hang by the arrows taped on the hull of the boat.

"Hey, Buddy!" Keith shouts from the deck. "You got the JACKS OFF yet?" And he smirks at me. Keith calls people he does not know Buddy.

His bushy gray beard makes it hard to see his mouth, but I know what it looks like. Keith is the biggest man I know. He is tall and husky.

"I'm a husky guy! Those are muscles, Per! Muscles!" He will point to the gut hanging over his belt. Husky is another name for muscles in your stomach.

I do not have a gut. I am not husky.

We painted the bottom of this boat yesterday and have to finish a light sand on its rail today. Light sand means working hard and sweating. The wooden parts of boats need to be sanded and varnished. It is hard work, but cool to see how beautiful they look when they are done. We make boats look very good. Keith says we bring them back from the dead.

"We bring them back, Per! They'd be dumped or sunk. We are defenders of a lost art. Look at those new boats, Per. No character! Not one piece of teak. What a waste." A lost art means we are the only ones doing the work. No character means easy to take care of.

When this boat goes into the water, it will be moved into a slip and tied up. The owner says he is going to put the varnish on his rail himself and save money.

"That's what they all say, Per!" Keith chortles. "Twenty minutes into the job, he'll be back here bellyaching about it being too hot or too cold or too hard on his knees, and you and I will have another thousand bucks under the table."

The first time I heard under the table, I thought it meant hide. I had to ask Keith for sure.

"It means we get to keep all the money ourselves instead of giving some of it to the government." When Keith talks into my ear, he gets it all wet. I hate that.

"You mean cheat?" I do not want to go to jail.

"No. No. It's okay, Per. We don't owe them a dime! They didn't do any of the work, did they? They didn't help us one bit. Just don't tell anybody, okay?"

Under the table is okay if you don't tell anybody. Keith and I make a lot of money under the table sanding and varnishing for people who are too lazy to do it themselves.

The boat we are working on is called *Playboy II*. People have no imagination, Keith says.

"No fucking imagination. You know how many *Playboy*s there are, Per?" He does not wait for me to answer. "About a gazillion!" He says this about every boat name.

"You know how many *My Prozac*s there are?"

"You know how many *Sea Dream*s there are?"

People sometimes hook together the first two letters of their wife and kids' names for their boat. This really annoys Keith.

"*Jo-bo-ha-ga-li?* What the fuck is that supposed to mean, Per? They're just lazy. That's what they are. Just fucking lazy!"

People either lack imagination or are lazy, according to Keith. He says the F-word more than anybody else I know. I do not say the F-word.

Keith has to drink beer and watch me work while he tells me about his adventures. He was a ferry captain until he ran his boat into a terminal. He told me the true story. It was not his fault. It was a passenger with really big tits.

"Tits so big, Per, they were more than boobs. They were tatas. They were jugs. They were so big, the end of the world could come and you wouldn't even notice." His eyes are very round and do not blink when he tells me this. "It was not my fault."

That is another thing people say when they make a mistake. *Not their fault.* It is like rethink.

"Well worth it, Per. Well worth it. Big. Big. Tits." Keith makes his hands look like he is itching somebody's back. Then he farts and laughs.

"Just doin' my part as a loyal citizen of Everett," he says.

5

≈

Every morning I get up, go to the bathroom, shave, and comb my hair. I wear jeans and a flannel shirt with an undershirt.

"You have an undershirt on, Perry?" Gram asks.

"Yeah."

"You sure?"

I lift up my shirt and check.

"Yeah, I'm sure."

Gram says only low-class people go without undershirts. I definitely like undershirts. Everett is too cold to be naked under a shirt anytime of the year even with a jacket.

I am a good cook. I make oatmeal and other stuff too, like macaroni and cheese, hamburger casserole, and toasted tuna sandwiches. Gram used to do all the cooking, but now she sits at the kitchen table, works on her crossword puzzle, and tells me what to do. She likes me to stretch. That means try new things.

"Don't get in a rut, Perry. Stretch yourself. Do something new," she says.

When she told me to make stew for dinner, I cut the meat in long strips. I never made stew before.

"Cut them up smaller. Once more across. Then again. That's right. Make them the same size so they'll cook even."

She always tells me to read instructions carefully.

"What's braising?" I ask. Cookbooks are like dictionaries. They use hard words.

"Cook in liquid," Gram says.

"Why don't they just say that then?" I complain.

"Don't be smart!" Gram does not even have to look up from her puzzle.

Oatmeal is easy now. It used to be difficult. Difficult means you have to work hard and sweat. Gram says life is difficult.

"Life is tough, Perry. It's full of rude surprises and obstacles to overcome. Sometimes misfortune just smashes you upside the head. It's difficult. Most things in life are difficult." She tells me this while she picks tiny balls off her wool sweater and throws them into the trash. They stick to everything, those little balls.

While I eat my breakfast, I do my words and write.

Gram gave me my own writing book when I was small. I used to write my words on tiny pieces of paper and lose them. She would have to bend down and pick them up. They would be scattered all over our house. Gram hates any messes she does not make herself.

"This is for the birds!" she complained.

I always laugh when Gram says this. It does not mean you will feed the birds, only that you would like to. She buys me big black books from the school supply aisle at Kmart. I remember the first one I got.

"What's this?" I asked. "It has nothing inside." The pages were blank. I thumbed through each one to make sure. Nothing.

"It's a journal. A scrapbook for words. You have to do the writing." Gram poked her skinny finger deep into my shoulder.

"What a gyp. Did it cost less than a book-book?"

"No, as a matter of fact, it costs more." People use matter of fact when they mean something is highly unlikely or probably untrue.

"You need to write, Perry, it will help you remember, develop your mind. Improve your thinking." Gram jabbed her finger again and it hurt.

"Oww!" I yelped.

"Quit your bellyaching! Now, write!" Gram said.

So that is what I do. I write. I do my words. I think. And I listen. I am an auditor.

There are times I forget I am slow. When I am riding my bike to Holsted's. When I scrub teak on the deck of a sailboat with Keith. When Gary lets me fill out paperwork in the office. When I am by myself. Without other people. They are the ones who are fast. They talk fast and think faster.

"Turning themselves into butter!" Gram thinks regular people are too speedy. "Around and around and around they turn. Watch, Perry!"

Gram is right. I see them on the bus as I look through the window. Driving, talking on their cell phones, eating a breakfast sandwich, all at the same time. I see them at the marina, clicking into tiny computers that they carry around. Gram calls them pets.

"Goddamn metallic pets! Look, Perry! Like they're attached to the end of their fingers." Then she will cackle and do her witch laugh.

There are times I am glad I am slow. I see things. I hear things. And there are times I don't think about it at all.

6

≈

Holsted's Marine Supply is a two-story white warehouse between the big commercial harbor and the brand-new Everett Marina. We sit right next door to Carroll's Boatyard. Keith says the new marina will force regular guys out of boating and make it only for rich slobs.

"They squeeze us tight like a horny guy's hand on a pretty girl's boob. That's what we are," Keith says, "the boobs," and he scrunches up his fingers.

I think this is funny and laugh. This makes Keith wriggle his eyebrows at me.

"Perry, can you inflate these two fenders?" Gary asks. He stares at Keith. "Some people have a job to do."

Keith goes back to the register.

People come into Holsted's to buy things like lines, which are ropes, and hatches, and fenders. Whatever they need. We have a lot of stuff packed into shelves and hanging up on walls. I have worked here longer than anybody, except for Gary. I am good at inflating fenders. It is my newest job and I have to concentrate. My hair gets in my eyes and I have to push it back. I need a haircut. A fat man with a cigar looks over my shoulder. I can see two spots of dark wet on his blue shirt under his armpits. I am afraid his ash will drop on me and sizzle a hole through my skin. Burns hurt and they leave a scar.

"You sure you know how to do that?" The man chews on his cigar. I think that is a very stupid question, but people ask stupid questions all the time.

They ask Keith, "Can I tie up here?" in front of the post labeled NO MOORING.

They ask Gary, "Can I fish here?" by the marker NO FISHING.

They ask Manuel, "Can I leave my car here?" by the sign NO PARKING.

Most people do not read. I read all the time.

The man asks me again if I know what I am doing.

"Hey! I'm talking to you!" he says.

"Yes, I know what I'm doing." It is the only answer I can give. When I talk, I talk slow. This worries people.

"Hey, is he okay?" The man looks at Gary. Being okay is very important.

"Yes!" Gary and I say this at the same time. This seems to worry the man even more. When people watch me, I go slower because it makes me nervous. All I have to do is hold the fender from moving, but the man stands very close. I smell his smoky breath. He pants in my ear. When I finish, I hand him his fender.

"Here you go, sir." It is important to be polite to customers so they will come back and spend more money.

The man chews his cigar, looks at his watch, squeezes his fender, and talks to Gary, all at the same time. "I need to get to the San Juans . . . Friday Harbor . . . Three weeks' vacation . . . Can we speed this up?" he asks. "I need to get going." He looks at his watch again.

Vacations are when you stop being in a hurry to go to work and start being in a hurry to go someplace else.

"My idiot son threw a fender off the stern and it wasn't tied on. Got all the way up here. You'd think he was retarded! Oh, sorry." The man looks at me.

Retarded. Idiot. These are words I know. They mean foolish or stupid. I am not foolish. I am not stupid. I am not retarded. I am slow. Gram says we are all idiots really, and that idiot comes from the Greek word *idios*.

"It means private citizen, Perry, a loner, someone just concerned with himself!" Gram says. "That pretty much sums up everybody I know." She first told me this the day I came home from school crying. Somebody called me an idiot.

"Teasing is a cross we all bear," Gram said. "A cross we all carry and suffer. It will make you a better person. Name-calling just proves the other guy is ignorant. Who called you that?" When she found out it was my teacher she spit nails. That is what she said.

"I could just spit nails!" and then she threw a dish. I remember I laughed at spit nails and the dish, and cried because I wanted my old teacher Miss Elk.

It was my last day of school. I was thirteen years old. I never went back. Gram taught me herself then. I learned more from Gram than anyone else in the world.

7

≈

Gram died on Tuesday, August 12. She did not linger, she just did not wake up. Gram said in an emergency to call the number 911 on the phone. It was our drill and we practiced.

"What do you do if I don't talk to you in the morning or can't wake up?" she would ask.

"Call nine-one-one," I would say.

"What do you do if I am lying on the floor and don't move?"

"Call nine-one-one," I would answer.

That morning she did not wake up or talk. I called 911. Her face was white and her cheek was cold when I touched it. Her mouth was stretched flat and her lips were blue. When the paramedics came, they covered Gram up in a cloth and took her away. They did not use their siren. I called Holsted's first.

"Gary? Gram died and I can't come into work today." I was shaking and crying so hard that snot came out my nose. Gary had to ask me three times what happened. My fingers would not work right. I could hardly hold the phone. It was all slippery from my snot.

It is very important to let Gary know anytime I cannot come to work.

Gram's address book sits right by the phone. It is blue and has mountains on it. She put every number we ever needed inside. The back cover has our family emergency phone number list. Emergency means something bad has happened or something you did not expect. Like the lights going out. Or a person dying.

The top number is my mother, Louise Crandall. She makes me nervous because she waves her hands around and does not ever look at me. The last time I saw her was when Gramp died. No one answers, so I leave a message. I hate that because machines go too fast. I just say *Call Gram*, but get confused because Gram is dead.

I am scared of calling because I do not know these people, not like I know Keith and Gary. My cousin-brother John is number two, but there is no answer, not even a recorder. Number three is my other cousin-brother, David. He answers on the second ring.

"David, this is Perry L. Crandall." It is important to identify yourself on the phone. If you do not it makes people mad. After I told him about Gram, he swore.

"Oh, hell!" That is what he said.

It sounded like he had a blanket in front of his mouth. I heard him talking to his wife.

What happened?

It's Perry. Gram died. Where did we put Mom's new number?

David comes to pick me up in his car and we go to get John and Louise. They say we are going to an arrangement place. Everybody talks except for me.

I become a problem.

This is a real problem. That is what I hear them say. *What are we going to do?*

What are we going to do about Perry? I hear them ask.

It's going to be a real problem now without Gram, they say.

I am it. I am a problem.

They thought Gram took care of me, but I was the one who took care of her. That is what she said. That is what I know.

"The two of us. We make a good pair. Just the two of us. I don't know what I would do if I didn't have you to take care of me, Perry." She said this every single day since Gramp died.

They say things behind my back. They think I do not understand what their words mean, but I am an auditor and I hear them clearly. Louise, John, and David are making arrangements. Arrangements are something nobody wants to do, and cost money nobody wants to spend.

In the arrangement place, I sit alone against the wall and wait. I am like those Greek people. An *idios,* I think. I can see what they are doing from my chair. I have two good eyes. I hear them talk. I have two good ears. Gram told me she wanted to be buried next to Gramp at Marysville Memorial Park. We made plans to buy the plot, but it cost over two thousand dollars, and we had to fix the roof instead.

Louise and John are talking to a man dressed in black and arguing with each other. The badge on his chest says *Funeral Director* and below that it says *Steven.* That is a nice name, I think, as I look at the buttons on his suit. They are shiny and gold. He looks like an actor, all sad, and talks low like it was his Gram. I thought he must have known her. His face looks so glum.

"Hey, Steven, did you know my Gram?" When I say this, his face turns red.

"Don't be stupid, Perry," John says. He sounds mean. "He

doesn't know any better." John's hand covers his mouth. People do that just before they say something rude.

She had money set aside for a funeral. We don't have to use it all. The minister is free. He owes me a favor. I handled his divorce. We don't want anybody to think we aren't doing what we should.

Didn't Grandma say not to make a fuss?

Don't worry, Mom. You'll get something out of this. We won't spend it all.

"Eight hundred bucks to cremate. What about an urn? Jesus! This brass one is over a hundred!" John's voice is squeaky.

David pulls my hand and I get up. We walk around the room looking at dead-people stuff, like caskets and vases.

"This wood box is pretty. She would like that," I say. It is square and glossy. The tag says it is made of walnut. The wood is smooth and cool like the door on our refrigerator.

"It's called an urn. It's for ashes. You're probably the only one who knows what Gram would like." David speaks very soft and looks at me. He does not scare me as much as John and Louise.

"We should buy this box," I say.

The others stop talking and look at me.

"Yeah. Well. You're not paying for it," John says. I expect him to stick his tongue out at me, but he does not.

"I can. I can pay for it." My voice comes out much louder than I want. It echoes around the room. I have five hundred and seventeen dollars in my checking account and payday is next week. My checkbook with my own name on it is in my pocket. I do not tell them about my savings account. Gram said not to.

"Perry, your savings account is your own goddamn business! Don't you say a thing! Ever! It's for your future," Gram warned. "Our family's a bunch of vultures and don't you forget it! Don't you say one word!"

Vultures are animals, but they can be people too. Gram said that when she was alive. She is dead now. I keep forgetting this and start to worry. I know this because I reach up to my forehead with my fingers and feel wrinkles. Gram called them worry lines. I worry because none of these people are on my list. I do not have to do what they say, but I am afraid not to.

"Put your checkbook away. You're going to need all your money to live on, Perry," David says. He is the only one besides me who looks sad.

Louise sits in a chair, putting on more red lipstick and using a tiny little mirror. Her hair is now whitish-gold. It is pulled back from her face so tight her eyes have to squint.

"Too bad about Grandma, Perry," she says, and blots her lips on a tissue.

Gram. Her name is Gram, but I do not tell Louise this. It is something she should know.

They keep talking. That is okay.

I can't believe Elaine let you out of the house on your own, David. Where is she anyway?

Shut up, John! She has a trial. We need to decide about Perry.

What's to decide?

What's he going to do?

Well, he can't live with us and Mom's not exactly known for her care and feeding of children.

Isn't he on disability? Doesn't he get checks?

I thought he worked.

Well, his employer should be the one to take care of him. They should be responsible.

Somebody has to be responsible, but it doesn't have to be us. We shouldn't have to take care of him.

I chose the most beautiful box for Gram while my cousin-brothers argued. I chose the one I knew she would like. And wrote the check to Steven.

Later that night, when I am home alone, I look at Gram's picture and wonder where she is.

I remember asking questions when Gramp passed away.

"Where do we go? Where do we go when we die, Gram?"

She grabbed me tight to her chest and said, "We go into wind and rain. We turn into the sea and the fog. That's where we go, Perry. Each time it rains, think of Gramp. Each time the wind blows he will be there, and when I die, I'll be there too."

I think that is true. I hear drips on the roof as it starts to rain.

I think of Gram.

And I wait for the wind to blow.

8

≈

Gram's memorial service was held at Sullivan Park on Silver Lake. It was most appropriate, John said. That meant it was close to where everyone had to get to that day and it was free. All of the family came, except for my mother, Louise, and David's wife, Elaine.

I do not have suit pants that fit. I wear clean blue jeans and my black suit jacket. It is too tight over my shoulders, but that is okay because I do not plan to wear it ever again.

My cousin-brothers come by an hour early to pick me up. They have two cars. While I talk to David, John takes a lady carrying a pink poodle around to look at Gram's house. They walk across the lawn and stare into the front window, but do not go inside. I am glad because it is a mess. Gram and I have a lot of crap. The lady trips in the long grass and says a bad word.

"Who is she?" I ask David.

"John's new wife, CeCe," he says.

"What does she do? Is she a lawyer?" Almost everybody in my family is a lawyer.

"No, she shops." David gives a short laugh.

There's nothing of any value. The property is a gold mine though.

How long are we staying? I have a hair appointment.

Only as long as we have to. Twenty minutes max.

Even though it is not winter, the park is wet. It is always wet. Rain falls out of the sky. Rain always falls out of the sky. Kids and dogs run in the muddy grass. One big brown collie jumps up on John and gets dirt on his pants. Gram would have done her cackle laugh and slapped her knee. My cousin-brothers stand together. John's wife, CeCe, sits in his car with her poodle. She does not want it to get wet. I never knew dogs could be pink. David says it is dyed, but it looks alive to me. It even barked once.

The minister guy talks about Gram and Jesus.

Dorothea Crandall is at home with the Lord. . . .

Gram would have been mad. "It's my own goddamned business, Perry! I hate all that holier-than-thou stuff. All that crap! Turn the other cheek! He wasn't that much of a wuss!" She would roll her eyes. "WWJD? Now what the hell is that supposed to mean, Perry? What would Jesus do? What do you think he'd do? He'd walk away and be disgusted! That's what!"

The minister shakes my hand and says he is very sorry for my loss. He tells me Gram is in a much better place. What a crock, I think. Gram would have wanted to be at our house. At our place. Crock means untrue or a lie. It can also mean a pot you cook beans in.

I am happy because I get to take Gram home with me in her box.

"You can put her up in the mountains," David says to me. "Come on, Perry, I'll take you back to Gram's house."

Gram would not want to be in a park or in the mountains. She wanted to be next to Gramp at Marysville Memorial Park. I do not tell them this. They do not seem to care where Gram wants to be.

They all talk above my head in the parking lot, before David drives me home. I listen carefully. They get confused. Sometimes they are my cousins and other times my brothers. They cannot make up their minds. But I know who they are. They are cousin-brothers.

I don't have time for this! CeCe has an appointment.

How is he going to live?

What do you care?

What provisions did Gram make for Perry?

There's no will. It will be up to us.

But John, she said—

David! Shut up about it. There IS NO WILL. You think Grandma trusted lawyers after what happened? The estate will be split between us!

That's right. It will bypass Mom. She's not related to Gram. The money from the house will come directly to us. That's really going to piss her off. She probably thinks she'll get something out of all this.

You know very well we'll end up giving her something or she'll throw a fit . . . like last time.

And they both laugh. They talk about me as if I am not there. That is okay. I am an auditor. I listen to John and David. Gram always told me she was concerned about what would happen to me when she was gone and I would be left alone.

"You're so goddamned suggestible," she said. "Suggestible and honest! A terrible combination! Terrible! They'll take advantage of you."

She would shake her head and click her tongue like an alarm clock. Advantage means up to no good. That was why she would not put any of them on our list. But it made me wonder. Can I still use our list now that Gram is dead?

John drives behind us all the way to Gram's house and follows us to the door. CeCe stays in the car and complains through the open window. Her voice is squeaky just like John's.

I'm going to be late! You have to wrap this up!

David and John go from room to room looking for papers. We have to find papers. I help.

Here we go. Christ! Hardly anything in the accounts. What did they live on?

Social Security . . . Perry's job . . . What does he do, anyway?

Christ, David, I don't know! What does it matter? Here it is. The title. Thank God THAT wasn't mortgaged. He's on the title to the house. Jesus! What'd she do that for?

Developers have been buying up all around the harbor. We could sell it and invest the proceeds for him. We'll need to have him sign a Power of Attorney. Elaine can take care of it.

Elaine! That bitch. Just because you listen to her doesn't mean I have to! And why would I take legal advice from you? You're not even a lawyer. Perry can't be trusted to handle his own money, that's for sure. Besides, it should be split between all of us. It's only fair.

BLAH! BLAH! A car horn blares and John opens the front door.

"We have to leave now!" CeCe screams. She is very loud.

"You coming over to the house, David?" John says as he pulls out his keys.

"Yeah. I'll drop by later with Elaine. She wants to be there."

"It's a *Family* Meeting, David, to decide what to do about the house. Elaine doesn't *need* to be there."

"Yeah, well, I'll let you tell her that," David mutters, and turns to me. "Don't worry, we'll take care of you," and pats me on the shoulder.

I say okay, and go back inside.

9

≈

When a person dies, their body goes away, but their voice stays. I hear Gram every day. Every day I hear her voice.

Be careful, Perry, she says. *Don't be smart,* she warns. *This is for the birds,* she tells me.

I would rather have her with me.

My family says they will be over to dispose of the assets. Assets are things that can be used to pay debts. They are also an advantage, the dictionary says. This is most likely what Gram meant when she told me John, David, and Louise would take advantage.

Louise comes by first. Her hair is now red and matches her lipstick.

"I just wanted a couple things to remind me of Grandma." She holds a Kleenex to her face, but her eyes are not wet. Louise takes Gram's jewelry box, her wedding rings, and the mother-of-pearl brush and mirror set. She sets these things carefully in the front seat of her car. I watch her through the curtains. When she comes back inside, she goes straight to the dining room and opens the china cabinet.

"Is this real or fake?" Louise lifts plates up and looks underneath. She picks up all of Gram's things, and turns them over and over in her hands. Feeling them. Rubbing them. The china. The crystal.

"Is this all there is?" she asks me. "I thought there was a Limoges? I'm almost positive there was a Limoges. Or maybe some Waterford?" She looks at me closely when she says this. I can see the dishes in her eyes, but the names that she says, I do not know. They are not on my list or in my book.

"I'll have to take these with me. Find me a box, Perry. I'll have an expert decide. Have them all appraised. Is this it? Is this all there is?" she says again, and drops Kleenex on the floor. I guess she does not need tissues anymore.

It is important to appraise things. To make sure things are real. But I know they are. All I have to do is touch them. I stand on the porch and watch her drive away. Her car taillights are two red eyes.

John comes next. He brings his own boxes. CeCe and her poodle are not with him.

"Where's the model?" he asks. "Where's the boat model? That's an original. I'd like to have that. What about the watercolors? I thought Gramp had a Winslow Homer. I was sure it was somewhere around here. How about those signed prints? Do you know where they are?"

I have trouble answering all his questions. He kicks over our pile of *Reader's Digest*s and I have to stack them up again.

"Forget that!" he yells. "Give me a hand over here."

I help him wrap Gramp's model so it does not break or get scratched. I look at his hands. His fingernails are all bit down. I look at mine. I do not bite mine anymore. Gram made me stop. John's eyes are dry. As dry as mine are wet. I have to wipe my nose on my sleeve.

"For Christ's sake, use a handkerchief and stop sniffing." John's mouth is turned down and his eyes move from side to side. Looking. I do not know what he is looking for. I hope he finds it and leaves. He fills all his boxes and I help carry them to the trunk of his car. When his car rolls out of the driveway, he does not wave good-bye.

I sweep the kitchen and put the dishes that Louise did not take back into the cupboard. A car horn honks outside. BEEP! BEEP! It is David. He is alone. Elaine is not with him.

"You are last, David." I say this as he walks through the door. David stops in front of me and looks around.

"God, this takes me back." He walks slowly from room to room, touching the walls, rubbing a doorframe. "Where's Gramp's boat model? Did you know I helped with that? I did the masts and cut the sails."

When he sees my face, he says, "John took it, didn't he? What about the watercolors? Who took the china?"

"We could not find Homer," I tell him, "but John took the signed prints and the model. He didn't know what it was, but said it might be worth a lot of money. It was not just a boat model. It was a schooner," I say.

David shakes his head. "Jesus!" he says, and turns away. "I should have gotten here sooner. What's left? Nothing but a bunch of crap!" He kicks a box. I jump. The box tips over and papers fly out. David squats on his heels, picks them up one by one, and looks at them.

"Hell," he says, and sits hard on the floor. "Oh hell," he says again, and lifts page after page. I sit down next to him and watch.

"One lousy point! Did you know that?" He looks at me. "No, of course you don't."

"What?" I ask.

"The bar exam," he says. "I missed it by one point. I failed it twice. That's why I went back to school. That's why I got my MBA. One point." He shakes his head. "Mom and John never let me forget it. Neither does Elaine. We were in law school together. Did you know that? Graduated the same year. Elaine passed on her first try. She's brilliant. Really brilliant."

He does not look like he thinks she is brilliant. He sounds sad.

"Of course, they all had to let Gram and Gramp know. They never let me forget it for an instant. Not for a goddamned minute." He sounds like Gram.

David crumples the papers into a giant ball and gets to his feet. I follow him to the kitchen and he stuffs them into the trash. He walks into the living room, to Gram's bedroom, and back again. I follow behind.

He opens drawers and cupboards.

"Isn't there anything left? Who took the jewelry? Elaine wondered about the necklaces and rings," he says.

"Louise took the jewelry, but the coin collection is still here," I tell him. I just remembered this. Neither John nor Louise asked about it.

"Well, that's something," he says. "At least that's something. Cash. That might satisfy her." He smiles slowly. "Did you know I sorted all Gramp's pennies and dimes when I was little? I used to bring Gramp all my change from my lunch money at school. He'd look through it and pick out the ones he wanted."

I listen to David talk. I am not afraid of him, but I still hear Gram say, *Careful.*

"David is weak," Gram used to say. "More like his father than John is. He's a weak, weak man. Exactly like your father. That's why they married the same kind of woman. The kind that wears the pants and spends the money."

I have never seen Elaine or Louise wear pants, but I do not see them very often so I do not know what they wear when I am not around. "He looks strong to me," I would say, but Gram would chew her lip and frown.

"Just remember, Perry, he's weak. The weak are more dangerous in the end. You remember that."

I help divide the coin collection into three brown paper sacks and carry them out to his BMW. David gives me a hard hug around the shoulders and leaves whistling.

I think it is funny his car has BM for a name. BM means taking a poop, but I did not tell him this. It would not be nice. Gram always laughed.

"Crap, Perry. BM's another name for crap." She would hit her knee and howl. "His car's a crapper!"

Thinking about what Gram used to say makes me laugh, and then cry again.

I feel a little better, and call Holsted's to leave a message for Keith. He does not have a phone on his boat. I will need more help to empty the house before it is sold. There is a lot of stuff to clear out and pack. Gram's housedresses and aprons. Her underwear. Her shoes. I set one dress aside to keep. The yellow one with green stripes. It smells like Gram. I love that dress. She always wore it to bingo.

Keith is my friend and gives me a hand when it is time to move.

"Why are you selling the house?" Keith asks this for the eighth or twelfth time. I have lost count. He does not understand my family. He tells me this over and over.

"I sure don't understand your family," he says, and shakes his head. "That wife of your brother's. What's her name? Elaine? She's a bitch on wheels!"

I looked at Elaine's feet the last time I saw her and I did not see any roller skates. I think he has her mixed up with someone else.

Keith is picking his nose. I wish he would not do that, but I do not tell him to stop. If a person wants to pick their nose, I guess they should be able to.

"They say it's for the best. It will be more secure for me. Better for my future." I have to remember all the different words David, John, and Elaine used.

"Better for them maybe." Keith is what Gram used to call cynical. Cynical means you are honest in a nasty way.

Keith has a 1982 Toyota truck that has rust spots and is painted with gray primer. He calls his truck Yo because the To and Ta are rubbed off the tailgate. Yo carries five loads to the dump. Yo is good for hauling crap. Gram and I had a lot of crap.

"A hell of a crap hauler!" he says, and slaps Yo's dashboard with his hand. When he does that, the knob to the heater falls off.

"Get that, Per!" Keith yells. I have to bend down quick and grab it so it does not fall through the hole in the floor. The hole is fun to look through because I can see how fast Yo goes without looking at the speedometer.

It took Keith and me two weeks to finish because we could only work on the house after getting off work at Holsted's. We had to hurry, because John said the house would close soon. That did not mean the doors would shut, it meant I would have to move out.

"You'll have to find somewhere else to live." John told me this.

He got mad when I called him to let him know we needed more time.

"Come on, Perry. How much time does it take to get rid of all that garbage?" John yelled. "Christ! Just use a backhoe!" and he laughed over the phone. I did not know what was funny about a backhoe.

"What's a backhoe?" I asked Keith. "Is that like a tractor?"

He got pissed.

"The shits!" he said. "The moneygrubbers!" he snorted.

Keith asked why he wasn't invited to Gram's funeral.

"John said it was just for the family," I said. "Gary wasn't invited either." I feel bad about that.

"Your family is a bunch of *fucks.* You hear me, Per?"

I start to cry again.

"Don't worry, Per. You'll get through this. Everybody does," he says, and pats my back. "Life goes on, Per. It surely does go on."

Keith and I pile old crossword puzzle books in boxes for the dump.

I take one to keep. Gram's handwriting is like a spider's web, all wavy and thin. I like to look at it and think of her doing the crosswords.

"Why'd you let them take all the valuable things?" Keith is my friend. Friends are people who get mad when they think someone does something unfair to you. He does not understand.

"I got all the things I wanted," I tell him. "I got the really good stuff. The melamine dishes decorated with anchors and flags that Gram and Gramp used to have on their boat, the free silverware from when we bought groceries at QFC."

I also have my clothes, four shoeboxes of Gram's papers and pictures, and two large boxes of stuff marked SAVE.

He just shakes his head.

I can keep all the dictionaries and crossword puzzle books I want. I find three thesauruses. I do not know what a thesaurus is. I have to look it up in the dictionary.

"The-saur-us," I say, and look inside.

"Sounds like a frigging dinosaur." Keith does not act like he cares about words.

"It means treasure. A book of words," I say. "Gram always said words are the key to life. She would want me to keep these." Treasure. I like that.

I am responsible for Gram's house until it is sold. I mow the lawn and wash the windows until they shine. I vacuum the living room carpet, scrub the kitchen floor tiles, and hose off the driveway. Keith helps me.

Being responsible means that you work for a thing that you love. I loved Gram's house. Gram and I had Christmas stockings, Easter baskets, and Thanksgiving dinners there. It was perfect for the two of us. I had my own bedroom and Gram had hers. The rest of the house was filled with crap. Even Gram said that. But it was okay because the only person who came over after Gramp died was Keith. We did not need anyone else. It was a wonderful house.

John said we would not get much money for it. We did escrow. I think it has something to do with birds. Gram would say it was for the birds. That is what she would say.

John told me there would be a lot of paperwork, but I had to go to work at Holsted's. It was not my day off.

"We can handle it for you. Sign here." He gave me a paper. It gave him my Power to the house so he could write my name thirty-two times. That is what he said. Escrow is when you have to write your name thirty-two times. He told me this.

Keith takes me back to Gram's house for the last time. I hear Yo's engine run. RATTLE. RATTLE. John hands me an envelope with a five-hundred-dollar check inside marked HOUSE SALE. I will put two hundred and fifty dollars in my checking account and two hundred and fifty in my savings account. Spend half and save half, Gram always said. I would rather have had Gram and our house than five hundred dollars. It does not seem like much money for a house.

"That's it!" John smiles over my head. Elaine stands behind him, next to David, and Louise stands on the other side. I hand David the key to Gram's house. Elaine grabs it out of his hand and John grabs it out of hers.

They make me sweat and my armpits smell. Gram always said she knew when they were up to something.

"They have that look!" she would say.

"What look?" I always asked.

"Don't be smart," Gram would say. Her lips would stretch tight and her brown eyes would squint.

They have that look, I hear her say inside my ear.

They have that look now.

10

~~

I have no place to live so Gary let me move into the apartment right above Holsted's where Otis the security guard used to stay. He stole money out of the cash register and was arrested.

"Serves him right, Per! He's in jail now! Monroe Penitentiary, with wife beaters, baby killers, and perverts!" Keith said.

"This will work fine, Perry. You need a place to live and I need someone to live over the store at night," Gary said.

To get to my apartment I have to climb up a long outside stairway right above Holsted's main entry. My front door opens into a large space. Half is the kitchen and half is the living room. The kitchen side has a stove, refrigerator, and counter.

"The sink leaks so you have to keep a bucket underneath," Gary warns. I have four cupboards. I put my cans and cereal in the top ones and keep dishes in the bottom ones. The living room is neat because it has a big picture window that has a view of the parking lot and marina. I can look down and see who comes into Holsted's. That is so cool. I have to keep a towel on the sill because rain leaks around the edges.

A long wall across from the door fits Gram's couch perfectly. My table and chairs sit next to the window. I put Gram's double bed in the bedroom and scoot it against the wall. Gram's old white night-stand is on one side with my clock radio on top. The radio part does not work and the alarm sometimes does not ring, but the clock keeps good time. It flashes and is digital. That means it has numbers instead of hands.

There is a short hall off the living room with a washer and dryer at the end, a bathroom on one side, and my bedroom door on the other. I have a toilet, sink, and shower, but no tub. That is okay. I do not like bathtubs because that is where they put murdered people on TV.

Keith helped me move into my apartment, but he would not help me clean.

"I have to draw the line somewhere, Per! I've never cleaned a kitchen in my life and don't intend to start now." Keith helped me carry all of my furniture up the long stairway to my apartment. He only said the F-word twice and the S-word once when he pinched his finger between the doorframe and the sofa.

"This will be really convenient having you so close, Perry," Gary said. Convenient means that other people do not have to work so hard.

Keith's twenty-seven-foot Catalina sailboat *Diamond Girl* is moored in the first slip on C dock. I can see his boat from my window and when he sees me he waves. I like to visit Keith, but he sleeps a lot and I do not want to bother him. I would like to live on a twenty-seven-foot Catalina. That would be cool.

The first time I met Keith was the first time I saw *Diamond Girl*. I cannot think of one without the other. I saw them coming into the harbor and I watched as Keith steered her to the slip. He did not do a good job and almost crashed *Diamond Girl*'s bow into the dock. That's okay. People make mistakes when they drive boats.

"Grab my line, will you?" I heard Keith before I saw him and before I knew he was Keith. He did not need to tell me what to do. I was already holding *Diamond Girl* off the dock with my foot. Keith threw out a fender and I wrapped his bowline on a cleat.

"She's beautiful," I said. "Catalinas are great boats." And I helped him secure his aft line.

Most people look at me hard when they first hear me talk. Keith is not most people.

He double-checked *Diamond Girl*'s lines and said, "Good job there, matey!" Then he stuck out his hand and said, "Keith!"

I shook it and said, "Perry."

Then he farted twice really loud and walked across the parking lot to Holsted's. I followed him because my lunch break was over. The next day he started working at Holsted's. I like Keith. He is my friend.

I have Gram's ashes with me. Her wooden urn stays on the bottom shelf of my bedside table. My books are on top and she is underneath. It is like us being together again, but she does not talk out loud. She is only in my head now.

My life is different with Gram gone. I do not go to bingo anymore on Tuesdays. I have no one to play with because Keith does not like bingo. I only asked him to go once.

"You want to go to bingo, Keith?"

"Stick needles in my eye, Per! Go inside a Catholic church? Not on your life!" That is what Keith says when he really does not want to do something. He says he would rather have needles in his eye. I just say okay.

I go to Gilly's, Marina Handy Mart, and KFC. I do not go to the movies. I would have to take a bus and it is hard to choose which movie to see, so I stay home. On Sunday morning, I wake up early, walk to Marina Handy Mart, and get a paper and box of powdered-sugar doughnuts or cinnamon rolls. It gives me a chance to see Cherry. When I get home, I sit upstairs and watch out my window until Keith wakes up. If he wants me to come over, he will wave. Then we will sit together in his cockpit and eat cinnamon rolls or doughnuts. It does not matter if it is cold or raining. I feed seagulls pieces of my doughnut, which makes Keith mad.

"Jesus, Per! Don't encourage the little shits!" He throws empty beer cans at them, but never hits any because aluminum beer cans are too light. They end up in the water and he has to get a net with a long handle and scoop them up out of the Sound so the harbormaster doesn't get pissed off.

"Don't feed them, Per!" he says. "Please?"

"Okay." I like seagulls except when they crap on things. Their crap is powerful and can corrode paint off a car.

"See what happened to Yo? That's all from seagull shit!" Keith says.

"I didn't know bird crap could rot, rust, and dent trucks. I think that is amazing," I say.

"Don't be smart, Per!" Keith sounds just like Gram, and I laugh.

I do not have to share the Sunday paper at home, because Keith is not interested in the newspaper except for sports. That makes me sad because I like to share. It takes me all week to read the paper. Gram used to say I got my money's worth. Getting your money's worth is funny. I mean, you mostly get something for money, except maybe when you sell a house.

Cherry works the register at Marina Handy Mart. She has a pretty smile and a beautiful face. I like to take my time and visit on Sundays. It is hard not to stare. Sometimes there is lipstick on her teeth, but it is rude to tell her that. You can only look and wish she would take her fingernail and peel it off.

"I'm sorry about your Gram," she says, and plays with the silver ball on her tongue. Cherry looks sorry. I hear her click the stud against her teeth. Gram would always make her laugh. She would call her Apple or Banana for fun.

"That's what you get for having fruit as a name!" Gram would cackle and Cherry would giggle.

But Gram is not here.

"Give me five Lotto tickets and a Slurpee, please." I set a bag of Hershey's Kisses on the counter. I do not pick up the *Enquirer*.

"Don't you want the paper?" Cherry's hair is very colorful. It is green and blue stripes with brown.

"No." My throat is tight and my eyes fill with water like from sad movies.

"You can do the puzzle, you know. It might make you feel better," she says. Her eyes are dark brown like a seal except they are not wet.

"Okay, then." I have a hard time getting words out of my mouth.

"Cherry is a very nice girl," Gram would say. "Even though she has earrings all over her face and tattoos up her butt!"

Nice is when you look like you mean the things you say. I do not think Cherry has tattoos up her butt. She has a flower on her shoulder, a cat on one arm, and a chain thing around her ankle. Cherry told me the only one that hurt was the one on her foot. That is because it was on bone.

"The ones that hurt are close to the bone," she says.

Being without Gram is close to the bone, I think. I want to stay and talk to Cherry, but I do not know what to say. There are other people in line, so I leave. I pretend that Gram is walking along with me so I do not get lonely. I imagine her just behind.

"Come on, Gram," I say. "Hurry up. We need to get home."

It is hard to turn around and see that she is not there.

Like bone, I think.

I check my lottery tickets on Sunday. When no numbers match, I throw the tickets into the trash. I work on the crossword for six days straight. I get three answers, but it is harder without Gram. I answer seven down, three down, and two across.

Downs are always easier than acrosses. Crossword puzzles are difficult when there is no one to help. Most things in life are difficult, Gram used to say.

Everything is harder without Gram.

I ran out of milk for my oatmeal, so I wanted to go to QFC grocery store. My bus pass was no good and I did not have exact change. I rode my bike to Marina Handy Mart instead, even though it was raining hard. I bought milk, a can of SpaghettiOs, and bread.

Handy Mart is more expensive and SpaghettiOs are not as good as Saturday night spaghetti like Gram, Keith, and I used to make. Cherry was not working at the counter, so I did not stay to talk. I hooked the plastic bags on the handlebars of my bike and they swung and hit my knees all the way back to my apartment.

11

~~

I still have to do my wash on Wednesdays, but it is only my clothes and not Gram's. I only have two small loads. I used to do four loads. I would have sheets, towels, Gram's underwear, and her pajamas. Those are the whites. My shirts, jeans, and Gram's dresses are the darks. Thinking of this makes me sad, so I have to cry again.

Gram said it was very important to have the dark clothes together and the white ones separate so they do not run or change colors. Gram taught me. The first time I washed clothes, I accidentally put her red top with my underpants.

"Goddamn, Perry! All your underwear's pink! So are my bras. Well, that's okay. I don't mind pink bras, but you better start growing or you're going to wear pink underwear for a long, long time. We can't afford to buy new," and Gram made me keep them until I needed the next larger size. After that, we used them for rags. Pink underwear is definitely not cool and I would have been embarrassed if anybody found out.

I stayed in my pajamas and put all my other clothes into the washer. I dumped soap in, turned the dial, and closed the lid. It was bathroom-cleaning day. At Gram's house on days off, I always cleaned the bathroom and Gram did the kitchen floor. Now I have to do all the chores. It takes a long time.

The first thing I do is clean the shower with Comet. It is all scratchy on the tile and my back gets sore. I am scrubbing the toilet bowl with a brush when I hear BANG! CRASH! CRASH! I run into the hall. There is soapy water all over the floor. I slip and fall on my butt and slide all the way to my bedroom. It hurts. I hit my arm on the door. I crawl on my hands and knees and have to use all my clean towels to mop it up. The washer is still leaking and I turn it off quick so it does not explode and kill me.

It is a very bad day.

My pajama bottoms are soaked. I must have made a lot of noise because Keith and Gary come running upstairs and bang on my door. I hear their voices so I know who it is. I am embarrassed, all dripping wet, and covered with Comet and laundry soap. I do not want to answer their knocks, but it is rude to pretend you are not home. I open the door and tell them what happened.

"My clothes are dirty. The washer is broken. There's water all over the floor. I have nothing to wear. Gram is dead and there's no one to help me."

I cannot stop crying and get the hiccups. My eyes are swollen shut and I cannot see. Gary goes into my kitchen and brings me back a glass of water. He makes me sit on the couch and hands me a paper towel to wipe my face. Paper towels are rough and they hurt. It is better to use toilet paper, but I do not tell him that. It would hurt his feelings.

"Have you had anything to eat?" Keith asks. He looks around at the mess in my apartment. I am ashamed at my dirty place. My elbow throbs and my knee prickles.

"No," I tell him. That is the truth. I forgot to buy my cereal.

Keith is my friend. He goes down to his boat and brings me back a Snickers candy bar and a navy blue sweatshirt and pair of jeans. Gary finds Gramp's old belt in my drawer. Keith's pants are too big for me. They drag on the floor, but I do not care. He helps throw my wet laundry in the back of Yo and drives me to Nick's Laundromat. He keeps me company and we eat Cheetos while my laundry washes and dries. He even helps me fold everything.

"You let me know when you need help like this. You hear, Per?" Keith has to clear his throat three times.

"You getting a cold, Keith?" I ask.

"No, Per."

He tells me it's going to take a while for me to adjust. "Gary and I will be here to help you. Call us. Okay?"

Adjust means that you have to change because things are different. When things are different, even though you do not like them, you have to adjust. This is true.

Gary ordered a new washer-dryer from Sears and had them take the old ones away. The new one is tall and white. The dryer is on top and the washer part is on the bottom. It is a Kenmore and I know how to make it work.

"Hey, Keith! Can I wash your clothes? I can wash your clothes." This is my first good idea since Gram died.

"Yeah, that would be great, Per. Thanks!" He smiles and gives me a pat on the back.

Now we are both happy.

I guess I just needed to wash more than just my own clothes to not be so sad. Gary gives me all the rags and towels from Holsted's to clean too. I have lots of clothes to wash now. I can pretend they are Gram's except there are no dresses, just big dirty jeans, extra large T-shirts, and stained, stretched-out men's underpants.

Gram would never have been caught dead in men's underwear.

But that's okay.

Life goes on. Gram's voice is in my ear.

Cherry chews gum, blows bubbles, and makes a snapping sound. I lean against the Handy Mart counter and spread my things out in front of her so she can ring them up. I like to take my time when Cherry is working. She has dimples on her elbows. That is so cool.

"No PayDay?" she asks. Cherry remembers everything I buy.

"No. I have to watch my pennies now," I say. That is what Gram always said. Watching your pennies means you cannot spend too much on extra things like PayDay candy bars and big bags of Hershey's Kisses.

The utility company sent me the last electric bill from the house. It was $216.94. John mailed it and wrote a letter saying that it was my responsibility because Gram and I were the last ones who lived there. It took almost half my check from Holsted's.

"Watch out, Perry! They electrocute people for less! If your bill's late they shock you!" Manuel whispered this in my ear. Most of the time he lies, so I am not sure. I did not want to make the electric company mad.

The bill from Gram's ambulance ride was $1,198.32. They told me to send what I could, so I talked to Gary. He helped me figure it out. I mail them a check for fifty-six dollars and twenty-eight cents each month. It is still an unexpected expense. This means I can run out of money before my next check if I am not careful.

"What do David and John say? Can't they give you a hand?" Gary asked. He helped me fill out all the papers for the ambulance company.

"It is my responsibility," I say.

"Use some of your savings, Perry. You do have savings, don't you?" he asks.

I do not talk about my savings account.

"Gram said it's for my future." I cannot use it for electric bills.

"Your future is now!" Gary sputters when he is excited. I can tell he does not understand Gram's rules. She was ahead of him on my list. Even dead, she comes first. It is very important to have rules and save for the future.

I like to buy the *Enquirer* now because it reminds me of Gram, and that is important. It is only seventy-five cents. That is not quite a dollar. I buy a tuna sandwich from Marina Handy Mart because it is cheaper than Gilly's fake crab. I buy five Lotto tickets because Gram would want me to. I buy a much smaller bag of Hershey's Kisses. I save them as treats and only eat them when I miss Gram too much. I have to make them last a long time because there are lots of times I miss her, like on bingo nights or when I walk past KFC.

Cherry puts everything in a plastic bag for me. Her fingernails are interesting. They have little pictures of animals on them.

"I do them myself with a kit from the drugstore. You like them?" Cherry wriggles them in front of me. She makes them dance on the counter. One is a zebra. It has teeny, tiny stripes. "So where's your friend, Keith?" she asks.

"At work." I know he will be by later for beer. Cherry knows this too, but she always asks where he is. I try to think of something else to say. "Your fingers are cool. Is it hard to do?"

"Nah . . . It's easy. You just paste them on. Well, you tell Keith hi from me. Okay?" She snaps her gum.

The door whooshes shut as I leave to go back to work. It is a busy day. We have another shipment to unload. After I eat my sandwich, I put my sack under the counter. Manuel pulls it out during break and tosses it into the trash.

"Manuel, where's my sack?" He likes to tease me.

"In the garbage." He laughs, until Keith sneaks up behind and smacks him on one ear.

"Manuel, don't be a jackass! Leave him alone!" Keith yells. He always calls him a jackass, and worse sometimes.

"Oww! Shit, Keith, we're just having fun!" Manuel pulls away and rubs his ear.

"It's okay, Keith." I wish Keith would not yell at Manuel. It makes it worse when he is not around.

Manuel asks Keith to call him Manny for short. I think he wants to be friends, but Keith will not call him Manny.

"Manny, my ass! You only give nicknames to friends, Per! And Manuel is no friend of mine. Listen to me, Per. There are some people you just can't be friends with. Remember that," Keith says.

I am lonely after work. It only takes me two minutes to leave Holsted's and walk up the stairs, but I miss Gram when I see the crossword puzzle on my table. I look for my Hershey's Kisses, and then remember I left my sack under the counter by the register.

Gary has gone for the day and Holsted's door is locked up tight, so I will have to wait and get it tomorrow.

The next day, the first thing I do is find my bag under the counter. Manuel throws it in the trash three more times and pours Coke on it during break. When I get home from work, I set the sack on my kitchen counter and spread the *Enquirer* out so it can dry off from the soda. It stays sticky.

Sunday morning, I go to Marina Handy Mart and buy the paper. It is heavy and full of ads. I like to read the ads. They are interesting and I learn a lot, like the Toyota Prius can get fifty-five miles to the gallon or 650 miles between fill-ups and there is a company that makes address labels with any picture you want on it. Stuff like that.

I also bought a box of powdered-sugar doughnuts, which I like better than cinnamon rolls. Gram always liked cinnamon rolls best. Keith does not wake up until late on Sundays because he does not have to be at Holsted's early to open up or run the register.

I eat my doughnuts, read my paper, and watch for Keith to move around on his boat. I have to watch carefully. I cannot visit him unless he waves.

He waves today so I come down.

It is cool, but there is no wind. Keith sits on a blanket in his cockpit and holds a full glass in his hand.

"What are you drinking?" I ask. It looks red. Like blood.

"The hair of the dog that bit me, Per! The hair of the dog," he says.

"What?" I ask. I do not see any hair in his drink and Keith does not look like he has a dog bite. There is no bandage on him that I can see.

"It's just tomato juice and vodka. Healthy, Per," he says. "Vegetables and cereal! Nothing healthier than that for breakfast! Especially if you have a hangover."

A hangover is when you drink too much alcohol all at once. Keith is almost always hungover. He gives me plain juice without the vodka. Gram never allowed me to drink vodka or any kind of alcohol.

"Cherry says hi," I say. It is hard to talk with doughnuts stuffed in my mouth.

"She's working today?" Keith sounds surprised.

"No, that was Wednesday, I think." I feel bad I did not remember to tell him.

"Thanks for nothing." Keith uses mad words, but laughs at the same time. He is my friend.

We sit on the rocking boat together. *Diamond Girl* has white fiberglass with dark blue trim. There is gray dirt smudged on the gelcoat. "I could wax and polish her for you." And I rub a spot with my sleeve. "Keith, you want me to clean your decks with a hose and scrub brush?" I ask. It is important to help your friends.

"Yeah sure," he says. "We'll get around to it one day."

It is quiet. I can hear waves plop against *Diamond Girl*.

DING! DING! DING! I look up and see Keith's halyards slapping his mast.

"Those need to be tightened," I say. "I can do that too, if you want," I offer, and continue chewing my doughnut.

"Anyone ever tell you you're a peaceful guy?" Keith leans back. His eyes are squinting even though it is cloudy. "You're like having a cat that talks. Company that doesn't take a lot of energy to maintain."

"No one ever says peaceful, but they call me retarded and other stuff," I say.

"Smack 'em the next time they call you that," Keith says.

"Why?"

"Why not?" Keith rubs one eye. It is all red and veiny.

"Gram said not to. She said it makes me just as bad as them."

It is quiet again and I remember when Gramp tried to teach me to defend myself. I was ten.

"No, Perry!" he would say. "Don't put your thumb inside your fist! You can break it that way!" He would put his hand in mine. "Like this! Now try to hit me! Come on, Perry!" But I could not.

"Poor hand-eye coordination," I tell Keith. "That's what Miss Elk, my teacher, said. She had me practice throwing foamy balls into a small hoop at the back of the classroom."

Keith blinks several times and says, "All you have to do is hit their fucking mouths! How hard is that?" He looks me up and down. "You're tall enough, Per, you could use a little meat on those bones, but if you swung hard, you'd sure as hell hurt somebody."

Keith is both a fighter and a lover. That is what he says.

I cannot punch. I am not a fighter.

But I love. I am someone who loves.

That makes me a lover.

"Okay," I say, and throw another piece of doughnut to the seagulls when I see Keith close his eyes.

12

≈

WINNING TICKET SOLD

That is the Monday-morning headline. I am happy for that person, but Keith and I have to paint underneath a boat. Bottom paint is very thick and we have to stir it with a paddle attached to an electric drill. That is Keith's job. Opening the lid is mine.

POUND! POUND! I use a hammer and a screwdriver. SPLAT! The lid flies off and splashes blue boat paint all over my jacket.

"Shit!" I put my hand over my mouth. I did not mean to say that word. It just flew out past my tongue. I hear Gram in my head. *Wash that mouth out with soap!*

"Perry, I'm surprised at you." Keith only uses Perry when I have done something wrong. He will say, "Perry, you threw away the invoice," or "Perry, you put the label gun in the wrong drawer," or "Perry, where the hell did I put my Camels?"

Painting boat bottoms is hard work because we have to use a roller and hold our arms up high.

"You missed a spot, Per," Keith says. He has to make sure I do a good job.

My shirt is dirty and stiff with paint when I get home. I am sad because it is my favorite shirt and used to be Gramp's. It even has his name written on the front pocket. *George Crandall.* I put it in the washer right away but the paint does not come out. I decide to keep it anyway, and say out loud, "This will be my paint shirt." I try to use Gram's voice.

Gram never threw anything away. I decide that I am just like her, and hang Gramp's shirt back up in my closet.

WINNER HAS NOT COME FORWARD
TO CLAIM 12 MILL PRIZE

The Tuesday headline is still on the front page, but higher. It is right next to the picture of the President of the United States.

How cool, I think. Right next to the President.

Gary has the paper on his desk. I read the story while I wait for him to call the guy to fix our air compressor. It broke after I inflated six fenders in a row. WHOOOSH! And then nothing. I jump and almost wet my pants. Gary calls Fritz Dias on the phone and has him come by. Fritz repairs all our machines.

"What you do, Perry? You broke it? How you do that?" Fritz says, and laughs. He is from Spain or Africa or maybe Germany and very smart about machines. He smiles all the time and has a gold tooth right in front. That is so cool, I think.

"Just the diaphragm. Here, see?" He spreads the parts to the compressor all over the floor.

"You press the button and here, see this? That moves and then over here, see this valve and this hose? The air comes out here."

He talks to me like a real person while he takes it apart. He never treats me like I am retarded. I help by handing him his tools.

"You're a great helper, Perry," he says, only he pronounces my name *Parreeee*.

It takes him all morning to tell Gary that he has to order a new part.

Gary is annoyed and asks, "Don't you have the right diaphragms with you?"

"Why would I have one with me? You're the distributor. Cheaper for you to order, yeah?" Fritz never loses his temper and always smiles showing his gold tooth.

He stays and eats lunch with us. We all buy tuna sandwiches from Marina Handy Mart.

WINNING TICKET COMES FROM
EVERETT MARINA HANDY MART

Wednesday's headline is right in the top middle. I have the day off and go downstairs to pick up Keith's dirty laundry and read the paper. Keith is working in the back office and Manuel is working the register. The newspaper is lying on the counter. Nobody is looking at it, so I borrow the front page and tromp back upstairs. I know Gary will not mind and I can give it back later. I read the story while I cook my oatmeal. It is all about the Marina Handy Mart and there is an interview with the manager, Peter Koslowski. I wonder if Peter and Cherry know the person who won. I fold the Wednesday paper and put it by the door so I do not forget to take it back downstairs to Gary. I can walk over to Handy Mart later and maybe buy a sandwich and talk to Cherry. She will be famous because she works there and they sold the ticket. That is so cool.

I have all my Wednesday chores to do. My oatmeal is too hot to eat, so I start the washer before breakfast. I hear the CHUG CHUG

CHUG of the machine as I pour milk and sprinkle sugar. It is like having company. Keith's jeans are in the first load along with two of my shirts. They are very dirty from all the sanding and painting we have done this week.

The Sunday paper is on my company TV tray and my cereal bowl is on my regular one. Sections of the paper are stacked in a neat pile. I set the comics on the floor and pick up the front page. There is a picture of a turkey farm. It is an interesting story, but sad because it will be Thanksgiving next month and the turkeys will all be dead. I decide that I will not eat turkey this year. I think about Gram. She made good turkey.

The Lotto numbers are in a line at the bottom of the front page.

I do not have to check mine because someone else has already won. I wonder why they have not picked up their money yet. If I won, I would get my money right away. I miss Gram. She would read the numbers and I would check them. I take a bite of oatmeal, then get up and look for my sack. It has flown off my counter and rolled next to the refrigerator. I pull out my Lotto ticket. One edge is still sticky from Manuel's spilled Coke. I go back to the sofa and sit at my TV tray. I make believe Gram is next to me.

"Gram, you want to read the numbers?" I ask.

"Okay," I say.

I pretend I am her.

"Here they are." I set them in front of me on the tray.

There are ten rows of numbers down and six across. Two of them start with 12, two start with 11, and the others are 05, 06, 02, 04, 15, and 09. It is hard to check. The numbers have to be the same and all on the right line. I check each row for the first number listed in the newspaper. It starts with 09.

"Hey, Gram! We have the first number right! Okay, here we go." I try to make my voice like Gram's for *yep*.

"Oh-nine."

"*Yep.*"

"One-oh."

"*Yep.*"

"One-nine."

"*Yep.*"

"Three-two."

"*Yep.*"

"Four-four."

"*Yep.*"

"Four-seven."

"*Yep.*"

"Oh! Oh! Gram! We got all the numbers!" The spit goes out of my mouth. All the numbers are there. I read them twice. I read them again just to make sure. My numbers. It was me all along. I am the winner.

I am lucky!

I jump up so high my cereal bowl flips off my tray. I can hear my feet hit the floor as I dance up and down. *Clump! Clump! Clump!* Oatmeal splashes all over and I slip.

"Holy cow!" I yell. It is okay to say cow. Cow is not a bad word.

Goddamn! I hear Gram say. *Goddamn!*

How much do I win?

Twelve million dollars, I hear her say.

How much is that?

I sit back down on the sofa and bounce.

Perry, it is important to think at times like these. I hear Gram's voice in my head.

Think.

What do you do when you have the lucky numbers? I have to look through all the papers. Sunday. Monday. Tuesday. Wednesday. The paper said no one came in to claim the prize yet. That is because it is me.

I laugh in my head. *Ha! Ha! Ha!* It is me! Then I start to worry. How long do I have before they give my money away? I turn my ticket over. There are instructions on the back.

Claim prizes in excess of $600 at the lottery office in Olympia.

What is excess? Where is the lottery office? I step in more oatmeal. Gram's dictionary is on the floor. Excess. *More than. Surplus.* That is like the Army-Navy Surplus Store where Gram and I used to buy our long underwear. They have more stuff than even Kmart.

"More stuff than you can shake a stick at!" Gram would say as we walked up and down their aisles. They had big dolls dressed up as Navy and Army guys, which are very cool.

I laugh again. "Ha!"

I know twelve million dollars is way more than six hundred.

I need to go to the office in Olympia. My armpits are wet and I am hot. I open my window to cool off. I do not know where to go in Olympia. I do not even know where Olympia is. I look at my ticket. *PO Box 2167, Olympia, WA 98507.* Where is Olympia?

Who should I talk to? Who should I call? I see Gram's blue phone book with the list of emergency numbers. I wonder if this is a family emergency. I wish I could ask Gram. Maybe John knows. He is smart. I dial his number.

"John, can you take me to Olympia?"

"Perry! Why the hell are you calling me? It's the middle of the week, for Christ's sake! I'm busy! Normal people are at work. I'm at work. Find someone else to take you to Olympia." He hangs up before I can take a breath and explain.

When I call David, his answering machine comes on. I drop the phone. It is hard to leave a message. His machine goes too fast. I do not have Louise's new phone number. She changed it after Gram died. Besides, she still scares me.

Be careful, Perry. I hear Gram's voice. I decide to bother Keith at Holsted's.

"Keith, I need to know where Olympia is. I have to go there. It's really important. Can you take me?" I ask.

Keith does not sound at all bothered. "Yeah, great! No problem, Per. Yo will need some gas, but sure, I can take you. Let me tell Gary I gotta take off." He sounds happy even though he is working. Keith is my friend. A friend is someone who does what you want without asking why. I think I have enough money for gas to get to Olympia, but I am not sure. I have written only three checks this week, one for sixteen dollars, one for twenty-seven dollars, and one for twelve ninety-five. Gram always made me use a calculator so I did not make a mistake. My balance is two hundred and forty-four dollars and five cents. This is true or *echt* because I used a calculator.

Echt is a word Gram and I found in *Reader's Digest* Word Power. It was answer C. True or genuine. I use it for important things. Like when I sailed by myself for the first time and when I first met Keith.

Today I won the lottery. That is *echt*.

I count twenty-three ones in my wallet. More dollar bills make me feel rich. Hey, I am rich, I think. I sing in my head and then out loud.

"I am rich. I am rich. I am rich," and bounce on the couch.

13

~~

Gram and I have not had a car since before Gramp died. I hope gas is not more than twenty-three dollars. I hear a honk below my window. BLAAAAH! BLAAAAH! I run down to Keith's truck, but have to run right back up again to get my jacket. Yo's heater does not work and fall is cold in Everett.

"I told Holsted it was an emergency." Keith calls Gary by his last name when he is in a good mood. He turns on the radio to the oldies station.

Keith used to be a hippie, then an army guy, then a ferry captain. Now he is a drunk. That is what he says. Gram used to call him a philosopher.

"That's a five-dollar word!" Keith told her. "A five-dollar word to describe someone who doesn't have a red cent."

Gram just laughed at him. She liked Keith.

We head south down the freeway. I am glad Keith knows which direction to go. Yo is heading south because Keith told me and that is what all the signs say as we whiz underneath. Keith drives extremely fast. Extremely is more than very and not as much as exceedingly. I feel for my lottery ticket through my shirt pocket. It is still there.

"Why do you need to go to Olympia?" he asks.

When I tell him he swerves into the other lane.

"Holy fucking shit! You're fucking kidding me! Right? Holy fuck!" He shakes his head and licks his lips like our collie, Reuben, used to do before we fed him and before he died.

That reminds me. "Hey, I can get a dog!" I tell him.

That is a good idea. I can get a dog again.

Keith's hands are shaking on the wheel.

"Are you sure? Fuck! You need some help on this. Shit!" He gets very quiet. I have my wallet out and lay ten one-dollar bills on the seat.

"Here is for gas. I hope it is enough," I say.

That is all it takes to make him go off again. "Jesus! Shit!"

I hear Gram's voice in my head. *Careful.*

Keith's gray hair is long, greasy, and tied in a ponytail. I think he looks like Willie Nelson from the back. From the front, he looks like an old fat white guy, but I do not tell him this. It would not be nice.

"Where do we have to go?" His hands squeeze the wheel like a sponge.

"PO Box two one six seven Olympia." I read this slowly off the ticket.

"That's only a box number, we need the address. We'll have to ask someone when we get to Olympia." Keith is as smart as John, maybe smarter, even though he is not on my list.

It takes three hours in traffic, plus we do not know exactly where we need to go. We stop at the Pancake House when we finally get to Olympia.

"Everybody knows where the lottery office is! It's just a few blocks over!" That is what Pamela, the cashier, says. We order something to drink and I bounce at the counter. She flutters her eyes at Keith and gives us free refills on our coffee. We are both grinning.

"Did you win or something?" she asks. Her teeth are yellow.

Keith gets quiet and looks at me. I stop bouncing. We push our lips straight.

"No, we just need to find out where it is, just in case," Keith says.

"Yeah, in case," I add.

"That'll be four ninety-eight." She frowns and rings us up. I do not finish my third cup of coffee because it can make you pee and I do not know if the lottery office has a bathroom.

The building we want is eight blocks away. I count. The outside is made of concrete painted light green. There is only a small sign above the door. I am surprised that it is not big and fancy, as they have all that money. The people at the lottery office are friendly and smile. They make me a giant cardboard check and take my picture while I hold it. They tell me I can take it home if I want.

"Won't this be cool to hang up on my wall?" I ask Keith.

"Yeah, it'll be cool all right," he agrees.

I get a copy of the picture right there from an instant camera. I am smiling, but my hair hangs over my eyes. I need a haircut. My ears stick out and my eyes look dark, like Gram's. I think I look pretty good, but Keith pushes my hair off my forehead and says I look goofy. I laugh. Keith is my friend.

He pulls my arm, bends down, whispers in my ear, and gets my neck wet. "You got to get some good financial advice, and not from those brothers of yours!"

"They like me to call them cousins." I feel important. Everybody is looking at me.

"Trust me, they won't after this. They'll be your fucking blood brothers." Keith's eyes are narrow and he has white spit in the corner of his mouth. He looks like that cool jungle guy hunting on Animal Planet. That was when Gram and I could still afford cable and had a TV that worked. This gives me an idea.

"Hey," I say. "I can get Animal Planet now." This makes me excited.

"Hey!" I think of something else. I have a lot of good ideas today. "I can get a TV!"

Margery from the lottery office wants to talk with me.

"Do you have family? I mean someone who helps you," she asks.

I know what she really means. She thinks I am retarded. She thinks I cannot take care of myself. I hate that, and it upsets me.

"Hey, he's not retarded if that's what you're getting at!" Keith yells.

I am glad Keith yelled because my words get jumbled and thick in my throat. I stop being angry and get embarrassed. I feel better when Margery apologizes. She leads us into another office when a bunch of people with cameras and microphones crowd into the main room.

Keith stands behind me full of advice. "Don't take the lump sum!" He hisses like a snake.

"I don't know what you're talking about," I say.

"Take the payments!" he says.

Winning the lottery is very complicated.

First, they ask to see my ticket and a man checks all the numbers. Next, I have to sign the back of the ticket with my address and phone number. Then I show my Washington State Picture ID, Social Security card, and fill out another paper.

I have to fill out lots of paperwork so that Uncle Sam gets his share. I do not have an Uncle Sam. People just say that when they mean taxes. Taxes are something you have to pay even though you do not want to. I ask the lottery people if they want to see anything else. They say no, that's fine. Finally, they ask me what I want to do. They tell me I can get my money once a year for twenty-five years, or all at once. If I take my money all at once, I only get half.

"It's a rip-off, Per. If you take it all you'd only get six mill, plus all the taxes! You'd only end up with three mill at the end."

Three million dollars sounds good to me, but Keith says payments are the way to go.

"You can take sixty days to decide," Margery says. I tell her I do not need sixty days, I can decide right now. Keith is pulling my elbow and patting my back.

"When does he get the money?" He sounds more excited than me. "Take the payments!" He yells this directly into my ear. I have to wipe his wet off my cheek again.

"I want the payments like Keith says so I can buy a TV," I tell her.

Margery looks like she does not think a TV is a good idea. She squeezes her lips tight like Gram used to as she gives me papers to sign. She tells me the amount I will get each year, but I am so excited I forget. Margery tells me to wait while they put a smaller check into an envelope.

Keith remembers for me. "Nearly four hundred fucking thousand dollars a year for twenty-five years!" Keith lectures me about taxes and says, "The fucking government will get a bunch of your money." He tells me I should invest. He says there will be a lot of people who will help me.

I am glad.

"You need to think about what you'll do when you quit working at Holsted's," Keith says. "You can travel. Go to school. Do whatever you want."

That makes me sad. "I don't want to quit my job. I don't want to go to school. I like working at Holsted's!" I say.

I like working with Gary and Keith, but I do not know if they will make me stop working. Maybe there is a rule when you win the lottery you have to give your job away to someone who needs it. I hope not.

Margery leads Keith and me out through a hidden door in the back, but all the men with cameras see us leave the parking lot. As we drive back home, they follow us from lane to lane in blue and silver cars. Keith is a great driver. We double back, make two very exciting turns, and run a red light. It is like a movie when guys are in a car getting away with money from a bank, then almost crashing. Just like that. Yo's tires squeal.

We would have escaped like those guys, except Keith forgets we need gas. We run out just after Tacoma. CHUG! CUNK! Yo went. The reporters from the newspapers and magazines are very nice. They give us a ride to the gas station and talk to me while Keith puts gas in an orange can.

What are you going to do with the money?

How will this change your life?

Do you plan to give any to charity, to your family, to the church?

Do you have brothers or sisters? A wife? A girlfriend?

What does your family think?

The questions come so fast all I can do is smile and nod.

Keith yells while he pumps. "Don't say anything, Per! They can turn what you say around until you don't recognize it. Don't say a word! No! Don't let them take pictures!"

Keith is a good boxer. He misses one reporter, but catches another full in the face and gives him a bloody nose. They don't seem to mind and take us back to Yo anyway. When we get there, a policeman is standing next to Yo writing a ticket.

"When's the last time you registered your truck?" he asks Keith.

I feel bad I got him into trouble. That ticket was probably a lot of money. Keith never told me how much.

"I'm not going to be one of those bloodsuckers," he said.

I wrote him a check for five hundred dollars right there.

"It's a loan," Keith said. "I consider it only a loan. I'll pay you back."

A loan to a friend means you don't have to pay it back. I know this.

"That's okay," I say.

And we get into Yo and drive away.

14

≈

Finding the sun in Washington state is hard, because you have to be in just the right place. The sun hides a lot of the time. I hear the people from California complain to Gary or Keith about never seeing it. But I know the sun is there. You just have to know where to look. I can sit in my room above the Everett Marina and see it in the water like a mirror. When I see extra brightness through the gray clouds, I can tell exactly where it is. It reminds me of how I have to look for Gram now. I look in those places for her.

The sun is red, orange, or maybe yellow and bounces through the sky when I look at it through Yo's back window. It is Yo bouncing, but I pretend it is the sun. I like to bounce.

It takes only two hours for us to get home from Olympia. There is not as much traffic. I look out Yo's window at the sun peeking through holes in the sky, and think about being rich.

I am rich. That is so cool.

When we get back to my apartment, we stomp up the stairs

together and Keith helps me nail my big check on the wall. We use long brass tacks and one of my heavy black dress shoes. POUND! POUND! POUND!

I hear thumps outside.

"Hey, someone's running up the stairs," Keith says.

It is Gary.

"What the hell are you guys doing up here? Sounds like a herd of elephants!" Gary's voice is loud and he looks upset. His office is right underneath my living room. Maybe he thinks the new washer broke down.

"The washer is fine and there are no elephants either," I say, and then I add, "Hey, Gary, guess what? I won the lottery."

He smiles at me. "That's very funny, Perry." Then he stops speaking and his eyes get big. He walks over and touches the check nailed to the wall. His face turns white. Big drops of sweat roll off his forehead. I have to help him sit down on my chair by the door.

His voice comes out hoarse. "Shit! You're kidding, right? Shit! You know what to do? Shit! You have to get some financial advice. Is that the only check they gave you? I mean did they give you a smaller one? They did, didn't they? Can I see it? You'd better put it right in the bank. Shit! We have to take him to the bank, Keith!" Gary has never said that many S-words in a row. His eyebrows are moving and he looks sick. Maybe he has indigestion or a heart attack. People can die from a heart attack.

"You need a Tums, Gary? I got a Tums." I always carried them for Gram. "You want Pepto-Bismol? I got Pepto-Bismol." I have everything. Even Listerine and Ex-Lax. "You need Ex-Lax, Gary?"

My big check is fixed high on the wall behind Gram's couch. The little one that Margery gave me is folded up tight in my wallet. Gary puts his head between his knees and takes deep breaths. Keith has to help me fill out my deposit slip there are so many zeros. I write big, but very neatly. Gram taught me. I have to make the zeros skinny so all of them fit inside the lines.

Gary refuses to ride in Yo, so we ride to Everett Federal in his Jeep Cherokee. Keith and Gary are in front and I sit by myself in the back. I feel important like I am a sports guy just like Tiger Woods, except I am not brown and I do not know how to play golf.

I like going to the bank. I usually walk and it takes twenty minutes. It is cool to ride. They know me at my bank. Every second Tuesday I deposit my check from Holsted's in Everett Federal. Judy, the teller, always smiles and gives me a red-and-white-striped mint along with my receipt. A receipt is a piece of paper that says the bank has your money. Gary gets a parking place right in front, which is very lucky. I watch cars circling around and around trying to find an empty space. Of course, if we had Yo, we could park in handicapped because Yo is a disabled vehicle. That is what Keith says.

The lobby of my bank is crowded, but we do not have to stand in line. Gary whispers to a teller and we cut right to the front. A lady I do not know leads us through a door. I look for Judy behind the counter, but I do not see her.

Maybe this is her day off.

People talk to each other and point. The lady, whose chest tag says *Norma,* gives me five mints. She takes us into a big room with a brown leather couch. It is soft and fluffy, but I am too nervous to bounce. We wait only a few minutes for Mr. Jordan. He is the president of the bank and I am just a little bit afraid.

I wonder if he is related to Michael Jordan.

When he shakes my hand, I have to look up at his face. I think he is just like the basketball player. He is tall, but does not wear Nikes. He has a huge stomach and curly blond hair like Mrs. Callahan's poodle Sparky. Mrs. Callahan lived next door to us before she went to a nursing home. After that, Gram died and I moved away. I do not know what happened to Sparky.

"Well, Mr. Crandall." Mr. Jordan sits down in his chair and leans back. He makes a steeple with his fingers and says, "Well . . . Well . . . Well . . ." over and over.

I sit in a chair across, and Keith and Gary are on either side of me. They are like bodyguards from that movie with the gangsters. This is so cool. I try to decide whether the bank president looks more like a priest or a spider. He smiles like Father Jacob at St. Augustine's. Like he knows me very well. It is spooky. He talks about what the bank can do with all my money. When he uncrosses his legs, I think he looks like a spider.

"We have some excellent and fiscally responsible ideas that would be to your benefit. I can recommend that you—" he says, but does not get to finish because Keith stands up.

"He's not interested," Keith interrupts.

He tells Mr. Jordan that I am considering my options. I like the sound of that. I decide to say I am considering my options, if anybody else asks me about what I am going to do with my money. It sounds really smart.

"Yeah, I'm considering my options," I repeat under my breath so I will remember. I wish I had known those words when the reporters talked to me. Maybe I can call them.

I deposit half of my money into my checking account and the other half into my savings account. That is what I do. Half in checking, half in savings. Gram told me always to use half and save half. Mr. Jordan does not quite look as happy when I leave as when I came. That is okay. I get one hundred dollars cash in ones, fives, and tens from the teller. This makes me feel rich. I have never had that much money at once. Mr. Jordan looks disappointed. He wanted me to buy CDs and T-bills, but I do not know what those are.

Gram said, "If you don't know what something is, don't buy it. Look at this, Perry! All these fools losing their money!" She would laugh and point to the newspaper. "They deserve what they get buying what they don't understand!"

Keith will not tell me what to do. "It's your call, Per, it's your call. You'll have plenty other people telling you what you should do with the money." He shakes his head. "Better you than me, Per, better you than me. I'd just spend it on booze and Mexican babes." Mexican babes cost a lot of dollars.

On the way back to my apartment, we swing by Gilly's and pick up sandwiches for everybody at the store. Keith runs into Marina Handy Mart for beer. Gary does not even frown. All of it is my treat. It makes me feel good that I get to buy beer and sandwiches for everybody.

"This is the best feeling in the world!" I tell them.

15

~~

Keith drinks beer while I straighten my bank papers in a pile on the kitchen counter.

I will need a desk, I decide. Rich people have desks. I chew on a sandwich, sit at my kitchen table, and do my words. I am careful not to spill crab and mayonnaise on my dictionary or in my journal.

"This is the first day that I am rich," I write. Then I remember I was so excited this morning I forgot to do any of my chores. I have to finish my laundry. I look over at Keith. His mouth is open wide, but he is not talking. I hear him grunt. He is stretched out sideways on my couch and his eyes are closed. I get up, remove the can of beer from his hand before it spills, and cover him with Gram's orange and brown knitted afghan. While Keith sleeps, I clean my bathroom and move clothes from the washer to the dryer. While it rumbles CHUG CHUG CHUG, I make a list of what I can buy with my lottery money:

1. Big flat-screen (twenty-seven inches) TV
2. Cable with Animal Planet
3. New jacket (green) with hood

That is as far as I get. My phone rings. I try to grab it fast before it wakes Keith, but he does not stir. His mouth is moving, like he is chewing. He grunts louder and turns over. He sounds more like a pig than a motorcycle. He keeps snoring on the couch. It makes it hard to hear. I put the receiver to my head and cover my other ear.

It is John. I am surprised. I hear the sound of traffic behind his voice.

"I'm in Everett. Where do you live?" He never asked where my apartment was when I moved. John thinks so fast he cannot keep details in his mind. That is what Gram used to say.

"That boy's mind is like a steel trap with the hinges hanging half off," she said.

"My place is above the store," I tell him.

"Where's the store?" He has never come to see me at Holsted's. I tell him it is next door to Gramp's boatyard. He hangs up on me.

My phone rings again right away.

"Oh darling! I just saw the news on the television! Lucky, lucky boy! How is my precious?" I do not know who this is. I do not recognize the voice.

"Miss Elk?" It might be Miss Elk.

"No! Silly! It's your mother! When can I come see you? Tomorrow?" I can hear her breathing through the line. It sounds like she has been running.

"Louise? Are you running?" She has never called me on the phone before. Gram said she was allergic to consideration.

"Only her own feelings, Perry. That's all she ever cares about.

She's allergic to anyone else's but her own. I don't know what my son was thinking," Gram said. "The only thing she's considerate of is someone else's bank account."

Louise's laugh sounds like a tinkling bell. "Sweetie, don't be silly. It's just our little joke. You can call me Mother now. In fact, it's probably better if you do. People might get confused." She hangs up only after I promise to write her a check.

My phone rings again. It is my other cousin-brother, David. He says he is on his way.

"Where are you?" David's voice is hard to understand. He talks low. I hear his wife in the background. *You'd better get your ass over there. Get over there now!*

"Home," I say.

"I'm coming right over." David does not know where I live either. *Ask your brother if John is there.* That is what his wife says.

I look over at Keith. He is still sleeping on Gram's couch. My couch now. When John sat on it at Gram's he said it smelled like cat pee, but it does not. It smells like Gram. That is why I like it. Keith snorts again. I cannot decide whether he has passed out or is just taking a nap. It can be hard to tell sometimes. Seven beer cans are scattered on the floor. Seven is nothing for Keith. I have seen him drink more. I do not drink.

"Has John been there yet?" David asks. I think that is funny.

When John called he asked, "Has David been there?" And when Louise called she asked, "Have your brothers gotten there yet?"

I tell him they will have to talk to each other because I cannot remember where they all are or where they are going. I hear Elaine yelling at him through the phone and he takes a long, loud breath. Gram said that is what my brothers do when they want something and don't want anyone to know it.

"You listen to them breathe, Perry. That'll tell you all you need to know," Gram said.

"Where exactly"—David's words are slow—"is your apartment?" After I tell him, he hangs up.

My dryer buzzes, so I fold the clothes and put Keith's in a separate pile. I go get my Sears catalogue and page through to see what kind of televisions they have. I do not find flat screens, but my catalogue is five years old.

After our TV broke, Gram and I would take the bus to Kmart and watch *Wheel of Fortune* on the new televisions.

"It's the only goddamned thing worth watching on TV, now that *Let's Make a Deal* is off the air," Gram said. We would pretend to choose which one to buy. I wish I won the lottery when she was alive. She would really love having a TV again. Flat screen. A big twenty-seven-incher. Gram liked *The Price Is Right* and *Days of Our Lives* even though she would complain when she watched them.

"No, you're bidding too high!" she would yell.

"Lower! Lower! You'll go over!" She would motion with her thumb.

"Can't you see he's lying to you? Goddamned! They're all so ignorant!" She would shake her head, disgusted. Gram said most people have no common sense. "They just have no sense, Perry!"

She got so loud one time the Kmart guy asked us to leave. I was embarrassed, but Gram was not.

"Never feel bad when you have to leave somewhere," she would say. "The other person is only showing their lack of consideration."

Consideration is when other people want you around and do not ask you to leave. Even when you are loud. That is consideration. I do not have time to think about that anymore because there is a banging on my door so loud my teeth rattle.

"It's me. John! Open up!" I recognize John because his voice has a growling shout. I laugh because it is funny when people tell you things you already know.

"Ha!" I laugh. "Ha! Ha!"

"Don't play games!" John calls out through the door. "Open up!" I count to five then turn the knob. John sounds angry, but the kind of angry that he does not want me to know about. Like the time he found out about Gram's house.

Keith tells me I should be more careful of John.

"He's like a junkyard dog, fine until you have him trapped in a corner," Keith says.

I laugh to imagine John a dog.

"His wife, CeCe, has a dog," I said to Keith. "A tiny pink poodle named Gigi."

Keith snorted when I told him that. "It figures!" he said.

I hear Gram say *be careful* and *junkyard dog* in my head.

"Well, my brother is quite the lucky one." John's breath comes hard like he has been exercising. His smile reminds me of the piranha I saw on Discovery Channel, all pokey with teeth. "You need to pack a suitcase. On the other hand, don't bother. We'll get you new clothes. Yours smell like that old couch." He paces across the floor as he says this and chews on the end of one finger.

This surprises me. He has never offered to buy me anything. Gram always said when a person offers to do something it is usually to their advantage. I wait.

"We have the spare room all set up, you can stay with CeCe and me. You can't stay here. People are going to descend on you like a swarm of flies." He looks at his hand. Picks a finger and starts to nibble the nail.

When Gram died, John's spare room was torn up. I am happy for him it is fixed now.

"I'm okay." I stop speaking when I see John's face move. His eyebrows go down and his lips get small like they used to when he talked to Gram. Small and tight like when she told him she would not invest her savings in his projects or lend him money. Right now, I would rather decide which TV I want to buy than talk to John. He does not look like he is interested in what I want to do.

"Who's he?" John points to Keith asleep on the couch.

"My friend Keith." I tell him.

"See, they're after you already! You've got to be careful," John warns.

"Hey! That's what Gram said!" But he does not seem to hear me. I am uncomfortable. My neck itches. I do not know why John is here. He has never come for a visit before.

My knocker rattles again. John pushes past me to open the door. It is David. This makes me upset.

"It is not nice to open other people's doors," I tell John.

"I can't believe you won the lottery!" David smiles and tries to shake my hand, but John steps in front, blocking him.

"Don't you mean *we*?" John smiles so wide his teeth and gums show. He pokes David's shoulder.

"No, I mean Perry, you moron!" David pushes him away.

"Who are you calling a moron, you pipsqueak?" John says.

It is rude to call someone a moron.

It is also rude to call someone a pipsqueak.

They are both so loud Keith wakes up. "What the hell!" His eyes look like bottle caps, all round and white around the edges. Keith rolls off the couch onto the floor. That had to hurt. I do not have carpet on my floor, only brown speckled linoleum tile. I am afraid that David and John will fight with each other and I want them to go away.

Fighting is rude.

"Go away," I say. When they do not listen, I sit down on the couch. There is more room now that Keith has fallen off.

"I'm surprised that wife of yours let you out of her sight. As long as you're here, make yourself useful. Tell Perry he needs to come with me."

"Why you? Just what are you planning?" David's chin juts out. He pokes his brother in the chest.

John's teeth are bared. He looks like his wife's dog, Gigi, except he is bigger and does not have curly pink hair and a bow.

"We need to decide what to do. Take charge of this situation." His chin wiggles and shakes like Jell-O or maybe Santa, I decide. He is frowning like a Halloween pumpkin.

"Ha! He's got two holidays, Keith!" I laugh.

John scowls at me and David scowls at John. Keith is crawling around on the floor trying to wake up.

"What's so funny, Perry?" John yells.

"He's just nervous. He's not responsible. Someone has to take care of him, watch out for him," David says. "Elaine says he can stay with us."

"*Elaine says! Elaine says! Elaine says!*" John makes his voice high like a girl's and pushes David's shoulder. "Is that all you can say? Perry needs to stay with me and CeCe!"

I did not need to be taken care of or watched when Gram died. But now I do.

"I think you both have worn out your welcome." Keith is not tall when he is on his hands and knees, but when he gets to his feet, he looks fierce. Just like the Hulk, only he is not green and his shirt is not ripped.

John and David end up going out the door very fast. Keith's foot is right behind them. He is a good boxer even without his hands. Keith slams the door so hard the window shudders.

"I can sue you for assault! I can sue!" I hear John shout as his feet make loud tromps down the stairs. Sue means that you will get back at someone when they do something you do not like. Sue is also a girl's name.

"Over my dead body, assholes! Over my dead body! You two don't fool me!" Keith yells through the door. "No siree, Bob! I'm not fooled!"

Not being fooled is what everybody says when they are.

16

≈

Gram started a baby book, my first book, when I was born. It had my picture from the hospital when I looked like a monkey.

"All babies look like monkeys, Perry, every single one," Gram said.

"Do monkey babies look like humans to other monkeys?" It was something I wondered.

"Don't be smart!" Gram said.

I learned to print my name with Gram's help when I was six. Gram helped me write in my baby book. Inside we put pictures of me and Gram and Gramp. Each time we finished a page we would go on to the next. When I was seven my book was full and Gram bought another.

Now I have to buy my own books. I keep my words and ideas in them. I have lots of ideas and lots of books. Gram told me if I wrote smaller I would not need so many, but I like to write big. And pictures. I like to put pictures in. I have nineteen books. I am on book twenty.

With Gram gone I have to not forget. Not forgetting is hard. I have to work hard to not forget. Remembering is different than not forgetting. It is the opposite of. Remembering is like a little movie that comes back to you. It is something special and unexpected. Like when I remembered the first time Gramp took me sailing. A little movie.

Not forgetting is business. Like you have to not forget that your laundry is in the dryer or not forget to pay your bills. Remembering is fun. Not forgetting is hard. Writing helps me to not forget.

I came to live with Gram when I was just a baby. I do not remember when I was one year old, or two, or three, but Gram did. I like to read my first book again from the very beginning, whenever I miss Gram.

Sat up by himself—ten months.

Walked—two years.

First word Ga! for Gramp—two and a half years. George was so proud of him!

George was my Gramp. I like to know that he was proud of me.

I read silently but sometimes my lips move over the hard words. I can feel them.

Gram wrote chapters in my first book like this.

One year old.

Two   ”   ”

Three   ”   ”

Those little marks save time. They look like teeth. They are like words. That is so cool. They mean that things are all the same. Or they mean whatever you want them to. I do not remember much about when I was that little. It is fortunate that Gram wrote everything down in my baby book. That way I can read it over and over.

There are other things inside my book. Letters in Gram's handwriting stamped with *Return to sender* on the envelope.

> *Dear Louise,*
> *Gramp and I have no problem keeping Perry, but you have to be a part of his life. All boys need their mothers. . . .*

> *G.J.,*
> *We need to hear from you. We need to know why . . .*

G.J. is my father. That is what Gram said. I think his name was George too. But he was called G.J. His name is only letters.

"He's your father, but he's no son of mine. No son of mine!" Gram would say.

Louise was a lawyer's wife. That is different than a plain mother. They do not have to keep all of their children. Gram said she and Gramp needed me so Louise lent me to them. They liked me so much they kept me for good. That is cool.

There is a picture of me as a baby crawling. It is taped to one page. Gram's handwriting is underneath. *Perry loves his Gramp and follows him around like a puppy.* I laugh. I like to think of myself as a puppy. There is another one of me in our boat. I have a red hat with matching mittens. Gram's words are above. *Perry went sailing with Gramp. He's picked it up real fast and is learning to work the tiller.*

Gram wrote all the things I could do and how old I was.

Perry is reading words now. That teacher doesn't know what she is talking about. He reads signs and we do the crossword together. I tell him to print the words and which square to put them in and he does a real good job.

Doing things faster, better, and bigger is important to people.

"It's like a contest for moms if a baby weighs more, is taller, or walks first. A goddamn contest!" Gram said this when I had trouble reading and writing in school. My teachers would invite all the parents to meetings and Gram would come. She would collect my papers and bring them home and we would work together to make them better. Her voice would get soft and low when she told me about how mad she got during those school meetings. The teachers would call me names. School meetings are called conferences. Conferences are when the teacher tells you how bad your kid is. The teachers would all say different things.

Maybe Downs, but he doesn't look it.

He is borderline. Not developing normally.

You have to accept the fact that Perry is retarded ... mildly retarded.

"It's like they're talking about a goddamn cheese, Perry! Mild shmild my ass!" Gram said.

They put me in Special Ed.

"There's nothing special about it! It's just a bunch of names! Perry, you're just slow and that's not a bad thing. You'll still end up at the same place. People like names. It makes them feel superior," Gram said.

Superior is when somebody thinks they are better than you, only they are not.

Gram always laughed when she read all the stuff about schools and teaching in the news, especially when I got older.

"Education shmeducation. Those politicians don't know a goddamned thing! It's them that needs educating." And "Look, Perry, we could sue the sonsabitches if you were going to school now!" Then she would do her witch-cackle laugh. She made sure I knew all the new names. Each year they were different.

"Hey, Perry, you would be cognitively challenged now! Just like your brothers, only they're morally challenged!" She pointed to the articles in magazines or newspapers.

Challenged. I liked that. We are all challenged. Challenged means you have obstacles to overcome. Gram read up on something called learning disabilities.

"Perry, I bet you had some of those and we never even knew it."

I told her I did not think so. I was just slow. That was hard enough. I did not want her to give me anything else.

I keep looking through my book.

SCHOOL. MY FIRST memories of school. I was six years old. I know this because Gram wrote pages about it in my book. This is one of my first memories, but it was not a good one. I cried. You cannot go into school if you do not poop and pee in the toilet. I was scared. The teacher did not tell me where the potty room was and my poop went into my pants. I laughed because I was scared. It was all warm and runny. I laugh when I am scared or nervous. I do not know why it just comes out. Gram said I get anxious easily. Anxious is when you are not sure what other people will do. My teacher, Miss Kathy, called Gram on the phone. I went home with Gram and she cleaned me up. For a while I went to school only in the morning. Gram would meet me at the door of my class.

School was scary and fun. There were some kids who were fun to play with. I thought that was neat. But then there were other kids. Other kids who laughed and pushed me down in the dirt. I got a bloody nose once. No. Three times. Three times, I got my nose all bloody. Most of the kids in our neighborhood stopped playing with me when they went to school. Like Kenny. He lived down the street. After he made me eat dog biscuits, Gram would not let me go over to his house anymore.

I turn five pages in my book and I am eight years old.

Eight. Gram said eight is great. That was a poem. It sounded the same. Eight is great. I remember Gram gave me a card to celebrate. I still have it tucked inside my book as a marker. Celebrate. That is another word. It means good fun. Eight-is-great-we-celebrate. I went poop and pee in the toilet all the time. I could stay dry all day in school and not have an accident.

Gram said, "Goddamned that's amazing." I know this because of my card and Gram would tell me.

There is a picture of me standing on the sidewalk in front of our house. I am holding up my bike. It is way too big for me. Our house was on a long straight road with bushes and it was made of brick on the bottom and wood painted white on top. I helped paint the wood twice. The first time was when I helped Gramp. I was fourteen. The second time I was twenty-nine. Gramp was dead and our ladder broke. I was too heavy for it I think. We would have had to paint again when I turned forty-four. Gram would have been ninety-nine. But Gram is dead and our house is sold. Gone. It is torn down now. There was a big sign that said something else would be built. I forgot what. A computer store I think.

Thinking about these things reminds me of Gram and Gramp's boxes. They are still stacked in a corner of my bedroom. I go in, pick one up, and put it on the bed. It is heavy and the cardboard is all bent. I have to get a knife from the kitchen and cut the tape that holds it closed. Papers are on top. I lift them off. There is a scrapbook. I open it. Sailboat pictures. A man holding a trophy in the air and smiling. I look on the back. *George Crandall.* Gramp.

Gram always said I looked like him except my ears stuck out. I go into the bathroom to check. My eyes are dark brown like Gram's were. Gramp had blue eyes. My hair is the same color as Gramp's except his was gray too. He was taller than me when he was alive, but I have grown. Maybe we are the same tallness now, but I do not know. I put the picture up against the mirror and stare at both faces.

My face is fatter. I turn sideways. Gramp's belly stuck out, but mine does not. My legs are okay, but my arms look thinner. Am I skinny? I will have to ask Keith about that.

I walk back into the bedroom and set the picture on the bed. There are many pictures of boats. Yellow ones. Blue ones. Old newspaper clippings.

YOUNG COUPLE SAILS TO SOUTH PACIFIC
ON 32-FT CRAFT

The newspaper stories are cut out and pasted in order in a scrapbook.

LOCAL RACER VICTORIOUS

Victorious means you win stuff. There are plans of sailboats and drawings. The box is full of other things. A small flag. *Waikiki Yacht Club*, it says. That is in Hawaii. Keith told me. The logbooks are full of writing. I set them aside to read later. I start out sad, but now am happy. These were Gram and Gramp's things.

One carton is too heavy for me to carry. Keith dragged it from the back of Yo when he helped me move from the house.

"Keith is strong as a bull," Gram said. "You can always depend on Keith."

I cut it open. On top is a stack of envelopes with my name written on the outside. My school papers. I set these aside and lift out another box underneath. It is latched and feels soft like leather or plastic. I cannot tell the difference. Plastic is fake and leather comes from cows. They have to kill them to get their skin. This makes me sad again. I open the box. For a moment, I do not know what it is, then I remember. It is Gramp's record player. I unwind the cord and look at it closely.

Record players are very old. No one uses them anymore. Manuel carries an iPod and Keith has tapes. I do not know what Gary has.

I wonder if it works. There is an outlet on the wall and I set the player on the floor and plug it in. Nothing happens. Wait. There is an on-off switch on the side, and I push. The turntable spins.

"Ha!" I laugh and jump because I scared myself. I go back into the bigger box. Gramp's records. I take one out. The cardboard cover is stiff as I slide the black disk out. There is a picture of an orchestra on the front. A man playing the piano. *Vivaldi*, it says. *The Four Seasons* is written across the top.

I put the record on and place the needle like I remember Gramp doing.

It is music. His music.

It is wonderful music.

I sit and listen to the sounds until it is dark.

17

≈

"T his is the hard part," Keith says. He is talking to Gary. "It's hard to know who to trust. How much do you know about those brothers of his, anyway?" He takes a long drag of his cigarette. Keith smokes Camels. The package is very cool and has the picture of a camel and a pyramid. I eat Hershey's Kisses while Gary and Keith talk.

"John's a lawyer and David has some kind of accounting business. The wives are a couple of gold diggers. That's all Gram would say. I've only heard rumors through the grapevine. Nothing specific." Gary does not smoke. He coughs and tells me to open my window. It is late fall and I am cold, but I open the window anyway. He told me to. He is number three on my list.

"Then we have to keep our eyes open and make sure they don't try anything underhanded. I don't trust lawyers farther than I can kick them in the ass." Keith blows smoke up into the air.

Gary is searching through his pockets. I can tell he is looking for his bottle of Afrin.

"I can't imagine they'd try anything overtly illegal. Besides, they have money of their own. Why would they try to get Perry's?" he says.

"You're fucking naive, Gary. Those kind, they never have enough money. I think we should get Per his own lawyer."

"I think we should ask Perry. It's up to him." Gary turns to look at me. "Perry, what do you want to do?" he asks.

"Nothing. Eat my Kisses." Then I remember. "Let's go get my TV. I haven't bought a TV yet."

"Yeah, we'll get your TV." Keith squashes his cigarette out in my sink. I hope he will clean it up, but it looks like he won't.

Gary and Keith are my best friends. Gary has been my friend the longest even though he is my boss. He knew my Gramp and Gram from when they had the boatyard and he knew me when I was younger. I do not remember ever not knowing Gary Holsted, but I remember when I first met Keith. I even remember the second time. Keith's first day at Holsted's.

"Perry, you remember Keith? You'll be working together," Gary said.

I was nervous because I was still not used to Holsted's and the customers scared me.

"Of course he remembers. It was only yesterday. Come on, Per, help me unpack these boxes," Keith said. He called me Per for short. Right from the very first. Just like we were good friends. I felt better right away, because he remembered my name and helped me unpack boxes. Keith and I have been best friends ever since.

Right now Keith paces in a circle. His feet thump on my floor. We have to stay in my apartment for privacy. That is so no one else can hear our secrets. Manny is by himself downstairs watching the store.

He has asked me to call him Manny now. That is cool. He wants to be friends.

"When those brothers of yours call you, tell them you don't need their help." Keith puts another cigarette between his lips. I watch him hunt through his pockets.

"I don't need their help," I say.

"That's right!" Keith bends down and uses my stove for a light.

"Hey, Keith, that is dangerous. You can blow your face up like that!" I sound just like Gram. She used to say you could lose an arm out of a car. She would make me roll up Yo's passenger-side window so I could not wave my hand out in the air and make it fly around when Keith drove fast.

"That's a good way to lose a finger," she said whenever I used the blender.

Gram was very smart. She knew all the ways a person could get hurt and lose something. Gary lectures just like Gram used to while I eat my sandwich. He says I should invest the money for my future. Invest means you give other people your money. People worry a lot about the future. Gram told me to worry too, but I think the future is going to come whether you worry about it or not. If it does not come, then you are dead and you do not have to worry anymore. I think about my future, and I save, but I do not worry. I listen to Gary like I used to listen to Gram. He tells me what I can do with my money and asks me questions.

"There are things you can buy called mutual funds that invest in a lot of different businesses and you earn dividends or interest. For example, what kind of businesses are you interested in?" he asks.

"Stores where you buy things for boats," I tell him. "Like your store, Gary. I know a lot about your store."

I get a really good idea.

"Can't I invest in your store? How about I invest in your store?" I ask.

Gary shakes his head like our collie Reuben used to when he got wet. "No, Perry, I'm not looking for a partner. I mean, I'd like to expand. Who wouldn't? But a partner? I don't think so."

Keith stands up and puts his cigarette out in his empty beer can. It sizzles. I hope he will not just throw it in my garbage can. It might not be out. It could start a fire.

"Why not?" he asks. "Why not let him invest in your store?"

"Jeez! I don't know. I never thought about it. I don't know if the business could support another person. We're small. Things have been tough. The competition is getting tougher. I can't afford to go under like George." Gary sighs so loud his lips vibrate like a snore.

I know they are talking about Gramp. Keith walks back and forth in front of my couch. "No, Gary, think about it. It's a good plan. He likes it here. This is a good place. You think those brothers of his and their wives are ever going to leave him alone now?"

They are talking about me now. I want to remind them that I am still here listening, but I do not. Gary's head is slick and shiny. He used to have more hair. It was brown, the same color as mine. He takes it from the side and combs it up over the bald place, but it does not stay. He tells me his head is too hot for hair, but I think it is from him worrying. Worries just tumble in your head and can push hair out from the inside. This is what I believe. Keith stops to take a bite of his sandwich. This is unusual because he always talks with his mouth full.

Gary waves his hands around. "Look, I've known Perry ever since he was little. In fact, I've known the whole damn family even before the boatyard fiasco. You can't tell me G.J. didn't have a finger in that pie, for Pete's sake! I'm sure his sneaky wife, Louise, did." He is getting excited and has to use a spray bottle up his nose again. He is allergic to everything, especially excitement.

I do not think it is nice to call Louise sneaky. She does not like being called Mother and I am sure she would not like being called sneaky. Listening to Gary and Keith talk is interesting. I play auditor and say nothing.

"You should think about it seriously. I mean it. Look at all the improvements you could make. Maybe hook up with Carroll's Boatyard. There's a hell of an opportunity here, Gary. The Everett waterfront is going to take off soon. Look at what's happened in Seattle. You need to be able to take advantage when the time comes."

There is that word again. *Advantage.*

Keith sits back down on my couch. It makes a squeak like a fart and I laugh.

It is good to talk about investments and it makes me think. I could be a businessman. I could be an investor in Holsted's Marine Supply. Investor. That sounds so cool. I get up and walk around my apartment while Gary and Keith finish eating. I am excited. Way too excited to even bounce. I think about how much I like my apartment. I can look at the boats out my window. It does not have a yard, but that is okay because I definitely do not like mowing grass or pulling weeds. I would need a yard if I got a dog, unless I walked it every day, but then I could get a cat. Cats don't need yards. Cats are cool. I worry that Gary does not want me as an investor.

"Gary, let me be an investor. Please—" I do not finish because Keith interrupts me.

"At least think about it, Gary, okay?" Keith asks.

"I'll think about it." Gary rolls his sandwich paper into a ball and throws it into my trash can in the kitchen. He makes a basket. As he goes out the door, he asks, "You guys coming?"

Keith said, "Nope, we got a TV to buy. We'll be in later." Then he asks me, "You ready to go?"

I jump up on the end of my toes. "Sure!" I say.

I put on my jacket and we go downstairs to Yo.

When we get to Everett Mall, we have to park at the far end of the lot. All the handicapped spaces are taken. This pisses Keith off.

"You can't tell me there are this many crippled people at the mall! It's the middle of the day, for Pete's sake! Fuck! They should all be at work!"

"Crippled is like retarded, Keith. Don't say that," I tell him.

"Okay, then, gimps."

"No. That's not nice either. Say people who have trouble walking."

Keith does not care about being nice and he grumbles so I can hardly understand him, "People who . . . trouble . . . walking."

That's okay.

Everett Mall has Christmas decorations up already and it isn't even Halloween. At the entrance, there is a person dressed in red ringing a bell over a big pot hanging from a stand.

"Any change? Any spare change?" The man sings and his bell clangs.

"I have money," I say, and stop to dig in my pocket. Keith grabs my shoulder and my money misses the black kettle and falls to the ground.

As Keith drags me inside through the big double doors, the man picks up the bills and calls out, "Bless you! Merry Christmas! Bless you, my son!"

"We don't have time for that! Here's the directory. Where you want to go first?" Keith asks. A directory is a mall map.

"To a TV place," I say.

"There ya go, Per. Top Electronics. Second floor. Middle."

"I smell cookies." My stomach gurgles.

To get upstairs we have to pass the food court, where the cookie smell is coming from. We stop for hot cocoa and chocolate chip cookies while we watch the Christmas display with trains being set up. Afterward we had to watch aerobics on the stage.

"Look at them puppies bounce." Keith likes watching other people exercising, especially women. I have to push him along. We window-shop for a while, but when Keith stops talking and looks bored, I know it is time to get my TV.

The man at the TV store has a name tag that says *Patrick Perry*.

"Hey, my name's Perry L. Crandall. We have the same name," I say.

"Welcome to Top Electronics. How can I help you?" He looks at Keith.

"My friend here needs a TV. You probably should be talking to him." Keith rolls his eyes when he is annoyed.

Patrick shows us a small white television in the corner. "This is our least expensive model. It's a good value." He starts messing around with the dials.

I walk over to the big flat screens. "I need a bigger one. How about this?" I point to one hanging on the wall.

Patrick motions to another television. "These are probably more affordable for you."

I can tell Keith is getting even more annoyed.

"I have plenty of money," I say, and watch as Keith's mouth puckers.

Patrick smiles and winks at Keith. "I'm sure you do," he says.

"How about this one?" Keith walks over and touches the biggest plasma screen in the store.

Patrick looks confused. "It's over a thousand."

Keith points to me and says, "I see you haven't met my friend Perry Crandall. You know Perry L. Crandall? *The* Perry L. Crandall? *The brand-new lottery winner? That* Perry L. Crandall?" Keith's face ge ts closer to Patrick's with each word and his finger jabs his chest right under his shiny black name tag.

"You want a stand with that?" Patrick talks to me directly.

For one thousand eight hundred eighty-three dollars and forty-five cents, I buy a twenty-seven-inch plasma TV. For three hundred dollars, I get a stand to put it on.

"We got a sale on stereos. You want a stereo? A DVD player?" Patrick looks like he is dizzy.

He sits down on a console when I say, "Sure!"

"You need a Tums?" I ask. But he says no.

I have to write three checks because I keep finding things to buy. Patrick says he will have his helpers take everything out to Yo when we are finished shopping.

"Thank you very much, Mr. Crandall. Thank you very much." He shakes my hand hard. His palm is sweaty.

"Hey, Keith, I don't have any music except for Gramp's records." I remember this when we walk past a music store. Sam's Music and Movies. I have no idea what to buy, but Keith helps.

"You got to have the Doobie Brothers, and here, Per, some Eagles, the Beatles . . ." Keith collects an armful. "*Aha!* The Grateful Dead! Oh, and Jimmy Buffett!"

I walk over to the movie section and pick out ten right away. I have to go over to the register and set them down on the counter so I can go get more. The lady at the counter frowns and folds her arms.

"This is ridiculous. You're going to have to put all these back! You've got over five hundred dollars worth of stuff here!" She glares at me and her glasses slide down her nose. "Don't you look at prices? Can't you add?"

"Here's the number for Mr. Jordan at the bank. He'll tell you Perry's check is good." Keith is smiling like he is enjoying causing a scene. I am worried that I will not get to buy my movies. The cashier is on the phone to my bank when her manager comes out from the back room. He stops when he sees me and holds out his hand.

"Hey, aren't you the guy who just won the lottery? You are, aren't you? Perry? Perry Crandall from Holsted's?" He turns to the lady at the register. "His picture is in today's paper. He just won twelve million dollars in the lottery! Jesus! How lucky can you get!"

Other people in the store crowd around. I start to feel uncomfortable. One man taps my shoulder, for luck, he says. The cashier introduces herself as Shirley.

"Shirley Nelson, uh, you can call me. Here's my number if you, uh, need anything."

Keith grabs the paper. "I'll take that," he says.

The manager lets me buy whatever I want. He gives me two free movies he thinks I might like. I give Shirley a CD of Smashing Pumpkins to say thank you.

She smiles and says, "Come back again anytime."

She likes me now, even though she does not know me.

Everybody at the mall was nice and none of them even knew me.

18

≈

My teacher is Miss Elk. I like school. My words are *clone, clop, close, close, close, closed,* and *closed circuit,* which is like being on TV. It would be cool to be on TV."

This is what I said when I gave my report in Miss Elk's class. She was nice. I remember how smart she made me feel. I remember her class. It was small and special. That is what the other teachers called us. Special.

"*Close* is an interesting word. There are lots of them. They are spelled the same, but sound different. It can be confusing. For example, you can close the door or someone can be close to you. Or you can be close but no bananas. That is what my Gram says." I did show-and-tell on my dictionary words.

"Very good, Perry. You are smart to read the dictionary. Words are the key." Miss Elk and Gram had the same ideas about words.

Miss Elk was my best teacher. I was ten years old when I went to her special class. She was the best special teacher I ever had. Special means very good or better. Or it can mean a class that you go to at school. She liked me so much she kept me for two years. I was her helper. She taught me to read better and I loved her. I told her I would marry her when I got older. She laughed and said she was already married. It ended up being a good thing. She would have been way too old for me, Gram said.

School can be a scary place. I remember I wanted to go like all the other kids. You got to ride on a bus. It was yellow and the driver yelled and smoked cigarettes. He threw the butts out the window. You can say the word *butt* if it is a cigarette butt. If you mean rear end, it is not nice. Sometimes he would miss the window and they would fly down the aisle and make sparks. The big boys in the back would pick them up and try to smoke them. That was gross. They would punch me in the head as they got off the bus. Anytime they passed me, they shoved, pushed, and took my papers or called me retard. They did not know my class was special.

I always wondered why. It was one of my wonders when Gram and I would talk.

"Why are people mean?" I would ask. "Why do they call me names? Why?"

I still do not know.

Gram could not answer me either. "I don't know, Perry. I just don't know. People can be cruel."

"Everybody belongs to the world. Everybody has a right to be here," Miss Elk said. I like that. Everybody belongs. The end of my second year with Miss Elk I found out I liked to read. It was strange. Just like a mystery. One minute it was hard and the next it was fun. Gram was impressed and wanted me to stay with Miss Elk all the time, but the principal said no. Then Miss Elk went away.

My next teacher made me sit by myself in a regular class.

"This is Perry, everyone. He is special. He will be joining our class. Can you say hello to Perry? He will be sitting back here with Missus Kennedy. Perry? Have a seat."

"Can't I sit over there? Can't I sit with the other kids?"

She told me no. She said to be quiet and sit down.

I had something called pullout. When the class got too fast for me, I was pulled out so I would not slow the other kids down. Missus Kennedy helped me two times a week. The other times I just sat.

"Can I sit with the other kids?" I asked. The teacher sent notes home.

He is a disruption.

He is negatively influencing the classroom environment.

The other children are affected.

This is not working.

She said I was included.

We have inclusion here. No more Special Ed. This is the least re-strictive environment.

The other children cannot learn when you make faces in the back, Perry.

"Can I sit with the class?" I asked again. I only stuck my tongue out once. Maybe twice. I was bored.

"No! I have had enough! You are disruptive and disrespectful!"

The principal came to our class.

My teacher complained. "I simply cannot teach a student this cognitively challenged." She meant retarded.

I was thirteen. I was too tall to stay in elementary school, so Gram took me home. She did not want me to go to junior high. The school sent us letters. Gram wrote on them in felt pen.

MOVED.

NO LONGER AT THIS ADDRESS.

NO ONE HERE BY THAT NAME.

WE DON'T LIVE HERE ANYMORE.

I missed riding the bus to school, but Gram showed me how to ride the Everett city bus down the hill to Gramp's boatyard. I would go there to work for Gramp after my lessons with Gram. Gramp and I would come home together in time for dinner. We would have chicken or meat loaf or tuna casserole. Those were good times. Gram did not have the evil arthritis and Gramp was not dead.

One of my favorite things was doing knots with Gramp. I am a good knot person. I can do figure eight and slip and bowline. I can do all those knots. I liked to read about boats and sailing and I sat in Gramp's office and looked at books. It was my job to answer the phone.

"Crandall's Boatyard. Perry L. Crandall speaking," I would say. "Can I help you?"

After Gramp died, we had a problem. It had to do with money. We did not have the boatyard and we did not have the money.

"We lost the boatyard," Gram would say, and then she would throw a dish or plate. It was good that we had melamine. I did not see how we could have lost it because it was right where Gramp left it. But it had to be sold. Gary Holsted and Gram talked at our house and then I worked for him at Holsted's Marine Supply right next door to our old boatyard.

"He's the only friend we have, Perry," Gram would say, "the only friend." And she would not say anything more. Just like when I would ask her about my father.

"Never you mind, Perry. Never you mind," and her lips would disappear.

19

get a lot of mail. Six or twenty letters a day, sometimes more. I never got much mail before, but I get mail now. Some of them say the same thing. Some of them are different.

Dear Lottery Winner . . .

To the Lucky Lottery Winner . . .

To Mr. Perry Crandall, Lottery Winner . . .

I make a big pile on my counter because I do not know what to do with them all. Gram said that if someone you do not know sends you something, it is probably a bad thing. Some of the letters look important with big black writing. Others have lots of tiny print that is hard to read and have empty checks inside. Still others tell me sad stories. There is one about a kid with cancer. Another one is from a person who says we are cousins and he lost his job. Other letters tell me about dying orphans in Africa and Kentucky. That is sad. Orphans have a tough enough time without parents. It was sad that they have to die too.

There are people standing outside my door. Some of them I know, like my teacher Miss Elk from school. She wants to shake my hand and ask me to donate to her new school. That is cool.

"How much do you want?" I ask.

"How much can you give?" she asks.

"How much do you want?" I ask.

"How much can you give?" she asks.

I write her a check for five hundred dollars. That is all the zeros that I can fit in the line without Keith's help.

The guy Chuck, from bingo, with Mary Margaret from St. Augustine's, came over to say "Hi!" and that was cool too.

"The poor of our community need your help."

"How much help do they need?" I asked.

It was for church and church is good. I gave them a check for five hundred dollars. They wanted five thousand, but Gram always said you do not give people what they want. It is bad for them.

"Hey! Perry! Long time no see!"

I do not know this man. "Who are you?" I ask him.

"Kenny! Kenny Brandt! Don't you remember me? We were buddies growing up! You remember me now? I lived down the street from you in the yellow house. Remember?" His blond hair is thin on top and he is shorter and skinnier than me. He could be my ex-neighbor Kenny. I have not seen him for a long time and do not recognize him, but he says that is who he is.

"So you got anything to spare for old times' sake? I lost my job. My wife left me. I could use a few bucks." He looks like a squirrel. His lips are moving fast, like when they chew their nuts.

"I'm sorry," I say. Having no job is hard, but I have a good idea. "Hey! I know! You can talk to Gary. Gary Holsted? He finds jobs for people. Gary could find you a job." I go to get a pen out of my drawer. Kenny smiles when he sees me write.

"Here is Gary's phone number. Call him, okay? And then—" I do not have time to finish.

Kenny looks down at the piece of paper and then at me and then down at the paper.

"Screw you! Screw you, asshole! I need money, not a frigging number!" He throws the paper at me and stomps out the door slamming it behind him. I do not have time to write him a check. He leaves before I can.

When Keith and Gary come upstairs, they chase everybody away. Gary says we need a security guard to keep intruders out. I laugh. That is my job. I am security. I stay above Holsted's at night and listen for intruders. Intruders are like burglars. These people are not intruders. They knocked first and then I opened my door and let them in.

My family calls me all the time now.

Nobody shouts, except for John and sometimes Elaine. Keith says they will never leave me alone now, but I do not want to be left alone.

"This is disgusting!" Keith says. Disgusting means that people disappoint you and do things you do not like.

"Bloodsuckers! Vultures! Hyenas!" Keith's face is all red and blotched. "Listen, Perry, this is important. Are you listening?" I have to listen because Keith's mouth is in front of my face. His breath smells like dog poop and beer. I do not tell him this. It definitely would not be nice.

"Yeah." I am an auditor. I listen.

"Your family is up to no good! Your brothers are up to no good," Gary says.

"Ha! That's what Gram always told me."

Gary and Keith stare at me, and then look at each other. Keith grabs his hair with his hands. Gary sighs again very loud.

"Perry, I'm serious here. You have to promise me not to fill out or sign anything anybody sends you. *Anything!* Do you understand?" Gary's voice is low and he sounds worried.

"Yeah." I have to think about that for a minute. Do not sign anything means sign nothing.

"What about checks? I have to sign my checks. What about my checks?" I ask.

"Don't sign any *papers*. Do not write your name for them. I think your brothers are planning to take advantage of you. They want your money," Keith says.

"They can have some." That is a good idea. "I can give them some money." A very good idea. "Hey, Keith, I could give them some. That would be okay. Wouldn't that be okay?"

"*No!* No. No, Perry. Listen. They want all of it. They will not be satisfied. Oh damn!" Keith looks like he has indigestion.

"Do you want a Tums, Keith? I got Tums. Fruit-flavored. Hey, let's go visit Cherry!" I have not been to Marina Handy Mart for days. "Hey, let's all get Slurpees!"

Gary says I need a plan.

"Perry, calm down. This is important. You have a tremendous opportunity to help people and have a great future for yourself, but you have to be careful. Please let Keith or me know if someone wants something from you again. Okay?"

Gary is nice and has known me for a long time.

"What's all this?" Gary starts looking through papers on my counter. "Holy crap! Keith, look at this!" They put their heads close together so they look like those Siamese twin sisters from *Ripley's Believe It or Not!*

It is okay when your friends read your mail.

"Have you been sending these people money?" Gary asks. He holds up a letter from a Girl Scout leader.

"They want to go on a trip to Canada," I explain. "It's educational."

"How do they know where to send these letters? How do people find him?" Keith takes a pile of envelopes from Gary. His mouth is open. He looks like a guppy. I used to have guppies, until they all died and Gram flushed them down the toilet.

"I send money to people with cancer. That's sad," I say.

"That list is public information, Keith. Anybody can find out who won the lottery," Gary says.

"Per, these people are ripping you off! You've got to stop this! They'll only send you more of these!" Keith waves a letter in the air.

Gary agrees. "Keith is right. Look here. See this? If you deposited the check from this company, you would give up an interest in the rest of your lottery winnings forever. You could lose it all. You have to be careful."

Gram says careful too, deep inside my head. *Careful.* I remind myself to listen. To be an auditor.

"Okay," I say. They are right. I am too excited. I have not been thinking clearly. It is very important to think, Gram said. I need to start writing these things down. To not forget.

"You can't be giving everybody money. It's not a good idea," Keith says.

"He's right, Perry. You have to think of your future. This is a chance for you never to worry about money ever again." When Gary looks me straight in the eye I laugh.

"Ha! I never worry about money. You work at your job and you get money. You save half and you spend half. Half in savings. Half in checking. That is what I do. That is what Gram said. Other people worry about money. Money just is. I don't worry about it."

Gary frowns, then says, "Perry, you have to be careful."

"Okay," I say. That seems to make them both feel better.

"Just watch out for any of their funny business, Per. Let Gary and me help you with your mail," Keith says. Brown pieces of tobacco are stuck on his teeth from smoking, and stringy boogers hang out his nose, but I do not tell him this. It would not be nice. I hope someone tells me when I have boogers hanging out my nose. I would want to wipe them off. But people are funny. They do not tell you when they see your boogers. Gram always told me.

"You got stuff hanging out your nose, Perry! Use a Kleenex!" And she would hand me toilet paper or tissue or if she was in the kitchen a paper towel, which is very rough and hurts. I am out of both Kleenex and paper towels so I say nothing. Besides, Keith is not looking at me. He is very concerned about funny business.

Funny business is something bad and not at all funny.

20

~~

I miss Gram. I still do everything the same in the morning. I get up, go to the bathroom, use my electric razor, and comb my hair. I put on jeans with my flannel shirt and an undershirt underneath. I put on my Nike socks with the cool arrow and slip on my boat shoes. I cook my oatmeal and do my words while I eat.

I have been rich for almost a month.

My words are *nest, nestle, nestling*, and *net, net, net,* and *net*. There are many nets. They catch things. Gram said we had to make up our own rules about words. Sometimes people cannot decide what words mean. The same word can mean a lot of things. Words are like people's faces. They do not always mean what they look like. Gram said you just look for what you understand. If you come to a word that you do not know, you keep going until you find one you do.

I know the word *nest*. We had birds on our porch and they used grass and stuff for a nest. I watched them put twigs together and build it. It was like they had a plan. Gram said most animals have plans. Our birds had babies that grew up and flew away. I think they were robins or sparrows. I did not know for sure. A nest is a place that is high and safe from cats that you fly away from. My apartment is my nest.

I have good friends. I am lucky, just like Gram said. Keith is my best friend and then Gary. I have known them both the longest. They were my friends before. I have new friends now. Like in Holsted's when I am working. People I do not even know come in just to talk to me. Gary likes it because they buy stuff.

Are you Perry Crandall?

Are you that guy who won the lottery?

Hey, guys, it's him!

Yeah, he's the guy, all right.

You won the lottery?

How many tickets did you buy?

Did you have the computer pick or did you have your own lucky numbers?

Do you still play?

Do you still buy tickets?

Do you? Do you?

Shake my hand . . . Shake my hand . . . Shake my hand . . .

I am famous now and people listen carefully to what I have to say. They do not interrupt. They do not say I am slow. They listen. Before I won the lottery, people would always ask for Keith and Manny to help them instead of me. That is stupid because I am the one who knows where everything is. I unload the boxes and put things away on the shelves. Keith and Manny always had to ask me.

"Hey, Perry, where'd we put the snatch blocks?" They would be looking in the wrong aisle.

"Hey, Perry, do you know where the teak cleaner is?" It would be right in front of them.

"Hey, Perry, where are the LectraSan fuses?" They forgot we moved them to the front.

If I look into people's eyes deep down, I can almost tell what they are thinking. Their eyeballs sort of dart around like dropped screws on the floor. Before I won the lottery, they did not want to talk to me. Now they do, but their eyes look the same. It is spooky, but fun. I mean, I do not know how they really feel.

Gary listens to me say things now. It is like he can't help it. Even though he knows that I am the exact same person. When you have money, people listen to you.

Keith laughs and says our customers will buy whatever I suggest. "That guy just bought two pairs of Sperrys. He probably doesn't even have a boat. He just decided to buy the shoes from you, Per," he says.

"Those shoes are eighty dollars a pair. That's a lot of money for shoes," I say. I wear boat shoes, but I do not pay eighty dollars. I get an employee discount. I would not pay eighty dollars for shoes. That is stupid even for Top-Siders. "Besides, he told me he does not have a boat. He just wanted to wash his driveway. I told him you do not slip and fall in the wet when you wear boat shoes. He thought that was a good idea."

I tell Gary we need to have new things to buy in the store.

"Ladies like to buy cards and water. They want cards like Hallmark and ask for that special water in green bottles." Hallmark ads make me cry, especially the ones with dogs and old men that remind me of Gramp.

Do you have any cards for people with boats? That is what all the ladies ask.

Do you have Perrier?

Or they will ask, *Do you sell lattes?*

They say this as their husbands or boyfriends look at boat stuff.

Keith always growls behind his hand to me. "Where do they think they are? Seattle?" That is funny, because we are in Everett.

Running a store is easy. You just have to remember to get things other people want to buy. You have to listen. It helps if you are an auditor. People tell you what they want all the time.

We eat our lunch on Keith's boat to get away from all the people in the store. *Diamond Girl* is painted in blue on one side.

"She's named after the best song in the world," that's what Keith says. He first heard it the day he left Vietnam. He calls it 'Nam.

When I left 'Nam.

After I got back from 'Nam.

I was on my way home from 'Nam when I first heard that song.

If I shut my eyes and smell, I can pretend we are sailing, but we are just eating our sandwiches in the cockpit. *Diamond Girl* is tied to the dock, but I can still pretend.

Gramp taught me to sail for the first time at Mukilteo Park. It was March and cold. I remember. I shut my eyes tight. A movie plays just for me in my head. I am eight or maybe nine years old.

"Heads up, Perry!" Gramp cautioned. There was only room for the two of us. I wore a puffy orange life jacket and could not turn my neck.

"Hold this line. Now pull! Harder! That's right." We flew. As we hit small waves, I felt lumps underneath. BUMP! Bump bump. BUMP! Bump bump. They pushed against my bottom and I laughed. Our sail was white with a long red stripe and the number twelve painted at the top. I do not know why.

"Feel the wind, Perry! Feel it." Gramp put a chilled hand to my face. It was as cold as the Popsicles I sucked on in July. I lifted up my head and hit the edge of my life preserver. The wind stung my cheeks. They were wet from the spray. I licked my lips. It was salt without french fries. My hands were warm in my gloves.

"Pull, Perry! Pull the sheet. Quick now!" Gramp sat behind me working the tiller, guiding the boat.

I was too slow. My line tangled. The boat jibed, tipped, and Gramp and I fell into the water. The cold squeezed my chest. My eyes opened to a blur and my throat was tight. I gulped frigid air as soon as my head broke the surface of the water and I yelled. "Help me! Help!" I couldn't see Gramp anywhere. I was petrified.

"Help! Help!" Then he was there right in front of me.

"Stand up, Perry, for Pete's sake!"

The water was shallow. Gramp stood next to me and hung on to the collar of my jacket. I was shivering and wet, but I scrambled to my feet and cheered, "Yeah! Let's do it again!"

Gramp laughed and said. "You're a sailor, Perry. A real sailor."

And we did it again. And again. And again.

"Per?" a voice says.

I open my eyes. Keith is waving his hand in front of my face. "Woo hoo! Perry?" He sounds just like Fritz Dias the repair guy, but Keith does not have a gold tooth and his voice is deeper.

It is time for us to go back to work. When we sit on Keith's boat for lunch it always seems like a little trip. I like that. A vacation in my head. It is a place where I can think of Gramp and miss him along with Gram. But it is a good miss. They come back into my head like they are here with me, and then they leave again. I just say good-bye to them. I know they will be back.

Every day at Holsted's, more people come in to see me. They smile and ask me questions about the lottery. They talk to me like they want to be friends and then we talk about boats. I know a lot about boats. People have a hard time finding things they want for their boats. They tell me this. I just listen. They come into Holsted's to find out about the lottery and leave with what they need for their boat.

We sell out of all the T-shirts that say *Holsted's Marine Supply*. I fill out another catalogue order form.

"Hey, Gary, look, we can put anything on the back we want."
I point to a blank space on the order form.

"Go for it, Per. What do you want to put?" Gary is filling out
time sheets.

Keith comes over. "People are buying all sorts of crap now,
Per. If you hand it to them, they're buying it. Put whatever you
want."

"Can I put my name?"

"Sure. Why not?"

Keith sets out more pens that say *Holsted's for Your Boating Needs.*
We used to give them away, but I accidentally dumped them into a
box that was marked two dollars and we sold every one. Keith had to
go into the back room and get more. We ran out of everything.

I order more pens and key chains with floats. I mark RUSH ORDER
on the form. If we order a lot, we can get it in three days. I also order
T-shirts that say *Holsted's Marine Supply* on one side and *Perry L.
Crandall works here* on the other. That is so cool. Keith said I could
put anything. I always wanted my name on a shirt. I get one hundred larges and extra-larges, fifty mediums, and fifty smalls. It costs
extra, but Keith says it doesn't matter.

"This seems like a big order, but okay." Gary initials my order
form. It is the first one I have ever filled out. We had a good week
and sold a lot of stuff. Gary tells me I am an excellent employee.

Even though I won the lottery, I unpack all the boxes that come
in on Saturday. It is my job.

"This one is huge," I say to Manny.

"How come it's so big?" he asks.

"The key chain and pen company usually ships in smaller boxes,"
I say.

"No shit! Where's the invoice?" Manny throws packing popcorn
all over the floor while he looks.

"Hey stop that!" I say. I know I will have to sweep it up later.

He finds the paper and studies it closely. "Here's the problem. Right here. An extra zero. It's your name on the order sheet. It's your fault. What are we going to do with five hundred key chains? Holy cow! They all have your name on them! Look! Right underneath *Holsted's Marine Supply!* Gary's gonna be pissed at you!" Manny walks away and leaves me to do the rest of the unpacking. He will probably tell on me.

That's okay.

I take the key chains out and put them into a box next to the pens. They all say *Holsted's Marine Supply.* I make a sign: *Matching pen and key chain. Get both for five dollars.* The number five is a good number. Most people have five-dollar bills and it is easier to add up. Tons of people came in that morning and everything was gone by Sunday afternoon.

Gary laughs. "Per, I don't know about you. I think maybe you were holding out on us before."

I laugh with him and feel happy that he called me Per.

When Keith hands Gary another order form on Monday, he passes it over to me. "This is your job now," he says.

We sell out of T-shirts again. The white pens and floating key chains now have *Holsted's Marine Supply Home of Perry L. Crandall Lottery Winner* printed on the side in bright green letters. It is cool to have my name on things.

"Don't look at me!" Keith says to Gary as he unfolds more invoices. "Ask Perry. He seems to know what people want."

They want my name on stuff. I laugh again. It is so easy. I just ask the customers what they want. They always tell me.

"What would you like to see in our store?" I say, and carry a yellow pad and write down everything they tell me.

"It's wonderful what you're doing," they say to Gary before they walk out of the store. "Just wonderful."

"What am I doing?" Gary looks at Keith and shrugs.

Keith gets his cynical look and winks at me. "You've turned Per into a businessman, Gary. All he had to do was win the lottery and now he's a businessman." He slaps me so hard on the back that I cough.

That is what I want to be most of all. A businessman.

21

≋

On Wednesday morning, John comes over to my apartment.

"I tried to call. Your phone is busy. It must be off the hook," he says. His eyes move around like he is looking for something he lost.

"No, that was Franklin. He says I can call him Frank," I explain.

"Frank? Who the hell's Frank?" he asks.

"I don't know. He says he's a friend of Elaine's," I say.

Frank has a deep voice and says he is worried about me. He says he is my friend too, but I have never seen him. I am not sure you can be friends with someone you have never seen. Besides, he is not on my list.

"What does he want?" John asks.

"To help me with the money. To give me advice."

"You don't need a stranger's help. You don't need their advice. That's what David and I are here for," he says.

John, David, and Frank all want to help me with my money. Everybody wants to help me with the money.

John's gray coat is wet from the rain and drips all over my floor. He turns his head to look behind like he thinks someone is following.

"We're just trying to help you, Perry. You need to keep us in the loop," he says.

I do not know what *in the loop* means. I stare at his feet. They are bigger than mine.

"Where's your fat friend, Keith?" He peels off his black gloves one at a time. John looks just like Batman except he does not have a mask and I know his car is brown.

"He's not fat. Those are stomach muscles and he had to go to the vet hospital," I say.

Keith is a vet, which is not like a dog doctor. It has to do with the army, Vietnam, and a guy called Agent Orange, which I think is a spy.

My dryer buzzes and John jumps, then looks around.

"What's that?" he asks.

"My laundry."

"Where's your boss?"

"He's downstairs working the register."

"Where's your bank statement? I'd like to help with your accounting, check your numbers." John is already shuffling through papers on my kitchen counter. He holds something up. "Are these all your papers? You have anything else?"

"It's not nice to look at other people's stuff," I say, but he ignores me.

"What happened? Has Elaine been over here helping you? Where's the rest? You seem to have spent a great deal of money already. What's going on, Perry?" His voice gets louder, then he suddenly stops and takes a deep breath. "I'm just trying to watch out for you. To help you. We're all concerned about you." He is speaking softly. Like he is singing.

Maybe he really wants to help me now.

I try to think.

I rock back and forth on the sofa. It is almost time for *Judge Judy*. I already missed *Gilligan's Island*. I wonder when he will leave.

"Perry, what have you done?" John brings a kitchen chair over and plops down. He will not sit on Gram's couch. He says it smells like cat pee. It does not. Gram did not have a cat. He puts a hand on my shoulder. It is heavy. One of his fingernails is so short is has blood on the end.

"Investments," I tell him, and cover my ears, but he does not yell and this surprises me. Instead, he takes another deep breath and lets it out slowly. Like a balloon. He looks at his bloody finger.

"You want a Band-Aid?" I ask him. "I got Band-Aids." He shakes his head no.

Gram told me not to tell them about my savings account, so I do not. Everett Federal has a special place for savers like me so my money can make money. Like music. CDs. I do not tell him this either. I put my special savings-account papers in Gram and Gramp's cardboard box. I do not leave them out for anyone to see. They are private.

"CeCe and I would really like you to come over for a visit, spend the night," he says.

"Why?" I ask.

That makes him stare right through me and he licks his lips. He looks like a dog when you give it treats.

Keith told me to ask why, if John or David or Louise wanted me to go somewhere. He said Gram would want me to.

"Why?" I ask John again.

He smiles and looks at his nails. I do not think there is any that is long enough to bite but I do not tell him this.

"Well, Perry, we'd all like to get to know you better. Spend some time together. Plus it's time for a Family Meeting." John's voice sounds like Mr. Thompson's dog Dazy when there was a cat sneaking over the fence. Dazy was part firedog and did not like cats. She would growl and chase them.

When someone invites you to their house, you say yes so you do not hurt their feelings. Hurting people's feelings is rude. I go with John to his house. I do not have a suitcase, so John stuffs my clothes into a pillowcase. That is definitely not cool because I will have to fold them again when I unpack. They will be all wrinkled.

I try to tell him, but he says, "Don't worry about it, Perry."

But I do. I am the one who has to fold them.

He looks out my front window and tells me to hurry, but I have to write a note to Keith. I leave it on the table. It says, "GONE TO JOHN'S HOUSE."

Keith and I were going to get pizza and watch a DVD tonight. He can always watch a DVD without me. I have to lock the door to my apartment so no one will go inside and steal my TV. It is good that Keith has his own key.

"Your brother John lives in a big white house in Bellevue with all the other rich people." That is what Gram said.

It takes an hour to get there even though his car is faster than Yo. His front yard has green bushes with red flowers. There is a hot tub on the redwood deck behind the house and a tall stone wall around the backyard. He shows me around as he tells me the rules. I am not allowed to use the hot tub. I am not allowed to go outside. I am not allowed in the living room. There are many *not alloweds* at his house. John tells me to sit at the table and he goes to use his phone. I hear him from the kitchen.

We're having another Family Meeting tonight. Perry will be here.

He's here now. I'm sure we can get him to sign. I don't think he'll be any problem at all. He's very suggestible.

Eight o'clock tonight. Try to be on time would you?
I had no trouble getting him away from those friends of his.
We need to make some decisions.
Everybody needs to be there. You need to let Mom know. It's important.
He means Louise. He calls Louise Mom.

After he hangs up, he says, "I've got to go back to work. You have to amuse yourself until CeCe and I get home."

When people tell you to amuse yourself, it means you are bothering them.

22

$$\approx$$

John's first wife was Lenore and his second wife was Grace. I do not know who three and four were. Number five is CeCe. She used to be his receptionist. That is what David said. Gram said they are all the same person, just different names. I did not meet the others, only CeCe, and her poodle, so I do not know if they are really the same. John bites his nails and does not eat Tums. He drinks Maalox straight out of a bottle. It makes white specks on his mustache. I do not tell him this. It would not be nice. People who bite their nails and drink Maalox are nervous, Gram said.

He does not have any children. Neither does David.

Gram always told me that was good. "Get them both out of the gene pool! That's what I say." The gene pool is something you want other people out of.

I sit on the sofa in the family room with Gigi and watch bull riding, Animal Planet, and *Jeopardy!* If you do not scratch her just right, Gigi will bite you. She bit me twice already. You can get rabies from dogs if they are frothing at the mouth. I look carefully at Gigi's spit. It does not look like froth. She does not like bull riding because of the buzzers and snaps at me three more times. Her teeth click in the air. I love dogs even when they bite.

I decide to channel-hike. That is when you click the remote and go from channel 03 to channel 099 and back again. Gigi likes it when I channel-hike and growls at all the commercials.

I hope I do not have to stay long. I need to go to work tomorrow. Gary has golf on Thursdays and I have to help Keith close up. I want to go home right after the Family Meeting. A Family Meeting is always about money or when someone has died. We had one for Gramp and another for Gram.

I am by myself for the rest of the day. It is rude to leave guests alone in your house. John did not say I could open any cupboards, so I do not eat lunch. It is also rude not to feed your guests.

No one gets home until after eight. I have not had dinner and I am hungry. I do not go into John's refrigerator because you have to ask permission for that.

I am happy but a little nervous when everyone arrives. My stomach grumbles loud.

"So, Perry, how's it going?" David's wife, Elaine, asks. My mouth is dry. She has never wanted to know how it was going before. I do not know how to answer.

"It is going fine," I finally say. She makes me nervous and hugs me so tight it hurts.

"I hope you know we are going through a lot of trouble to help you," she whispers in my ear and makes bumps go up my arm. David pats me on the back and I cough.

John and CeCe are already sitting at the dining room table. I am hungry. There are crackers and weird yellow mush in a bowl. CeCe says it is hummus. I laugh. It tastes like nut pudding. I do not like it and eat crackers naked. I want a glass of water, but no one offers me anything and it is not polite to ask. They all have wineglasses and make something called a toast about money. I never drink wine. Gram would not let me.

We have to go slowly. Carefully.

I think we should initiate guardianship proceedings immediately.

John, we've gone over this before. I told you it's problematic.

Says who? I know a few judges. Don't you?

Don't be obtuse.

John, Elaine's firm specializes in these issues. We should at least listen to her.

Oh David, shut up! I don't need to be defended by you!

And we should listen to you because? Oh. That's right, David. You didn't actually PASS the bar.

You always bring that up!

Stop it all of you. We have decisions to make.

Be careful. He's L-I-S-E-N-I-N-G.

CeCe says this, but it is stupid because I am a very good speller and she is not.

Great! Where'd you find her, John? She's worse than your last one.

Shut up, Elaine!

Shut up, John!

Shut up, David!

It is after nine when Louise comes through the front door. I do not know who she is at first because her hair is now black.

"Louise." "Darling." "Mother." John and Elaine talk at the same time, but Louise ignores them and hugs me. She smells like old flowers and Gigi growls at her.

"Oh honey! Such a lucky boy! Lucky. Lucky. Boy! Now, what are we going to do with all that lovely money?" When she smiles, her big front teeth make her look like a beaver except she has curly hair and no brown fur. She does not touch my face but kisses something in the air next to me.

"All the lovely money that's left anyway," John says. He has papers in his hand. "I have your checking account statement, Perry."

I am mad because that is my private stuff. It is not nice to take someone's private stuff.

John stares at me and picks his nails and Elaine stands behind him looking over his shoulder at the papers. "If you've blown this much in a month nothing will be left in a year. What did you spend it on?" John asks. Pick. Pick. Pick. I hear his fingers click like Gram's egg timer.

Elaine licks her lips and puts a hand on his arm. "Shhhh. You'll scare him," she says. "You have to be gentle." Her eyes move like the lizards' at Pets R Us. She is much scarier than either John or David. "I think you need to hand over your checkbook, Perry. For safekeeping," she says.

"What'd you do, Perry? It's okay. It's really your money." David puts his hand on my shoulder.

"Now, that's the stupidest thing I've heard you say tonight, David. Try not to cause any more problems than we've got right now." Elaine rolls her eyes. "Perry needs to have us be in charge of his finances. A simple general Power of Attorney, Perry, and your problems will be over."

John squeezes his lips together and tells me, "I consider this everybody's money. You're wasting it. We're a family. Families share money. Don't you want to share? What could you possibly have spent it on?"

Be careful. Gram's voice.

"Investments," I say again. "Stuff. A TV." I already told them once. I am getting even madder.

They think I am stupid. I can see it in their faces.

"What investments?" They all ask this at the same time. It is like the choir in church where Gram, Gramp, and I used to go for Easter.

They do not wait for my answer and start to talk among themselves all at once.

That does it. He needs protection!

He won't know what to do. We need to declare him incompetent!

Guardianship is problematic. I keep telling you this!

We just need a judge on our side, don't we?

It's not that simple anymore, John! Listen and stop talking, for once in your life. The easiest thing, of course, would have been if we had gotten to him before he turned in the ticket. All of our names could have been on that check. We could have created an LLC to claim the money.

The EASIEST thing would have been not to put an end date on that Power of Attorney we got him to sign for the house sale.

John was the one who had the chance to take him to Olympia. Talk about missed opportunities!

Oh, like you not passing the bar and giving us financial advice? That's worked so well for us, don't you think?

Can't we set up the LLC now?

No. It's too late, Mom.

Guardianship is a no-go.

Why not?

Because the court blocks use of the funds and requires regular reporting. We'd need to be selected and bonded. It won't meet our needs.

Oh.

We'll never get anywhere with this if you all don't stop rehashing previous decisions.

We have to figure out another way. The best way to approach the situation.

I've already told you . . .

We have to gain his trust, get to know him so we know the best way to go about this. It shouldn't be that difficult. He's very suggestible. Very, very suggestible . . .

We'll need to decide how to invest the money when we do get it into a trust.

When we cash it out and sell the annuity I think it should go right into mutual funds. It's more liquid.

I disagree. We need to pick some stocks. I got a guy at Hawthorne Group who's sharp, a real hotshot.

I still think we should have a judge declare him incompetent.

That's real maternal, Mom.

I've been trying to tell you it's too difficult. There are too many safeguards.

I think real estate. The market is hot right now.

CeCe, forget real estate, you don't know what you're talking about. The stock market is really hopping.

We need liquid assets and we need them now. Look, we'll have to get going on this. I have obligations . . .

What's the matter, John? Dipping into the till again, are we?

You're a real bitch, Elaine. You know that?

I consider that a compliment, John.

Has he given you a check?

No. Why? Did you get one?

Just a little one . . . to help me out. He won't write one for more than five hundred dollars! Isn't that ridiculous? He says he can't fit all the zeros in.

That's not a problem. John can teach him to write extra zeros on a check. Can't you, John? At least that's what your clients are saying.

Shut up, David!

Stop it, you two! We should split it up between all of us, but I should get more! I'm his mother.

No. It should be split evenly. It's only fair.

We're just thinking of Perry's future. Our future.

We have to be responsible for him.

They are boring, so I decide to leave and go into the other room.

No one notices, or if they do, they say nothing. Animal Planet is not on, so I take a shower, put on my pajamas, and get into bed. The room is strange. The sounds are strange. I am uncomfortable and want to go home.

My dreams are real. Like movies.

I dream about the dog I want to get. He runs after a stick I throw. His fur is long and soft.

He runs and pants. I throw it again and he brings it back. The stick is smooth and brown in my hand. It gets longer, forms an end, turns gray, and changes into a winch handle. I turn it. I am turning. Around and around. I dream about sailing *Diamond Girl* by myself. The wind is fierce. It blows my hair. My cheeks puff out. I am holding a line between my fingers and pulling. The wind pushes in my face. I look up into a blue sky, into the sun, and I feel happy.

I am happy. I wake up. And it is morning.

23

≈

I wonder if John has oatmeal in his kitchen. I decide to ask him when I hear him moving around. He sounds grumpy and talks to me through his bedroom door.

"What! What do you want, Perry?"

"Do you have oatmeal, John? I eat oatmeal for breakfast. Can I have some breakfast?" I am embarrassed to ask, but I did not get dinner and I do not want to starve to death. People can die when they do not eat enough food.

"I don't know, Perry. Look for yourself! I don't have time to talk to you right now. I have to leave. Fix yourself some eggs or something. Watch TV in the family room. Stay out of the living room. Let Gigi out in the backyard to do her stuff, but make sure she comes right back inside. Wipe her feet with a towel so she doesn't get the carpet dirty. CeCe and I have to go. We'll be back this afternoon."

After they leave, I am lonely and bored. I wish Keith would come over. Ten minutes later, I hear banging at the front of the house. I do not know what I should do. It is not nice to answer other people's doors. There is a lot of pounding.

"Hey, Per!" When I recognize Keith's voice, I am happy and open the door. I am still in my pajamas and have to grab Gigi by the neck so she doesn't run out the front. She is growling so hard, drips come out of her mouth in long strings. I check her again for white froth.

"Drop the little fucker and I'll kick it across the room!"

"It's a her! No!" I hug Gigi tight to my chest. She reaches around and nips me hard in the arm and I drop her. She is smart enough to run into the other room.

"How did you get here? This is like magic, Keith! I was just thinking that I wish you were here, and you appeared. That is so cool," I say.

"Sorry, Per, I had a few beers last night or I would have been here sooner." Keith has to drink alone on *Diamond Girl* before he comes to visit me. He tells me what happened. It was like a spy movie and very fun to hear.

"I didn't see your note until this morning. I found John's address in the blue book by your phone. *No problemo.*" Keith walks into the living room and looks around. "I waited until I saw your brother and his wife getting into their car in the driveway. I counted to fifty, then drove around the block and parked Yo down the road behind some bushes. I ran the rest of the way down the street. I couldn't find his fucking bell, so I banged on the door. You ready to go?"

He is all sweaty from running. I do not think Keith should run. He could drop dead of a heart attack. People die of heart attacks.

"Yeah, I'm ready to go," I say. "Just let me put on my clothes. I'm still in my pajamas."

"No need to tell me that, Per. I got eyes." And he points to his brows with his middle finger and laughs at me.

The middle finger means the F-word and *No problemo* is Spanish.

Keith can talk foreign just like Manny. That is so cool. Spanish is like English only you cannot understand what people are saying. Keith does not wipe his feet and tracks mud all over the white living room carpet.

"Hey, Keith, you got mud all over your boots. John will get mad." I hope he takes them off, but he just sits on the white sofa, picks the dirt clumps stuck to his soles, and flicks them off onto the glass coffee table.

"So this is where that brother of yours lives." He stands up. "Holsted was worried when you didn't come home. Of course, I knew the *son of a bitch* would come back. Holsted is so naive."

Keith is smart. He is even smarter when he has not been drinking.

"Do you want some breakfast? I can make eggs," I offer. I am hungry and hope we can eat before we leave.

"Sure," he says, then adds, "Wait. No. I'll make the eggs and you get dressed. Make sure you pack up everything you want to take home." On his way to the kitchen, Keith opens the glass cupboard over the bar. He starts pulling out bottles.

"Courvoisier. Ahhhh. Cognac. That's a good one." He talks to himself. "I'll take this one and hmmm . . . Oh yeah! That's another good one." Then to me, "Hurry up, Per! We don't have all day."

I put on my underwear, pull on my jeans, and button my shirt. My hair sticks out. I have to wet it to make it lie down.

"Hey, Keith, I need a haircut today," I yell. When I walk into the kitchen, I smell something burning. The kitchen is empty. Smoke is pouring from a frying pan on the stove. There are four eggs burned hard to the bottom of a pan. I dump them into the disposal and get another pan. I am cooking four more eggs when Keith comes back into the kitchen.

"I found these in the office. There's papers and shit all over the place." Keith's mouth drips just like Gigi's. "Look at all these credit card bills! I've never seen such high limits. See? They're all maxed out. *Past due. Last notice. Final bill* . . . for such a fancy house your brother seems to owe a shitload of money. What's this? Hey, look here! He's being sued! Misappropriation of funds. More bills. Alimony past due. Sweet Jesus! How does a guy like that get five wives?"

"It's not nice to snoop." I set two plates out and butter toast.

"What did you do with them last night?"

"We had a Family Meeting."

"What about?"

"Stuff. Investments. Money. They want me to be responsible."

"Interesting. Here's a big one that defers payment. It says John expects to come into a pile of money soon." Keith sits at the table and reads while he shovels eggs and toast into his mouth. He uses a corner of one paper for a napkin. "Did either of your brothers ask for a loan?"

"No. A loan is when you borrow money and have to pay it back. They did not ask for a loan. They all just wanted checks. They do not want to pay me back," I say.

"It figures, the moneygrubbing creeps. When is John getting home?" Keith asks.

"He said this afternoon but I don't know. Why?"

"Because I want to sit in his hot tub. I have a bad back." He stands up and stretches.

"I'm not allowed." I start to worry. We have made a huge mess in John's house. Gigi is howling in the other room and there is a wet spot on the rug. I was supposed to let her out in the backyard to poop and pee. I forgot.

"Yeah? Well, they didn't say anything about me." Keith peels off his shirt and drops his pants.

His butt is big and white. I can see his crack and his privates.

He leaves his plate on the table, goes out onto the deck naked, and flips a switch that causes bubbles to spring up from the bottom of the tub. It is not nice to let people see your privates. I hope John's neighbors are not looking over the fence. Keith groans when he steps into the water. "Ahhh! *Sweet Jesus!* That feels good!"

Sitting in the hot tub is a very big *Not Allowed.*

My hands shake and my stomach is achy. I need Tums. My heart is pounding so loud I hear it in my ears. I pace back and forth from room to room. I forget about Gigi until I notice she did a poop on the carpet. I try to pick it up with a paper towel, but I drop one piece and it rolls under the sofa.

"Keith!" I do not want to be here when John and CeCe get home.

I hear Keith in the hot tub singing. *". . . Sure do shine . . . glad I love ya . . . glad you're mine . . .* Watch some TV, Per! I'll be done in a minute," he hollers.

"I am too upset to watch TV, Keith! We'll get in trouble!" I look through the kitchen window and can see him floating on his back. He takes up the whole tub. He is splashing water on the deck. John will see that someone has been in the hot tub and think it was me.

"No you won't." He holds his nose with two fingers and slides under the surface.

"Don't drown, Keith, okay?" I do not want to pull his big, fat, naked body out of the tub.

"Gigi! Oh, Gigi!" I call quietly. I hear her scratching and whining in the office. Long deep gouges line the bottom of the wood door. She must have gotten in there while Keith was snooping. Three piles of poop and two more pee spots are scattered over the carpet. I push the poop under the desk with a magazine and just leave the wet. My hands are trembling. Gigi bites my ankle, but I have my thick Nike socks and boat shoes on. I pick her up by the collar and throw her too hard into the bathroom. She hits the wall as I slam the door.

"Sorry!" I tell her, but she does not sound like she forgives me.

Her growls and barks echo off the tile. When I come back to the deck Keith is slowly crawling out of the hot tub.

"Hot damn! That felt good." He dries himself off with a kitchen dish towel and then folds it neatly, laying it back on the counter. I watch him slide his underwear up his wet legs and then I look away. It is not polite to watch naked people get dressed.

There are pieces of burnt egg in the sink, dishes all over the table, and crumbs on the floor. There is a giant yellow puddle bright like the sun on the white tile in the hall. Gigi must have peed there too. I open the cupboard below the sink, grab a garbage bag, run into the spare room, and stuff my clothes inside. THUD THUD THUD. My chest is pounding like it will explode.

"Keith!" I yell again. "We have to go!"

He is back in John's office, sitting at the desk, reading more papers. His wet bare feet are propped up on the desk. Water drips from his wet hair and lands in speckles on the carpet underneath. He starts to put his feet down.

"Be careful. There's poop under there!" I warn him.

Keith sits up so hard the chair bucks. I laugh. It is like bull riding.

"Shit, what's all this?"

"Call it dog poop, Keith. It is not nice to use the S-word."

"No, these other papers. It looks like notes." He pages through a long yellow tablet.

"Stop snooping, Keith."

"Look at this. . . . *Mutual funds. Financial services. . . . Guardianship* . . . I think they're up to something. It looks like your family is researching how to invest a whole pile of money. They want to create a family trust, it says here." He starts to rip a page off then stops, smooths it out, and lays the pad back on the desk. He picks up some other papers and stuffs them into his shirt.

"We have to go, Keith." I am scared that John will come back and catch us snooping.

"Okay. Okay. Find my boots for me, will you?" He waves at me like I am a mosquito and stares at the ceiling. He is thinking. That is how Keith thinks.

I run around the house searching for his boots and find them under the coffee table. My stomach is queasy. I look for a Tums in my jeans pocket. There are two tablets left, covered with foil. I unwrap one quickly and pop it into my mouth.

"Keith! Hurry. Put these on!" I drop his boots and socks on the desk.

Keith pulls on his socks and smooths the wrinkles carefully with his hands. He sticks his feet into his boots and wriggles his toes. I can see him feel for each boot string, poke them through the holes, and one by one, slowly lace them up.

My hands are sweating and my heart thumps even louder. What if John comes back early? I am in so much trouble. Their house is a mess. I want Keith to hurry up.

"Hurry!" I cry.

And then I know. I know how other people must feel around me and I am ashamed. I chew my last Tums and swing my bag of clothes over my back. I walk out the door. Keith follows behind carrying a sack of bottles.

"Hey, Keith, isn't that stealing?" I ask.

Keith pulls the door shut behind us with one hand.

"Nah. I'll ask him next time he comes over to your place," he says.

"Okay," I say, and we drive home.

24

≋

Gary and Keith are hard-talking. It is like they are fighting but not mad. Gary thinks everything will be fine and calls Keith cynical and overexcited. Keith's pants slide down and show his crack and he paces around the small back office. There is only room for three steps each way. We are both supposed to be unpacking boxes. Instead, I hang just outside the door and eavesdrop. That is like being an auditor without permission.

"One, John is telling creditors and clients he expects to get cash soon and look at this!" Keith waves papers in Gary's face. "He's got four ex-wives screaming for money. What if he tries to get guardianship? What if he does any of that legal shit?"

"How can he do that? The courts would have to declare Perry incompetent and he's obviously not." Gary sits up.

"Gary, don't be naive! They're a bunch of lawyers! They'll figure out a way!"

When they see me standing there they stop talking.

"Per, you've got to be careful around that family of yours!" Keith speaks slowly, but each word gets louder.

"Yeah, Per. He's right. You've got to be careful," Gary echoes.

"Okay," I say but they do not look convinced.

"No, I mean it. You don't even have to do what I say!" Keith is not making any sense.

"Okay," I say again. It is better to agree. Keith does not understand. Sometimes it is a good idea to do what people say. Like if a building is on fire or the line at the grocery store is shut down. They put that little sign up that says CLOSED. And then you go over to another line. Like that. For times like those, a list does not matter.

Keith pulls a tiny stool over and sits down across from Gary. His bottom hangs over each side like a big W. I have never seen Keith so excited. Well, maybe last July, when those girls from the yacht jumped naked off their aft deck into the Sound in broad daylight.

"Broad daylight, Per! It was so cold they were practically blue!"

The Sound is never warm, plus it is dirty. Keith had to help drag them out. That made him happy.

"I get rock hard just thinking about it!" he will say. "Rock hard!" And then he will grin. He is not grinning now.

"Gary, we have to do something."

"Okay. I'll talk to my lawyer about bringing Per in as an investor. Maybe I'll see if there's something we can do to protect him from that family of his." Gary squeezes his spray bottle into one nostril. He shuts his eyes and inhales.

"Oh boy!" I say, and bounce against the doorway.

"No promises, Per. We'll run the numbers, and then see what the lawyer says," Gary warns.

I hope the numbers will be good.

Keith leans back, farts, and falls off his stool.

25

~

Keith and I decide to take Friday afternoon off. It is cold even though the sky is blue. So cold it gets in your head and nose even with the sun out. We are on *Diamond Girl*. Boats are always girls. You call them *she* no matter what.

The sky is so bright I can see it in the water. I can also see huge sea anemones attached to the dock. They look like big white dinosaur flowers. They are really animals, Gramp told me. Keith turns the key and pushes a button to start his engine.

BROOOM! Brooom! Brooom! Brooom! Clunk. He tries again.

BROOOM! Brooom! Brooom! Brooom! Clunk. He says the F-word.

BROOOM! BROOOM! BROOOM! The engine starts. It sputters, pings, and sounds sick to me, but Keith laughs like he has just heard a good joke.

He tells me to toss him the aft lines. I know all about lines. I do not need to be told. I help boats into the fuel dock all the time. I love to sit on the bow of Keith's boat. I stretch out on my stomach as we head out into the Sound past the spit. I see a seal.

"Hey, Keith, a seal!" I point.

"Harbor seal, Per, that's a harbor seal."

I knew it was a harbor seal, but I didn't tell Keith that. I know the difference between sea lions and harbor seals. You can tell because one has earflaps and the other doesn't. Of course, you have to look real close. I lean down and put my hand into the water. It is so cold it hurts.

The engine quits. CONK! Keith says the F-word again.

Diamond Girl is a sloop, which means she only has one mast. She has two sails. The one in front is called a jib, or foresail. You can even call it a jenny. That is also a girl's name. Keith looks like he wants to use the jib and starts to unwind the sail from the forestay.

"Why are you pulling the sheet? There's no wind," I say. Gramp made me call everything on a boat the correct name. A sheet is a piece of rope that is attached to a sail and not something on a bed. Keith pulling the sheet is not a great idea because I do not feel the wind anymore. The sail just hangs off the stay.

"Shit!" Keith cannot see to steer with the sail hanging down like that. "Fucking line!" Keith calls everything lines.

"Hey, Keith, I'll get the oar." I try to be helpful.

He says the F-word again and growls while he furls the sail back up. Keith tells me he hates the guys to see us scull back. It is embarrassing. His inboard engine gives him trouble. We will go out, and the engine will quit. If there is any wind we can sail back, which is okay. If there is no wind, we have to paddle, or scull. We use a heavy long oar, which is a bitch, Keith says. It insults a sailor to scull, he says.

Every time I go out with him, I am the one who does the sculling. It looks like I get to scull again today. I am a very good sculler. The other thing that happens when we go out is that clouds come out of nowhere. I see them in the distance.

The water is flat and calm. That means it will be easier to get back, because there will be little current. We go faster with me sculling than we did with the engine. Keith smokes a cigarette while I work the oar. I dip it in and out of the water. The drips run down the pole and get my hands wet and cold. I am hot, so I take off my jacket. My shirt is damp from work sweat. Clouds cover up the sun and it starts to rain. I stop sculling for a minute and put my jacket back on.

"I need to get my tank scrubbed. I must have dirty fuel." Keith says this each time his engine quits.

"Why don't you get it repaired?" I ask this each time too. Right after he says he needs to get his tank scrubbed or his fuel polished.

"Money, Per, it costs money."

"Oh." Then I get one of my good ideas. "Hey, Keith, I have money now. Let's get the engine fixed."

"No, Per, that's not necessary."

People say it is not necessary when they really want to do something but think it may be a problem. It is not a problem for me. I get excited because it means we can go out on more sailing trips. It also means we might not have to scull anymore and embarrass Keith. Fixing up *Diamond Girl* was on Keith's lottery list, so it must be a good idea.

It takes two hours to get back to the slip. I jump off the bow, tie the line to the cleat, and catch the aft line. Gram used to say that sometimes I could be stubborn. I feel this is one of those times.

Lots of people do inboard engine repair in the harbor. My favorite is Marty. Mr. Martin really, but everyone calls him Marty. He is sixty-seven years old. I know this because he always tells me each time I bring him filters. He calls Gary on the phone at least twice a week.

"Holsted! I need Racor filters. Put it on my account!" He always expects me to bring them.

"I'm sixty-seven years old with a bum hip!" he complains. "I can't walk down the dock every time I need a damn filter!"

His shop is at the far end of the pier. It is dark and full of metal pieces and old motors.

He laughs when I ask him to fix Keith's engine.

"That'll be the day. What's he gonna use for money?" Marty asks.

"I'll pay for it. I want us to go out farther, maybe to Whidbey Island or all the way around Camano, but not into the flats." I know all about the mud flats. Gramp had to rescue people from flats and sandbars all the time.

"That'll be a job." He grinds his cigarette out on the dock. I worry about this because the dock is wood.

"Won't that catch on fire?" I ask. I always wonder about people who smoke, like Keith, Marty, and Gram, because their cigarettes go everywhere. Gram's trash can caught on fire once and Keith burns holes in every shirt he owns. I do not worry about Gram anymore because she is dead. I still worry about Marty and Keith.

Marty does not answer me and gets up. He puffs, huffs, and limps after me over to Keith's boat. We have to walk around mussel shells and seagull poop. Marty walks slow and uses a cane carved out of the rail of a boat he used to own. This gets me thinking. There are lots of slows and Marty is the walking kind. I have to stop and wait for him. Thinking slow is the worst slow, then there is the talking slow, and last is the walking slow. That is what old people have.

"Okay, Keith, turn her over." Marty leans forward and steps onto *Diamond Girl*. She sinks like a dog with a sore back. That's what Gram used to say. Marty weighs a lot.

I hear Keith mutter. Marty and Keith always growl at each other. It is hard to tell if they like each other. They bum cigarettes from each other and argue all the time, so they must. Gram always told me that smokers usually like each other.

"A goddamned filthy habit, Perry! Us smokers got to stick together," she always said.

I do not smoke. Gram would not let me. I do not drink either.

If Marty is going to fix Keith's engine, and they are going to argue and smoke, I do not need to be there. Keith and Marty have cigarettes hanging off their lips and do not notice when I walk away.

I decide to go to Marina Handy Mart and visit Cherry.

26

≋

think about Cherry a lot. Keith calls her a plus-sized girl with giant tits, and laughs. Gary says she has too many tattoos and earrings. I think she is neat, and beautiful, and smart.

I put my hands in my pockets to warm them up. It is not far, but
it is still a cold, wet walk.

"Hey, Cherry." The bell tinkles when I walk through the door. I
shake water off my hair and get dizzy.

"Hey, Perry. How you doing?" Cherry is reading a magazine
behind the counter.

I try to think of something to say. My mouth is dry so I decide to
buy a Coke.

"What are you reading?" I ask, and set my drink on the counter
along with two dollars. I want to say something funny. Something
that will make her laugh, but I cannot think of one thing.

"*People*. It's a good one this week. Hey, you should be in it. They do stuff about lottery winners. You could be famous." Cherry stands and rings up my soda.

"I am famous now. The guys at the fishing dock said so," I say.

"No kidding. You're the first person I ever knew who won anything. I don't even buy MegaBucks anymore," she says.

"Why not?" Cherry always plays MegaBucks. She even sends away for tickets to Powerball.

"Well, Perry, just think about it for a moment," she says. "What are the odds? A million or more to one, right? What are the odds that I win, and I have a friend who wins? That's practically impossible! You just saved me a pile of money. There's no point to playing anymore. No way I'd win now!"

"I'm sorry." Because of me, my friends have no chance at winning the lottery. I feel sad for them. I look at Cherry's face. She has black lipstick today and it matches her eyelashes.

"Where's your nose ring?" I can think of nothing else to say. I am sweating under my pits. Maybe I forgot deodorant. I quickly lift up my arm and smell when Cherry bends down to put her magazine under the counter.

"At home. Sometimes I don't feel like wearing it. I have my tongue one in, though." And she sticks it out to show me when she stands up. "My dad hates them."

Cherry's mouth shuts and makes a deep frown as she hands me my change. I try to think of something else to say as I pop open my Coke. It fizzes up and Cherry has to take a cloth and wipe my spill off the counter.

"I don't have a dad. I mean, I think my dad's dead," I say.

Cherry raises her brows and looks at me with interest. "You're lucky," she says. "I wish mine was dead."

I just nod, smile, and hope I do not look too goofy. I cannot think of anything else to say.

Shouts echo in the parking lot outside. Three guys stomp into the store. Their heavy sweatshirts hang down their arms. They look like motorcycle men, except they do not have helmets or bikes.

"Hey! Anybody here?" The man that says this has a scraggly beard and huge dirty hands.

"You got any beer in this dump?" The one next to him spits a long brown stream of liquid onto the tile floor and laughs with another man. They all have greasy blond hair. They scare me.

I put my change in my pocket and turn to leave. The man with the beard grabs me by the arm as I walk past and lifts me up.

"Do I know you?" he says, and breathes into my face. He smells like Keith, but he is not my friend. His fingers tighten on my arm and my Coke drips on his sneakers.

"Shit! You dumped Coke on me! He dumped Coke on my shoes! Tell me you're sorry you little screwup! You hear me?" He lifts me higher up off the floor. My shoulder is twisting. My arm burns. My soda can flips out of my numb hand, bounces across the tiles, and splashes over the legs of the two other men. They yell and dance backwards into the aisle.

"I'm sorry! I'm really sorry." I am. I am very sorry and I am very scared. My heart is beating. Thump THUMP THUMP thump. My arm is tingling with pins and needles. I swallow hard because I have to throw up. When the man hears my voice, he smiles so wide I see his gray teeth. It is not a nice smile at all. His eyes get smaller. He looks like Mrs. Jansen's cat hunting a bird.

"Well, well, well, we have a little retard here."

His two friends come closer. One of them starts laughing deep and slow. The hand on my arm loosens a tiny bit. My eyes get wet.

"LEAVE HIM ALONE, ASSHOLES!"

I did not know Cherry could holler that loud. I was impressed. The baseball bat she hit the man with was aluminum. It probably hurt a lot, even though she only swung with one arm.

"I called the POLICE, and if you don't get your sorry butts out of this store, I'm shooting you guys with THIS!" She waves a spray can in her other hand. "IN FACT! I think it's a good idea to use this NOW! YOU CREEPS! YOU FRIGGING BULLIES!" And she did.

Something comes out of the can with a *whoosh!* Even though I only get a little in my eyes I cannot see. The man lets go of my arm and drops me. I fall to the floor next to the cereal shelf. I can feel tears run down my face from the spray. I throw up again and again. I cannot help it my arm hurts so bad.

I hear thumps as Cherry smacks the men over and over with the bat. THWACK! THUNK! Sirens start soft and get louder.

Cherry told me afterwards there is a special button for the police under the counter at all Handy Marts. That is a good idea, I think.

"Mace is very hard on the mucous membranes." That is what the officer says. The police are not happy and tell Cherry it was dangerous to do what she did.

"They could have been armed. You did a very foolish thing." Officer Mallory looks at my arm, but he talks to Cherry. She sits behind the counter answering their questions and popping her gum. She does not look at all foolish or scared. She looks bored and blows a bubble.

All three men sit on the floor with handcuffs around their ankles and wrists and wait to go to jail. They have something called outstanding warrants. Outstanding warrants are not good things, or very outstanding. It means the police are looking for you and you do not want to make it easy for them to find out where you are.

The other officer writes my name on the police form, and then looks at my face. "Hey, aren't you the guy who won the lottery? You are, aren't you! You're the guy who just won twelve million bucks?"

"That's right!" Officer Mallory hoots at the three men sitting on the floor. "You idiots just assaulted Perry L. Crandall. He's a millionaire. He'll have your sorry asses in jail forever!" He is still laughing as he helps his partner load the men into a big police van in the Handy Mart parking lot.

"You need to go to the emergency room." Cherry's face is all shiny and her makeup runs down her cheeks from her sweat. It is hard work to swing a baseball bat and hit people with it. She looks like a raccoon. "Let me call Keith for you," she says. "He can take us to Everett General."

I am so upset I cannot remember the number for Holsted's. Cherry has to look it up in the phone book. I do not know why Cherry started to cry. I am the one who is hurt. When Keith peels into the parking lot with Yo, she hangs the CLOSED sign on the door and locks the store. She rides with us to the hospital and pats my shoulder the whole way. I do not tell her that makes it hurt worse.

Keith and Cherry talk while I get my X-ray. It is so cool. They have a big machine that takes a picture of inside my arm. The colors on my skin are blue and red, but I do not have a broken bone. The doctor gives me a sling anyway, which is cool. He tells me it is a bad sprain and that I am lucky. I know this. I know I am lucky.

"That's what the L stands for," I try to say after the doctor gives me a shot. But it comes out like *"Thash wash the ell shtanns foorrr."*

I cannot talk.

After we pick up my pain pills at the pharmacy, Keith drives us to Denny's. We have an early dinner together. I lean back against the booth while Keith and Cherry talk.

"I can't believe I did what I did. I know it was stupid." Cherry's voice is fuzzy and far, far away.

"We all do stupid things, but really, what else were you gonna do? You're quite a gal." Keith takes two pills out of my bottle and swallows them with his beer. "Quite a gal." He takes a hand and lifts Cherry's hair out of her face. "You've got beautiful eyes. Anybody ever tell you that you have beautiful eyes?"

Cherry sounds like Gigi when she whines to go outside. I want to say, *Let her out,* or something to make her feel better, but my words will not come out right. All I can say is sorry, but it comes out as *uhhuhh.*

"Per's flying high. Aren't you, Per?" Keith laughs.

"Uhhuhh?" I try to say *what do you mean* or maybe *I guess so* or maybe *Gram.* I do not know. I do not care.

"It's just so bizarre I can defend Perry, but I can't defend myself against my dad. Way he looks when he drinks, the yelling, and when he gets angry he smacks me around." Cherry's voice is there, but I have many ears. Many, many ears and no eyes.

My body is on Keith's boat. I feel it rocking. I try to tell Keith. *"Uhhuhh."*

"You tell me when that happens! Day or night, you let me know! Nobody deserves that shit! Nobody! You hear me? Where do you live anyway?" Keith's words are mad, but they come out soft. Like a hug. I feel Cherry's smile, but my eyes are closed. I just feel her smile and it makes me warm. Their voices murmur and surround me like a blanket.

I love Cherry. She saved my life.

27

≋

LOTTERY WINNER ASSAULTED AT MARINA
HANDY MART WHERE TICKET WAS PURCHASED

That was the headline in the paper. The next part made me really upset.

RETARDED MAN ATTACKED BY THUGS:
THREE ARRESTED

"I am not retarded," I tell Keith. "I am not retarded. My number is 76. They lied. Can I sue?"

"Why do you want to do that?" Keith is dense sometimes.

"They lied. It's a mistake. I'm not retarded, I'm slow." I am embarrassed. I hope Cherry does not see the paper. Gary listens to us talk from the back office. The door is open.

"If people sue other people each time somebody lies or makes a mistake we won't get any work done at all. You want to call the paper? Make them print a retraction? You can do that, but it'll just make a mountain out of a molehill," Gary says, and sniffs his nose bottle. He is practical. That means he thinks other people should not get upset. I bet he wouldn't be so practical if he was the one called retarded.

Whenever Gary says one thing, Keith does just the opposite.

"I think Per has a point. Hey, Per, gimme that article! What's the phone number of the paper anyway?" Keith grabs the newspaper from my hand and walks over to the phone.

He must know how I feel. He is my friend.

"I'd like to talk to the reporter who wrote the piece on the lottery winner." Keith uses his good voice first. He is on hold so long I have to help Manny restock the shelves. I can only use my good arm. My other one is in a sling and hurts. I take my pills only at night to help me sleep. If I take them during the day, it makes me even slower. They are almost gone because I am sharing them with Keith.

"Yeah. This is a friend of Perry Crandall and, yeah, I'll hold." Keith has to lean on the counter and all the customers have to go around him. Gary comes out from the back office to ring up.

"Keith, we need that phone. Don't tie it up," Gary warns.

"No I don't want to e-mail! I have been on hold for thirty fucking minutes!" Keith can sound like he is yelling even though he talks normal.

"Watch your language, Keith!" Gary is waiting on Toby, who is a fisherman. I laugh because Toby swears far worse than Keith.

Keith ignores them. "Who do I need to talk to? Well, put her on!"

When it was time for me to get the sandwiches for lunch, Manny came with me because I could not carry them with only one good arm.

I buy everybody lunch on the days I work. It is so cool. I mean when a person can buy lunch for everybody, every day, it makes that person feel rich inside no matter how much money they have. That's why I like to do it. It makes me feel rich.

"How you feeling, Perry?" Cherry talks to me while Manny picks up beer and soft drinks. The Gilly's guy is making our sandwiches. We have to go back over and pick them up.

"Fine. I'm feeling fine." There are at least twenty people in Marina Handy Mart all shaking Cherry's hand and patting her on the back. She does not really have time to talk to me. Her hair is one more color than usual. Orange or maroon maybe. She is so beautiful, I just stare.

Manny carries the heavy stuff. "You like her, don't you?" He has that weasel sound in his voice.

"Yeah." I am uncomfortable telling him this.

When we get back to the store Gary is still waiting on customers. Keith hangs up the phone just as we walk up. He hands me a piece of paper with the name *Marleen Rafters*. There is a phone number written underneath.

"She's a top reporter. She's going to do a story on us." Keith looks excited. He has to pull up his pants twice.

"What kind of a story?" I hand him his sandwich. Keith does not look me in the eye and takes a big bite. He talks with his mouth full.

"You know, having money, being famous and all."

It sounds like Keith would like to be famous and have his picture in the paper. I know how it is being famous now. I know how it is and I tell him that being famous is not all it's cracked up to be.

"Be careful, Keith. It's not what you think it is. It can be embarrassing." Keith does not look like he believes me.

"Don't you want your picture in the paper?" he asks. Tuna pieces hang off his beard.

"Yeah, I guess. I don't know." I am confused. That is different from having my name on T-shirts, pens, and key chains. People would know my face.

Keith chews so loud I can hear his jaw crack.

I try to explain it to him and find the words I need out of my head. "It's just that, before, people didn't like me when they didn't know me. Then other people decided they didn't like me even when they did know me. Now it's just the opposite. People like me and they don't even know me at all. Sometimes they haven't ever met me and they like me." I am thinking about all the letters I get now. All the letters that people write asking me for things.

"It is the same thing, only the opposite of before," I say. "The opposite of before."

It is hard to put it into words. It is complicated. That means your feelings have many parts to them, but Keith seems to understand. A smile slowly comes across his face and he stops chewing.

It takes a lot to make Keith stop chewing.

"You're wise, Per," he says finally. "Fucking wise."

"For a slow guy, you mean," I correct him. "F-word wise for a slow guy."

28

≈

John and David come to visit Wednesday on my day off. They have someone with them. I am doing laundry so I do not hear them knock. They walk right in. That is so rude.

"We need to talk. We saw the papers. This is exactly what we were telling you about. You need protection." John is pacing. He talks softly but his fingers are bunched into tight fists. His face is shiny with sweat and there is white on his lips. I think it is from his Maalox.

"How is your arm?" David asks. He does not scare me as much as John does. There is a short, heavy man with black hair carrying a six-pack of Coke and a bag of potato chips. He hands me a can of Coke and offers me chips. I sit down on my couch. David stands in front of me. John paces. I think he will start biting his nails soon. The stranger sits next to me.

"This is our friend Mike Dinelli," David says. "He will be coming around to check on you. He's here for your protection."

Mike grabs my hand and shakes it hard up and down. He is strong. His brown eyes look all shiny like chocolate pudding in the can, which I like because it is fast. You just have to pop the top off and use a spoon.

"How you doing, Perry? Good to meet you," he says.

"Hello, Mike," I say.

"I'll be coming around to chat with you from time to time, Perry. See how you're doing. Make sure you're all right." Mike's teeth are small. Like Gigi's.

"We worry that you may be attacked again," David says.

"How come Keith or Gary didn't help you out?" John asks. He is still pacing slowly. "If we had known about it we could have protected you. Maybe you can't depend on those friends of yours," he says. "You need to start depending on us more."

This must be another Family Meeting, I think. Family Meetings should have all the family there. We are missing Louise, Elaine, and CeCe.

They start to talk among themselves.

Did you get the police record of the assault?

Why do we need that?

For evidence. To prove incompetence.

Can you leave that alone, John? Didn't you listen to Elaine? We're wasting time even thinking about it.

Listen to her and be pussy-whipped the way you are? No, thanks! What do you think I'm doing anyway? Sitting on my ass? Like you?

Screw you, John!

Screw you, David!

ENOUGH! Look, John. You played fast and loose with the wrong client's money. David, we won't stop with one brother if we see our way clear to get the other, if you get my drift. So you both need to get a grip and stop bickering. It won't get you anywhere and you don't need to frighten your brother. Am I making myself clear?

Mike rises, walks up to John, grabs his arm, and twists. John drops to his knees. David backs up. It is very interesting.

Now, I listened to you both. You assured me he would sign by now. It is obvious to me you don't have the influence you think you do. It's time for me to get involved. You need to do what I say, and stop wasting time arguing. If this doesn't work out you are going to have much more to worry about than each other.

Capisce?

I do not know that word.

Capisce?

Mike says this again and releases John's arm. He sits back down next to me. John and David close their mouths and nod their heads. Mike speaks in a whisper but I can hear him clearly. I feel shivers down my back.

Mike turns to me and smiles.

"Perry. I'm a financial adviser. Do you know what that is?" He leans back. "Nice couch," he says, and pats the back. "This afghan looks homemade. It's nice work. I have an aunt that crochets like this. Did your Gram make it? That's her name right? Gram?"

Mike is cool. He likes Gram's couch. He also likes Hershey's Kisses. He is just like me except he has black hair, sunglasses, and wears polo shirts. We sit and talk while David and John look out my window and hiss at each other. They sound like hoses.

When they leave, I go back downstairs.

"Who were your visitors?" Manny asks loudly. He is so nosy.

"Visitors? What visitors?" Gary's head lifts up.

"Probably those fucking brothers of his again," Keith snorts. "Am I right, Per?"

"No, there was also a guy named Mike," I say.

Gary and Keith sit with me in the back office, while Manny is in charge at the front of the store watching the register.

"You're so suggestible, Perry." Gary says this just like Gram used to.

"Damn right!" Keith pounds the desk with his fist. It does not scare me. Keith likes to pound tables with his hand. That is how he broke it once. His hand, not the table.

He comes over to me and says, "You have to *not* talk with your brothers or let them into your house unless one of us is around! Okay?" He holds my cheeks together just like Gram.

"They're my cousin-brothers," I tell him.

"Keith, you may be overreacting," Gary says.

"And you may be fucking naive," Keith says. He squeezes my face harder. "Just be careful, okay?"

"Okay," I say, and laugh because he still has a hold of my face and it is hard talking through fish lips.

Gary hands me a piece of paper at the same time Keith lets go of me.

"Here, Per, I have your new phone number. It's unlisted."

"I don't want a new number. I like my old one. It's got only twos, threes, and eights." I am upset. It takes me a long time to not forget my numbers.

"Complete strangers are calling collect and you're accepting all the charges! The bill last month was over eight hundred dollars! The apartment phone is a Holsted number. It goes to the company. I had to change it and pay extra to have it unlisted. Here. I wrote it down for you." Gary puts the paper in my hand and closes my fingers around it.

"This is such a gyp! Those people said they knew me!"

"Get back to work." Gary waves me out of the office. I put the paper into my pocket and go back to work unpacking boxes. Taking advantage is something other people do a lot of. I grumble to myself and complain.

It is good nobody can read my mind.

29

～～

There is a lot of unpacking to do, and it gives me ideas for where to put things on the shelves so they are easier to find. This cheers me up.

"We need to put the covers and short lines by the fenders. It makes it easier," I say to Manny.

He just says, "Whatever." And gives me his nasty look. I know he does not like to listen to me. He walks away even though there are still three more boxes to unpack.

I make a little place and organize fender covers by color and size. I look for a piece of cardboard and some colored markers to make a sign.

DON'T FORGET! I write big block letters. DO YOU HAVE LINES? And then underneath, DO YOU HAVE COVERS? YOUR FENDERS WILL LAST LONGER IF YOU DO. This is true. Gramp told me. I do not have room for anything else and I tack up my sign with a strip of duct tape.

Manny snickers and rolls his eyes at me. I stick my tongue out at him and quickly walk back to where Keith stands behind the counter so he won't come after me.

I heard Gary complaining to Manny three days later.

"Where'd all the lines and fender covers go? I can't find any more in the back."

"Perry moved them by the fenders. Talk to him." Manny looks like he hopes I will get into trouble. But I know I won't. The fender covers are all gone. Sold. Two customers told me it reminded them they needed new lines too, and thanked me.

"We sold out," I say to Gary. He looks at my signs, then at me, and then back at my signs.

"This is a really good idea." He sounds surprised. "How about we order some more?"

"I already did." I have good ideas. Gary and Keith both say so.

During lunch, I have some more ideas.

"People like to eat and drink when they buy things," I announce.

"How do you figure?" Gary usually eats his lunch at his desk. Sandy, his wife, always tries to make him eat healthy and fixes him salads in plastic bowls.

"That's fucking rabbit food, Gary. Eat like a real man!" Keith says, and buys him a Gilly's BLT, then threatens to tattle on him after he eats it.

After unpacking boxes all morning, I was too busy doing trash duty to go buy our sandwiches. I gave Keith a fifty-dollar bill and he went to Marina Handy Mart and then to Gilly's. He was gone for a long time. He brought me back a fake crab sandwich.

"At the grocery store customers buy stuff and walk around eating it and then they have cups in their cars and McDonald's and stuff. People eat all the time." I say this to Gary while I eat. Gram said eating was for mealtimes and at tables. I do not eat when I shop. Gram would not like it.

"Kitchen tables, Perry! That's what kitchen tables are for!" Gram said. Gram and I ate only at our kitchen table unless we went out to somebody's house and then we ate at theirs.

"He's got a point." Keith pulls open a beer and it makes a *pop* sound. Gary sticks his lip out. He looks like the boxer, Tandy, from Carroll's Boatyard, except he is not brown and white, and he is alive. Tandy was hit by a car last year and died. I liked Tandy.

Keith does not let me drink beer because Gram told him not to. Gary lets Keith drink one beer for lunch, but I know he drinks more outside Marina Handy Mart because Cherry tells me.

"I swear if you give my grandson any alcoholic beverage I will lambaste you from breakfast to Sunday!" Whenever Gram called me her grandson in front of Keith, we both knew she was serious. Lambaste means beat up. It does not have anything to do with lambs or with cooking. I do not drink alcoholic beverages because they taste like crap, Gram said.

"Drinking is something other people do a lot of." Gram would preach like she was Father Jacob.

"If you drink too much and are rich, then you are an alcoholic. If you drink too much and are poor, you're a drunk. Being an alcoholic is a disease and being a drunk is because you're weak and have regrets. Our friend Keith is a drunk," she would say.

After lunch, I take pieces of my sandwich and feed the birds. Nobody likes it when I do this. I do not know why. Birds have to eat too, especially seagulls. They eat a lot. I watch them fight with each other over my sandwich. One big white-and-gray one looks like the meanest and has a hook and line on his foot. I try to pull it off, but he flutters away, flapping his wings.

"Rats with wings, Perry! Rats with wings. You shouldn't feed them." I didn't hear Marty come up behind me and I jump.

"I know," I say. I always feel guilty, but feed the birds anyway.

"You can tell Keith his engine is fixed. You want to take him my bill?" Marty staggers like he is drunk only he is not. He has a bad hip.

"I get the bill. It goes to me," I tell him.

"Okay. Well, I replaced all the filters. I scrubbed the tank and practically had to rebuild the whole thing. The guts were all screwed up." Marty always calls the inside of an engine the guts. He hands me a paper with Keith's name at the top and a list of all the parts he used for Keith's engine.

I pull my checkbook out of my back pocket and write Marty a check for one thousand one hundred three dollars and seventy-three cents for parts and labor. He has to help me with the zeros.

"Parts and labor." I laugh. "That is funny. I mean, can you just have parts or just have labor? Would someone buy only parts?" I ask him. Marty does not answer and just shakes his head. I walk back to the store and give Keith the copy of Marty's bill. It is marked *paid* in Marty's cramped handwriting.

"Shit! You didn't need to spend all that money! He ripped you off!" Keith blows up, but he is still in one piece. He checks everything on the invoice. "I probably needed the filters, but holy fuck! He charged us extra for our own gaskets. Look!" Keith is always happiest when he can yell and complain about something. He looks almost cheerful and gives me a slap on the back. That is his way of saying thank you. He raps me on the back again two more times, burps, and looks satisfied.

"Keith, let's sail to Kingston or up to Anacortes or somewhere." I want to go on a sailing trip. It will be like being with Gramp again.

"It's pretty cold now, but yeah, when the weather clears we'll go up to Whidbey and anchor out." Keith starts looking at rope for new lines on his boat. His are chafed. That means they could break at any time. I laugh to imagine Keith's face one morning if he woke up and found himself and *Diamond Girl* floating free in the middle of the Sound.

I was so excited about fixing *Diamond Girl* that I made him take

Yo up to Ron's gas station at the corner to repair the heater and get a tune-up. It was one of the things on Gram's lottery list. She always told me that it was important to show people that you appreciate them. Keith always took us places in Yo. It was only fair.

"It's the first time Yo has been worked on since I bought him." Keith sounds amazed. Like he won a prize. Yo is a *him* and *Diamond Girl* is a *her*.

"Are all cars *hes* and boats *shes?*" I ask Keith.

"Pretty much."

"No, I don't think so. Some cars are *shes*. Gary's Jeep Cherokee is a *she*," I say.

"Manuel's Dodge is a *he*," Keith says back.

I cannot think of any *he* boats.

"What about Marty's car? What's that?" Marty's car has not been out of the parking lot in two years.

"That's an *it*. When cars don't run they're *its*. Like *it's* a lemon or *it* won't run." Keith is very smart.

When I show Keith the final bill from Ron's, he gets all upset again. He jumps up and down then rips the invoice up into tiny pieces. They scatter all over the floor.

"You going to sweep those up?" Gary looks disapproving. I run to get the broom and dustpan.

"Shit! Five hundred dollars for a fucking tune-up!" Keith's face is purple.

"Watch your language, Keith," Gary says for about the hundred millionth time. He wants us to be polite around customers. We can be as rude as we like around each other.

"It's okay, Keith, I took care of it. It's a fair thing. Gram would want me to," I say while I sweep the pieces up and put them in the trash.

"I'm doing this for Gram! It was something she always wanted to do for you," I say. "It was on her lottery list."

Keith would take her to the doctor whenever she needed to go.

We could ask him to take us to Costco for TP and paper towels. Those things are very hard to carry on the bus because they are so big. We both always appreciated the rides even though Gram would complain about Yo's heater. We offered money for gas, but Keith would never take it.

"If we won the lottery, I'd fix that goddamn heater!" Gram would promise him. In Everett, you always need a heater. It is cold even in the summer, especially early in the morning or when it rains, which is most of the time. Gram would be happy that Yo's heater is fixed. I start to wonder how it was before. Before I had the lottery money. I almost forget.

Marleen Rafters, the reporter, calls Keith back and schedules an interview for the following week. Keith starts combing his hair and tucking in his shirt. He even shaves every day, which is both strange and a miracle. That is what Gary says.

"It's a miracle! You're starting to look presentable. I may even make you manager." Gary looks pleased, like he is responsible for Keith's new appearance. I do not tell him it is because of Marleen the reporter. That would be tattling and it is not nice to tattle.

"You got to hear her voice, Per! It's deep and sexy. We got along great. Right from the get-go. She asked a lot of questions. How long I'd known you. How long we've been buddies. She said it must be something to have your friend be a millionaire." Keith keeps Marleen's number in his wallet. He pulls it out every so often like he wants to call.

But he does not.

30

≈

We end up rescheduling Marleen Rafter's appointment.

"I want to ride on an airplane and I want to see the candy factory where they make Hershey's Kisses," I tell Gary. This is another thing from our lottery-list game.

He types it into his computer.

"Here you go! Hershey's Theme Park. You can even go on a ride that shows you how chocolate is made. They have replicas of all the machinery."

"What do you mean replica? Where's the factory?"

"Replica. Uh. It means just like real. It isn't the factory, actually."

"But I want to see the real factory. I want a real tour." When people say "actually," it means they are telling you something you do not want to hear.

"I have bad news for you, Perry," Gary says. "They don't do real tours anymore. All they have is a theme park. There's no tour of the actual candy factory. There's a movie and a diorama tour ride, but no real factory there."

Theme parks are when you think you are doing something real and it ends up being pretend.

"I don't want a pretend factory. That's a gyp!"

Keith tries to make me feel better and orders a Meat Eaters Special from Pizza Bob's.

"I know you're disappointed, Per, but those things always turn out not as good as you think."

People always say this when you cannot do what you want to do. I really want to ride on an airplane, I think, and I look outside. It is frosty and there is ice on my window. It sparkles in the dark and looks like sugar. Winter is very cold in Everett.

"It's as cold as a witch's titty!" Keith says.

"Hey! Why would a witch have a cold titty? They wear all those black robes, so they have to be pretty warm under there," I say.

"It's all that broom riding they do," Keith says.

That makes me think about Gram. She was always cold and did good witch laughs.

"Hey, let's go to Hawaii!" I say. "Let's take Gram to Hawaii."

"What?" Keith sits up straight.

"It was on Gram's lottery list. Gram wanted to go somewhere warm."

Keith looks dizzy and says, "Gram is dead, Per."

"I know that, but you should be able to do the things you want even if you're dead."

Keith hands me a slice of pizza.

"Remember the movie, Keith? The one where those guys drag around their dead friend and take him to parties and stuff? That's my favorite movie. It's like that. Even though she is dead, I think Gram would still like to go to Hawaii. The three of us could go together," I say.

"You mean like spread her ashes?" Keith smiles when he says this. Meat Eaters has peppers and tomatoes, so he has red and green between his teeth.

"You spread mayonnaise and you spread peanut butter. It does not make sense to spread ashes," I tell him.

"You sprinkle them," he says.

"Like sugar on cereal? Like my oatmeal?"

"No! You throw them in the air off a mountain or toss them into the ocean. When I die, I want my ashes spread out into the Sound. Right off *Diamond Girl*, if she's still afloat," Keith says.

"Just dump them in the water?"

"Yeah! Then the water will just take me away. I'd go all over the world and it wouldn't cost me a dime!" Going around the world for free seems to impress Keith.

"I don't think Gram would want to be floating around in the water even in Hawaii. I never ever saw her in a bathing suit."

"So Waikiki, huh? Let's check it out." He grabs the phone book and phone. "Gram sure would get a hoot out of this!" Keith says.

A hoot is a thing that is much funnier after you're dead.

We fly first-class.

I did not know there were classes of plane seats. It is very cool. There is coach and there is first-class. First-class is when you pay a lot of money to cut in line. People mutter and stare when we go ahead of them. Nobody believes we are first-class. The seats are bigger, which is a good thing for Keith. We also get real silverware and free drinks.

Keith told me that the people in coach get no silverware and have to pay for food. In first-class, the food costs nothing. The stewardess lady checks our tickets so often that Keith asks her if she has a problem with us.

"Is there a problem?" Keith looks like he is going to get mad, but then he smiles kind of nasty and says, "I don't think you've met my friend Perry L. Crandall." He introduces me.

"You might have seen him in the newspaper when he WON THE WASHINGTON STATE LOTTERY?" He says this very loud and looks around.

Boy, people were interested. The nice man sitting across talks to us both and gives me his card. He sells insurance. The stewardess stops checking our tickets and instead gives us packages of mixed nuts and cookies, as many as we want. They act like they like me.

Then I remember.

These people like me because I won the lottery.

The stewardess hands me a tiny plastic pin.

"Look! Airplane wings, Keith!" I think they are totally cool.

"Do you want a pair?" the stewardess asks Keith, then hands him a package too.

"Do you think she thinks I'm retarded?" I whisper in Keith's ear. "Are these just for kids?"

"Nah, Per. She gave me a pair too. She doesn't think that."

That would have spoiled the whole trip for me, but it is okay. Keith says.

Going pee in the air was the best part.

"Keith, this is the highest I ever peed!" I say when I come back from the lavatory. Then I remember. "Is Mount Rainier higher? I peed there, too, in one of those little blue toilet houses. I went there on a field trip in Miss Elk's class."

Keith knows all about Miss Elk.

"I don't think that counts," Keith tells me.

"Why not?"

"One, because the one at Mount Rainier is still on the ground and two those portable ones don't flush. This plane has a flushing toilet."

"Where does it go, Keith?"

"What do you mean?" Keith is on his third umbrella drink.

"Where does all that poop and pee go?"

"I guess it just falls out of the plane. You know what they say. Shit happens."

I decide that I like flying so much I would do it even if I did not go anywhere. Like if I just went up and came down or even if maybe there was a restaurant on an airplane. That would be cool.

When we land in Hawaii, my ears pop like going down a big hill. I notice two things right away. One is that it is very hot when we get off the plane. The other thing is that all the signs have words with lots of aaas, eees, iiis, and ooos. Those are vowels. I am so excited I laugh. "Ha!"

"What's the matter?" Keith is sweating like a pig. Of course, I never saw a real pig except at the petting zoo at Woodland Park. If one did sweat, it would look like Keith. All pink and dripping.

"I am really happy, Keith."

"That's why I like you, Per. That's why I like you. That and you have money now." And he laughs back at me.

There are crowds of people around when we pick up our suitcases. Some guys have flowers in a ring around their necks. They smell good.

"Where did they get those from?" I ask.

"They're *lays*. So hookers know who to go to for money." Then he laughs and farts at the same time. "First-class, Per, we're going first-class all the way."

Riding in the cab is exciting. The drivers open the car door even though they know we probably can. When I was on the plane I wondered what Hawaii would be like, but it is just like Everett except that it has palm trees, is warmer, and everybody says, "Aloha." Nobody says Aloha in Everett. Our hotel is right on the beach. I can hear the ocean roar, like a machine.

"Hey, Keith, doesn't it sound like a washer?" I can feel myself start to bounce, I am so happy. "Hey! I have an idea! Let's buy swimsuits!"

"Shorts, Per, we just need shorts," but he follows me into a gift shop anyway. There is one in the lobby of our hotel. A lobby is a place where they keep anything you might need to buy like coconut bras, hula girl lamps, or towels with dolphins.

I absolutely do not understand the lady in the store and it really shakes me up.

"I thought you said we were in America?" I have to put my hand over my mouth when I whisper this to Keith so I do not hurt her feelings. I totally do not understand the language. It is probably Hawaiian, with all those extra vowels.

"We *are* in America, Per. It's called an accent," Keith whispers back.

Accents are when people speak and they don't sound like you.

The ocean in Hawaii is wonderful. I never saw anything like it. So blue and warm like a bath. I stand waist-deep in the water.

"Hey, you can float on your back!" I point at Keith. His stomach is like a giant ball.

"Go ahead! You can too!" he says.

"I can't swim. I don't want to drown."

"You're kidding, right?"

"Why would I kid about drowning?" I ask him.

Keith is my friend and tries to teach me to dog-paddle. I sink, flip over, and then float on my back. "Hey, look at me! I can float! I can't even swim. This is so cool! Hawaii sure is great!"

"You will be swimming for real before we go home. I swear!" Keith says.

People say I swear when they are not sure that they can do something, but they want to convince you they will.

We stay in the water until dinnertime. I float on my stomach, hold my breath, and open my eyes under water. I even see fish! I am so excited that I start to tell Keith and drown, but I do not die. I just get water up my nose.

"Per, calm down! Just because you get water up your nose doesn't mean you're drowning."

I stand up again. There are fish right at my feet. "This is like being in a giant aquarium!" I try to bounce on the ocean, but I get more water up my nose and splash Keith, which is not at all cool.

"Cut it out!" he says.

Nobody cares that we drip water and sand all the way back to our hotel room.

We can do anything we want.

That is so cool.

31

≈≈

The brightest sun in the world comes up in Hawaii. Part of our balcony faces the ocean and the other part faces a big rock called Diamond Head. That is like *Diamond Girl*, I think. It used to be a volcano, but it was shut off or something. I think they should turn it back on. That would be exciting.

I imagine yelling at Keith. "Hey, Keith! Volcano! You better run!"

Down in the lobby they have papers that tell all the things tourists can do in Hawaii. Tourists are people that visit places and do not live there. I am a tourist in Hawaii but not a tourist in Everett. I might be a tourist if I went to Seattle. I do not know for sure because you might not be if you are in the same state. All the papers are very colorful and I have trouble deciding which ones I want. They are free and are just like postcards, but have interesting things to read. Like: *This is the best luau in Hawaii* or *Save the endangered sea turtle* or *Rent a limousine for a day*. We get pages and pages of stuff and take them up to our room. I look at pictures of boats and dolphins.

"Okay, Per, what do you want to do?" Keith asks.

I am lucky he has been to Waikiki for something called R&R when he was in Vietnam. He tells me he likes to reminisce. Gram always told me reminiscing was different than remembering.

"Reminisce! Ha! That's when you lie about things that happened a long time ago," Gram would snort.

"God, the babes, Per! I used to have to beat 'em off with a stick!" Keith was a good-looking guy when he was young. That is what he says.

"Horseshit!" Gram would say when she heard Keith say this. "He's full of horseshit!" I do not say the S-word.

Gram's box is on the dresser. It is turned so she can see through the sliding glass door out to the ocean.

"So where you going to scatter her ashes?" Keith moves Gram an inch over so she has a better view.

"What do you mean scatter?" I ask.

"You know. Like we talked about. Spread. Sprinkle. Throw out," Keith says.

"Nowhere. I don't want to scatter Gram in Hawaii, just give her a little visit."

"You mean we're taking her back with us?"

"Yeah."

"Don't you want to leave even any of her ashes here?"

"Keith, that would be gross! She needs to be kept together! You wouldn't bury a body in two places." I can feel myself getting a teeny bit upset. I miss Gram. I do not want to leave even a little piece of her in Hawaii.

"Okay. Okay. I get it. Just a little trip. Don't get all wound up."

Keith always tells me not to get wound up. I never tell him not to drink, pick his nose, or fart.

Keith asks the valet guy at the front of the hotel, "My buddy and I are here for a few days. What should we do?"

A valet takes people's cars and parks them in different places. His name is Francisco. Like half of San Francisco. He looks just like Gary except he is brown, short, and has a lot of hair. "Go on the Arizona Memorial Tour," Francisco says.

He puts us on a bus and we take a motorboat ride across the water.

"Hey, Keith! Look! Fish!" I scream.

"Shhhhhh! Don't yell," he hisses.

I notice everybody on the boat is quiet.

Arizona is a dead ship from a war that makes everybody sad.

"Hey, Keith! Look at this stuff." There are lots of names of people who died in a war and a tiny church room with blue-and-yellow-glass windows that sparkle like glitter. The lady next to me looks like Gram except she is shorter and has kind of fuzzy hair. Her skin is dark brown. Gram's was white or maybe gray.

"Hi. I'm Perry. What's your name? You look like my Gram," I say.

"I'm Myrtle. Is your Gram here?" She looks around.

"No, she's back in the hotel room. She's dead," I tell her.

Myrtle raises her eyebrows and her mouth falls open. She looks better after I tell her Gram is just ashes in a box now.

"We aren't going to spread her around though," I say.

Myrtle calls me unique. Unique means you are not like other people in a good way. It is not like different, which means you are not like other people in a bad way.

We talk about war.

"I think war is bad. People get killed. That is my opinion." Gram always told me to tell people my opinion.

"Perry, make sure you say it is only your opinion. Remember everybody doesn't think the same," Gram would say.

"Yeah, war is bad all right." Myrtle has to wipe wet out of her eyes.

Blue, shiny pieces of oil bubble up from the wreck. They look like puddles in the rain when cars drive through them after the sun comes out. All ripples and full of shimmers.

During the bus ride back, I ask Keith about war.

"Keith, you were in a war, right?"

"Yeah." He has wet in his eyes too.

"What's it like?" I ask.

"You don't want to know," he says, and leans his head back against the seat.

"Yeah, Keith. Yeah I do."

He turns to me and his voice is thunder. "No, Perry," he says. *"No you don't."*

I sit and think.

And I think it is Keith who doesn't want to know.

32

≈

learned three things in Hawaii.

One, that people like me because I won the lottery. Two, that you can do things you want to do even if you're dead. And three, if I want Cherry to be my girlfriend I will have to buy her presents. I learned that last thing at the airport. You can learn a lot at an airport.

We were waiting to get on the airplane and Keith and I were looking at all the cool things for sale like coconuts you can mail and shark jaws. I saw a girl who looked just like Cherry. She had blond hair, not colored like Cherry's. She was taller and had a bigger nose, but she had earrings in her face and tattoos just like Cherry.

"Hey, that looks like Cherry," I tell Keith.

"Look at the guy with her. He's old enough to be her fucking grandfather," Keith growls. He is trying to peek inside a coconut bra on a plastic hula girl.

The Cherry-girl is trying on bracelets and smiling.

"Sometimes that's the only way a guy can get a girlfriend," Keith tells me.

I get an idea.

"Do you think Cherry would like this?" I show him a necklace.

"Sure, yeah. Girls like that kind of shit."

I bought Cherry the necklace and a box of chocolate-covered macadamia nuts.

Keith bought a box of pens that—when you click them on—make a hula girl naked.

That is cool.

I was way too tired to bounce on the plane. I felt like I had used up all my fun for the rest of my life. I thought about this the whole trip back. That all of us are given so much fun in life, kind of like brains. Some people save theirs until they are old and some people use it all up at the beginning of their lives. I'm using my fun up in the middle. That is so cool.

I was back two days before I saw Cherry. I went to get a Slurpee, but she had the day off. I had to buy another Slurpee the next day.

"Hey, Cherry, I'm back from HAWAII!" My sunburn is peeling off my forehead. Keith said everybody would either think I went on vacation or had a grungy skin disease.

I hope Cherry does not think I have a disease.

"I went on vacation and got you something." I hand her a white and green plastic sack that says HAWAII on it. She smiles when she sees the chocolate. She smiles even bigger when she sees the necklace. I help her put it on right there in the store.

"Awesome! Thanks." She has to bend down next to the metal wall of the refrigerator to see how the necklace looks around her neck. She could have asked me. I would have told her she looked beautiful.

"It's called puka shell. Puka means hole. Ha!" I think that is funny.

Cherry says she thinks it's funny too. She grabs me by the neck, pulls my head over, and gives me a big smacking kiss on my cheek.

Keith was right. Presents are a good way to get a girlfriend.

When I get home later, I have to sit on Gram's couch and bounce I am so happy.

33

≋

Mike Dinelli comes into the store on Thursdays to make sure I am all right. On Thursday afternoon, Gary plays golf and has lunch with his brother-in-law Leslie, which is totally a girl's name even though he goes by Les. I do not tell him this. It would not be nice. Keith goes to Pacific Marine Supply for our orders. He has more responsibility now. That is what Gary says.

John calls to see if Mike has come by and asks for a check.

David calls to see if John has called and asks for a check.

Elaine calls to see if David or John has called and tells me to send her a check.

Louise just calls and asks for a check.

Mike gives me a card with his name on it each time he comes. Sometimes he brings me lunch. He always brings me a giant bag of Hershey's Kisses. It is so cool that I do not need to buy them anymore. The bags have to go in my refrigerator because I cannot eat the Kisses fast enough. It is not good to eat too much candy.

I can't go out to eat lunch with Mike because I have to watch the store with Manny. He says we can just stand and talk. "We need to get to know each other, Perry. I'm a friend of John and David's and want to be your friend too."

"Okay," I say.

He is a protector and wants my Power. He brings a piece of paper each time he comes.

You need to sign this paper.

Can you write your name here on this line?

Let me see your signature.

It's important that you sign.

This will protect you.

It is for Power. That is what he says.

I do not want to give my Power away when I am working at Holsted's. I am too busy.

Manny runs the register and helps customers at the same time. We can get a lot of people on Thursdays. I look through catalogues to find stuff for the store.

"So, Mr. Crandall," Mike says, and laughs.

"Perry. Call me Perry," I say. This is our joke. I told him when people call me Mr. Crandall it makes me feel like I am in trouble, and so he teases me. This is a good tease. I like it when I have jokes with people. Keith and I have lots of jokes.

"My company has a specific plan for lottery winners who have selected the annuity option. It allows access to the money now instead of waiting for the yearly payments. Both your brothers think it would be a wise investment for you." Mike looks hungry.

"Do you want to buy a cookie or some coffee?" I ask. He does not ever eat with me even though he brings food.

Now that Holsted's has a corner for drinks and snacks, all the fishermen come in. They sit in chairs, drink coffee, and talk with each other. Gary complains that they never buy stuff, but I know they do. They are taking up all the seats so we have to stand while I finish my lunch. Mike buys a cup of decaf. I think decaf is stupid. I mean, the whole point of coffee is to keep you awake, but I do not tell him this.

"It's a good deal for you, Perry. We would actually be doing you a big favor. You could invest the cash and earn a lot more." Mike's voice stays very low. He keeps looking at the door like he expects it to open.

"How much money would you give me?" It is so funny. People always want to talk about my lottery money more than I do.

"Well, we take the rest of your payments and you would get four million cash right now." Mike talks fast, his pink gums show.

"But I won twelve million." Four for twelve does not sound fair.

"If you do it any other way you will have enormous tax consequences. Enormous. This way, since you could invest all your money at once, it's really to your advantage. You need to talk to your brothers and Elaine. They all think it's the best plan."

When he says that word *advantage*, it makes me think of Gram.

Each time Gram heard that word, she would tell me, "Whenever anyone ever says *it's to your advantage*, Perry? It is to theirs. You remember that. It's really to theirs."

"Well, I don't think that would be fair to you. I mean it would be unfair of me to take advantage of you just because I won the lottery. You probably ought to invest your money for yourself," I say. He is my friend. You do not take advantage of your friends.

Gram would be proud of me. Mike does not look happy. In fact, he looks like he needs a Tums.

"Hey, Mike. You need a Tums?" I ask. I worry. Mike is my friend and I do not want my friends to be sick.

This is always when Mike stops talking. When he sighs loud and when he leaves.

He looks like he has worries.

One time he said the F-word. Even though it was real soft, I heard it. I have two good ears.

"It's not nice to say the F-word," I told him, and he apologized. I do not say this word out loud, but lots of people do. Like the paperboy who throws the Sunday paper and it misses the mat. He yells the F-word. Or if Keith is just talking, he says F-something practically every sentence. Gram always warned that she would wash his mouth out with soap. She would too. That is what she did to me whenever I said a bad word. She said being drunk was no excuse for being crude or rude. That is what she would tell Keith.

But I know I am not crude or rude. Ha! That rhymes. I just noticed. Rhyme means sound the same, like Cherry and Perry.

Anyway, it was naphtha soap. She would use it to wash my mouth out. It is brown and tastes just like brussels sprouts if I ate them, which I totally do not because they make me throw up. Naphtha soap made me throw up too, so Gram only threatened to wash my mouth out if I did anything dirty. That was all she had to do. She was so smart.

When Keith came back, Manny told him I had a visitor. He is such a tattletale.

"Who was it, Per?" Keith wraps up his beer in a brown paper sack so he can drink and wait on customers at the same time.

"A guy named Mike. He is a protector."

"You need to stop talking to these guys. It's going to get you into trouble. Did he give you a card? What's his name?" I give Keith the card Mike gave me. He gives me one each Thursday. I have plenty.

"What the fuck's a protector?" Keith gives me a look that makes me happy he is my friend. I know he thinks he has to watch out for me just like Mike, but I can watch out for myself. Keith takes a long drink of his beer, crumbles the card up, and tosses it into the trash.

I have Power.

Mike says.

34

≈

"Marleen called this morning," Keith says. "She'll be out at three. We can take off work early and talk to her on *Diamond Girl*."

"Marleen?" I do not know a Marleen.

"She's that reporter," Keith says. "Remember? She's doing a story on us."

Now I know why he is wearing a tie and clean pants.

Gary is not upset about us taking extra time off for our interview. "Advertising, Keith!" he says. "Make sure you talk about the store and make sure they get the address right in the paper. Here. Give her a Holsted's Marine Supply pen and key chain."

"Hell, I'll give her five!" Keith says.

Marleen is tall, has a deep gravelly voice, and wears jeans with a flannel shirt. She has heavy black boots like Keith's that she unlaces and removes in order to come onto *Diamond Girl*. No one is supposed to wear boots on boats because they make black marks on the fiberglass. Marleen looks a lot like Keith. Her hair is the same gray-brown pulled back into a ponytail just like his.

"Hi, Perry. I'm Marleen. That's Arleen with an M." She shakes my hand hard and squeezes my fingers together until they tingle.

I laugh. "Ha! I'm Perry with a P!" I say, and rub my fingers so the feeling comes back. "Hey, I've seen you on TV!"

"You probably have. I do features on the news." Marleen smiles at me.

I whisper to Keith, "A TV star. Cool!"

Keith looks disappointed and whispers back, "A dyke, Per! Just my luck!"

A dike is both something to keep back water and a girl who likes other girls instead of boys. That is interesting, I think. A dam is strong and holds back water. Maybe that is why girls who like girls are called dikes. They must be strong. Marleen is nice. I count the hairs on her chin while she talks to me.

"People take advantage and jump to conclusions, I see . . ." and her voice trails off like the end of a song. She says *I see* sixteen times. I know because I keep track.

Then she asks the wrong thing.

"So do people treat you differently when they find out you're retarded?"

I do not say a word at first. If I were a cartoon, I would have steam shooting out of my ears.

"I don't know. Do they?" Spit drops fly out my mouth. I am really mad.

"Well . . ." Marleen looks at Keith. "Did I say something wrong?"

"Bingo!" Keith says. He pinches out his cigarette and tosses the end overboard. "Per's not retarded. He's slow. That's different than retarded."

"What's your number?" I ask Marleen. My hands are shaking.

She looks confused. "You mean my phone number? What do you mean?"

"No. Your number. My number is 76. I am not retarded. What is your number?" I ask.

"I don't know my number."

"Ha!" I say. "Then how do you know you're not retarded?"

"I'm not."

"How do you know?"

"I just know I'm not." She looks at Keith like she expects him to help.

"Hey, don't look at me. He's got a point. I have no idea what my number is. Shit! I let myself be drafted. I could very well be re-tarded." Keith bends down to light another smoke.

Marleen writes down everything I say and some other things that I don't. I look over her shoulder at her notebook.

Keith knows I am still mad and mouths *I'm sorry.*

Even though Keith seems disappointed that Marleen likes girls, they get along pretty well. They are laughing and drinking. Marleen keeps a cooler full of beer in the bed of her truck. They are bottles, not cans. She offers one to me.

"Nope, Perry doesn't drink any alcohol at all. *Nada!* He's an honest-to-God teetotaler," Keith says.

That means I do not drink beer.

"Look at that quad cab, Per! With duallys too!" He points to where Marleen's green truck is parked. "God, I love a good truck!" Keith says.

"So do I!" agrees Marleen, and she takes another swig of beer.

It does not look like she will be leaving anytime soon. My stom-ach is growling like Gigi. It is almost dinnertime. Keith looks like he has forgotten all about giving Marleen the Holsted's pen and key chain or anything about work. I think hard about what to tell her next so she will leave.

"That guy in prison. His number was only sixty-nine," I say.

"Who are you talking about?" Marleen stops writing and looks up.

"Russell. His name was Russell," I say. "His friends probably called him Rusty for short. That's what Keith and I decided."

"Russell James Cook. That was his name. There are more of them. A bunch more. Look them up in your paper," Keith told her. "It happens a lot. Especially in Texas."

"What do you mean?"

While Keith explained about Rusty to Marleen, I remember back to when he and I first found out about it. Ten years ago. He was reading the paper to me at work. He thought I would be interested to hear about Russell.

"Hey, Per! Look at this. Here's a guy on death row. His IQ is sixty-nine. He won't admit to being retarded. If he did, he'd probably just get life in prison. Instead, he's going to fry. What do you think about that?" Keith thought it was stupid and told me so. Russell lived in Texas. If you do murder in Texas, you fry.

"I can't understand why a guy would go to prison and rather be on death row than admit he's retarded!" he said.

Marleen is now saying the same thing that Keith said.

"I don't understand why he would do that," she says. "I mean he would be executed, right?"

People can be dumb sometimes.

"Russell would rather die than say he was retarded and so would I."

The sound of my voice flies up to *Diamond Girl*'s sails as I talk to Keith and Marleen.

I still remember the headlines. It made the front page of the newspaper every day for two weeks. And then they killed him.

35

~~

People would ask Gram questions.

Didn't his mother know?

Was she over forty?

Didn't she get tested?

Terminate? Couldn't she terminate?

Gram would get angry. "So you'd kill him just because he's slow? You'd do that?"

My first IQ number test was not good. It came out a bad number and both Gram and Gramp were upset. Gram asked me about it and I told her. Two things. First, I was scared. I thought I was in trouble. And second I had to pee really, really bad. I was worried that I would wet my pants and the other kids would laugh. I could not concentrate. Concentrate means do your best job. I could not do my best job. When my IQ number was not good, I could not be in class with Kenny and the other kids. Gram helped me with my homework.

"You're slow, Perry! There's not a goddamned thing wrong with you that time won't fix." When Gram clicked her tongue this time, it sounded like the sprinkler at school. She tried to make my teacher give me the number test again, but she said no.

The IQ score will not change appreciably from one test to another. There's a range of about ten percent. My teacher did not want to give me another test.

Gram was mad. "You mean to tell me you could be wrong? His test could be ten points higher?"

"That is unlikely." People say this when they are wrong and they don't want to argue anymore.

It was different with my next teacher, Miss Elk. She helped me take a new number test. She told me I could be anything I wanted. She said if I did not want to be retarded, then I did not have to be. I stayed after school and practiced doing tests until I was not scared. She told me how important IQ number tests are. I tried hard to do my best job. My number came out 76. It was bigger than 75. It was a good number, Gram said. The best number, and she and Gramp cheered.

We were happy, but the school did not care. They said the second test did not count, and took me out of Miss Elk's class and put me in *inclusion.* I cried every day. Then Gram said I didn't have to go to school anymore.

I told this to Keith when he asked. We talked about lots of things. About school. About what I like to eat. About sailing. He is my friend. Friends want to know all about you.

"Gram was a good teacher. She didn't mind that I was slow, but lots of people do." I name each one. I know them all by heart.

"First, there is the bus driver. He gets cranky if you do not get your bus pass out fast enough or have the right change. Then there is the grocery store lady at checkout in the fifteen-things-or-less line." I have to take deep breaths because it is hard to talk about being slow.

"If you are in that line and lose track of how many things you have, maybe you have extra milks or orange juice, and people think you are retarded, they stare at you and say mean things. If you have twenty things and go in the fifteen-things-or-less line and you are in a suit and talking on your cell phone and look very important, then you are just rude. That is okay. It is better to be rude than retarded," I tell him.

I explain things to Keith that he did not know. He did not know there are many numbers that mean retarded. Retarded is lower than 70 or it can be lower than 75.

But it is not 76. It is never 76.

36

≈

like the walk to Marina Handy Mart. It calms me down. I can
think. Sometimes I hum. There is a sidewalk the whole way and it
is easy to get to anytime of the day or night. It is close to the water. I
sometimes go there to get Chef Boyardee ravioli for dinner. Ravioli
are little meat pieces in dough covered with spaghetti sauce. They
taste good, are easy to fix, and are better than SpaghettiOs. You just
put them in a pan and heat them up until you see little tiny bubbles.
It is important to not look too close because they explode and hit
your face and hurt. Kind of like backwards pimples. When I walk in
the Marina Handy Mart door, the bell tinkles.

"Hey, Cherry!" I call.

Cherry can make anybody feel better. She is so pretty. I want to
ask her if she is my girlfriend today, but I stop when I see her. Something is very wrong. She is slumped behind the cash counter crying.
I can tell because her eyes are red and there is snot hanging from her
nose ring. She has a Kleenex and is blowing, which is good.

"Hey, Perry." When she wipes her face, I can see she has purple and blue all around one eye and a long scrape on her cheek. It looks like my arm after I got beat up.

"Cherry. Wow! Did you get in an accident?" Maybe she was in a car wreck. If she was in a car wreck, she would be lucky to be alive. Car wrecks can be very bad. You can die in a car wreck.

"No. Well. Yeah. Yeah, I guess you could say that." She blows her nose again and sounds like a duck, or maybe a goose like at Woodland Park Zoo. "My life is a car wreck," and she starts crying again hard.

"Please don't cry, Cherry." I pat her hand and her shoulder. She wipes her nose.

Boyfriends help girlfriends when they are in trouble but I do not know what to do.

I decide to buy lunch sandwiches from Marina Handy Mart instead of Gilly's so I can talk to Cherry longer. Cherry walks with me to the back and helps me find the right sandwiches.

"Manny likes cheese. Do you have cheese?" I know they don't have fake crab. They have tuna, which is okay. I like tuna. When I am done choosing sandwiches Cherry looks a little happier except for her black eye. She touches my hand when she gives me back my change.

"Thanks, Perry," she says. "Thanks a lot."

I walk back to work and wonder what kind of accident she had.

Keith is out of Gary's office and standing talking to a customer when I carry the lunches into the back room. Manny is leaning against the wall reading the paper.

"Marina Handy Mart? I hate their sandwiches," Manny complains. He always complains about Marina Handy Mart sandwiches, but he always eats his, even the crusts.

I can hear a man talking to Keith through the office door. His voice is loud and flat. Like the announcer guy on TV. I stand by the opening. I want to tell Keith about his sandwich, but I do not want to interrupt. It is not polite.

"So you know him?" the man says. He rolls an empty cart back and forth over the floor. The wheels go THWUNK. THWUNK. I wonder who the man is talking about.

"Yeah," says Keith, "I know him."

"Are you good friends?" The man looks over at me, then back at his cart, and then at Keith. He looks like Manny except he has silver hair and bigger feet.

"Yeah, we've known each other for a long time." Keith waves me over.

"It must be nice to have a friend who's a millionaire," the man says.

I get it. They are talking about me. I am embarrassed.

"Here, meet Perry Crandall. Perry, this is Ernie. Ernie, Perry." Keith puts a hand on my shoulder.

"Nice to meet you, Ernie." I hold out my hand.

Ernie looks from Keith to me. "Interesting. So . . . are you sharing your winnings with your family and friends?"

"Yeah, sure," I say. Sharing is a good idea and it is a nice thing to do.

Keith sweeps the air with his hand. "Hey, he does what he wants."

"I bet he does, I bet he does. Lucky you." Ernie gives a sharp barking laugh. He walks to the door and shoves the cart with one hand. It crashes into the wall and bounces back.

"Hot damn!" says Keith. "Not only do people get excited to meet a lottery winner, they get excited to meet the friend of one. And jealous too." He follows me into the back room to get his sandwich.

That is another thing. People are jealous of the lottery.

I did not buy Keith a beer. I only bought Cokes, but he did not seem to notice.

When I take a bite of my sandwich I remember to tell Keith something.

"Cherry has a black eye and scratched cheek," I say.

"What? How?" Keith sits straight up.

"An accident," I answer.

"Shit! God *damn* him!" Keith growls. He rips his sandwich apart and shoves it into the trash. "I'll be back!"

He sounds like Terminator. That is cool. I get up to follow. Maybe Keith has diarrhea. People leave a place real quick when they have the trots.

"Keith, you need Pepto-Bismol?" I ask. "I got Pepto-Bismol."

But he does not say a word. He does not go into the bathroom.

Instead, he grabs his jacket off the wall and rushes out the front door.

37

≈

When a dad beats up his daughter, he does not necessarily go to jail. But when a guy beats a dad up for beating up his daughter, they both go to jail. It is very confusing. A person only gets to make one phone call when they are arrested. I learned this from Keith. He was able to make one right away because Officer Ray Mallory recognized him at the station. Keith called me.

"I need to be bailed out. You need to pick me up. Yo's over at Marina Handy Mart," Keith says.

"I do not have a driver's license," I tell him.

"I know that. Cherry should be on her way. I need five hundred bucks. Bring your checkbook."

Bail can be what you do to water that gets in your boat or it can be money to get out of jail. After I hang up the phone, there is a knock at my door. It is Cherry carrying a backpack.

"Perry. We have to get Keith out of jail." She is panting from running up my stairs.

"I know. He called me," I tell her. "I wonder what jail is like. It would be scary. I wonder if Keith is scared."

"Nah! I don't think Keith is scared of anything," she says.

I am surprised Cherry knows where I live, but then I remember the time I got hurt at her store and she helped Keith bring me home. Her shirt is ripped on the bottom and her jeans drag on the floor. Her stomach hangs over her belt. It looks soft and white. There is a gold ring hooked through her belly button. She is so beautiful I can only just stare into her eyes. They are brown, red, and wet.

"I need to take Keith some money for bail," I say.

"I can drive. We can take Yo. Keith threw his keys to me just before the cops took him." Cherry sniffs and wipes her eyes with her sleeve. I think she should use a Kleenex because her black makeup is all over her shirt.

"I need someplace to stay," she says. "I can't go back home now. I can never go back." She takes a breath like it is hard for her to talk. "I could only think of you or Keith. I have no one else I can ask. There is no one else." She says this low, soft, and really fast. Her face is pointed down like she is sad, or like she expects me to say no.

"Yes," I say. "Yes, you can stay here."

Why would anyone say no, I wonder. I could never say no to Cherry.

She is shorter than me and looks like a kitten that needs to be held. Her foot scuffs my floor. Her toenails are painted purple. I think it is too cold to have feet showing through shoes, but Cherry looks like she does not mind.

"Let's go get Keith." When Cherry hears me say this, she drops her backpack on my floor and smiles. Her eyes are still wet, but her smile is so beautiful I cannot speak. My face feels hot. I bend down to tie my shoes, put on my jacket, and shove my wallet into my back pocket.

It is a good thing Cherry is with me because she is the one who has to figure out where the Everett Police Station is downtown. I do not know how to drive. I am impressed that Cherry can drive a stick shift. Yo shudders to a stop twice when she forgets to step on the clutch.

"It's easy to get confused because there are three pedals down there, Cherry. You're doing a good job." It is important to tell people they are doing a good job.

She talks to me all the way to the station.

"I had just gotten off. I had early shift. I left right after you bought your sandwiches. My dad was already home from work. I didn't expect him that early and I told him that if he touched me again I would call the police. For real this time. He thought I was kidding. He screamed at me and slapped me around so hard he gave me a bloody nose. I ran into the bedroom, grabbed the phone, and dialed nine-one-one. And then Keith just blew through our front door like the Hulk, fists flying! It was so awesome. He punched my dad in the face, threw him into the wall, and knocked him out. He was amazing." Cherry sighs. "I was so bummed because I had already made my call. It was the first time I ever called the cops when he beat me. They took both Keith *and* my dad in."

"I wish I had been there." I missed everything. It would have been very exciting.

Cherry and I both like Hulk comics. We like Slurpees and Pay-Days too.

Officer Mallory recognizes Cherry and me, and takes us around personally while the other officers get Keith out of jail. He shows me how the fingerprint station works and I get black ink on my hands. He told me that they don't usually take checks, but they know mine is good. That is so cool.

Keith is very glad to see us. He only has one tiny cut over his eye, a bump on his lip, and a bloody shirt.

"Hey thanks, Per." Keith slaps me on the back. He says thank you ten more times. Cherry hugs Keith and says thank you about twenty times. I do not slap anybody on the back. I just pay Keith's fine. Keith stuffs a bunch of papers in his pocket and we walk out to Yo. He slides into the driver's seat and I squeeze next to Cherry by the passenger door. Nobody talks much on the way home. Cherry just sniffs every once in a while. She sounds like Gigi when she looks for food on the floor.

Gary is waiting for us in front of Holsted's.

"What the hell is going on, Keith? I got a call from Ray Mallory! He said something about you being in a fight?"

"It's taken care of. Don't get your girdle in a knot."

That is funny. Only girls wear girdles. Gary does not laugh and talks low to Keith, then drives away.

We stand in the parking lot looking at each other and then Keith tells us good night. He strolls to his boat patting his pockets. I can tell he is looking for his Camels. Cherry follows me upstairs to my front door. She keeps looking back at Keith as we climb the steps, but he does not turn around. She bites her lip while I unlock my door.

I give her a tour of my place.

"You can sleep in my bed and I can sleep on Gram's couch. Here is my bathroom and a clean towel." I have never had a guest before except Keith and I don't tell him anything.

When I show her my TV, I can tell she is impressed.

"Oh, wow! That's awesome!" And she runs her hand over the top just like I do when I can't believe I finally have a TV.

I let Cherry take a shower first. She comes out with wet hair that snaps when she combs it. She wears pink sweatpants, a fleece shirt, and sits down on Gram's sofa. I take my turn in the bathroom. When I come out in my pajamas and robe Cherry is standing at the window looking out. Keith is sitting in his cockpit smoking a cigarette. *Diamond Girl* is very still in the water. I can see her hull reflected in the smooth black surface like there are two boats. I am feeling strange as I stand next to Cherry. Kind of excited, nervous, bouncy. My hands are sweating. My privates are hard. I grab the blanket Gram made, wrap it around my middle, and lie down on the couch. I squeeze my eyelids shut tight. I do not know what else to do. Cherry walks into the bedroom.

As she passes me, she puts out her hand, pats my cheek, and says, "Night, Perry," and "Thanks." I hear the door shut and try to go to sleep. It takes me a long, long time. I can still feel her touch on my face. Noises echo through the wall and the clock in the kitchen is ticking. *Click. Click. Click.*

I must have gone to sleep because I had a dream-story about Cherry. She was crying and then laughing. I beat up her dad with one punch, but I did not go to jail. I was like the Hulk, only handsome and tall with yellow hair. In my dream-story, Cherry put one arm around my waist and touched my privates.

I do not remember anything that happened after that.

When I wake up, my pajama bottoms are wet, but I did not pee my pants.

Cherry is still asleep. My clothes from yesterday are still on my bathroom floor. I put them on because I do not want to go into the bedroom for my clean ones.

I put my nightclothes in the washer, then make oatmeal and do my words.

I really, really like Cherry.

38

≈

So you have a roommate now." That is what Gary says. Then he always asks, "How's it working out?"

I say fine, but it is not just me, it is Keith. We both have a roommate. It is like we share Cherry. She spends a lot of time on *Diamond Girl*. Cherry and Keith talk and smoke in his cockpit. She tells me that since I do not smoke it's not fair for them to puff away in my apartment, but I tell them I do not mind. It reminds me of Gram except their cigarettes are not menthol, and they smoke more than just two.

Keith and I eat good dinners now. Cherry cooks Hamburger Helper, chili, Chicken Tenders, and makes us both eat salads. We have good desserts too, like Ho Hos, Twinkies, and canned pudding. She cleans my bathroom and mops my floor. It is so cool. I do not have to do anything. She even washes all our clothes. On Wednesday mornings, I have to remember to put all my dirty ones in the laundry bag.

"I am not searching through every frigging room in the apartment to find your wash, Perry!" Even when Cherry is pissed, she is beautiful. Pissed is not a bad word because you can say *I have to take a piss* or *I am pissed off*, or *piss on it* to make someone go faster.

She folds my clothes and everything. I only have to set the table. Keith eats with us every night. I tell Cherry I can cook, but she says she has to earn her keep. She still works at Marina Handy Mart, but I do not let her pay rent.

She is a hard worker like me. Sometimes she answers my phone.

"Who's Elaine?" she asks me.

"My cousin-brother David's wife."

"She left a message for you. Says she has papers for you to sign. What's her problem? She called me a slut on the phone. She doesn't even know me! I hung up on her. What a bitch!"

When Keith and Cherry are on *Diamond Girl*, I go into my bedroom. Cherry has her things neatly folded in my dresser. We share, but I only go into the bedroom to look at Gram and Gramp's boxes. When I miss them, I can bring them back by looking at pictures and sorting through their things. I spread everything around.

It is almost dinnertime and I hear my front door open.

"Perry? Are you here?" It is Cherry's voice. It always sounds like she is singing. I love her voice.

"You want roni-cheese for dinner? I bought hot dogs too! Keith and I went to the store," she calls out.

I slide the box back against the wall just as she walks into the room. She smells like smoke. I like that because it reminds me of Gram. I do not have time to take my mess off the bed.

"Perry? What are all these?"

"Gram and Gramp's stuff. It is mine now."

"Cool," she says. "You're so lucky. I don't have anything like this. I have nothing from my family."

She sits on the edge of the bed and looks at my memory things. I get Gramp's record player out and put on one of Gramp's records.

"This one is Sousa. Army guys march to this," I tell her.

We both kick our feet in time to the music.

"What's this?" she asks, and unfolds a piece of paper. "It looks like a list."

I take it from her hand. It has all the names of the people I am supposed to listen to: Gary, Officer Ray Mallory, firemen.

I read all the names.

I can do what they say, Gram said.

I have not looked at this list for a long time. I have not needed it. It is like I can decide who to listen to on my own now.

"Nothing. It is nothing," I say.

I fold it back up and put it into Gram's box.

39

≈

My first Christmas after the lottery was cool-sad. Cool because Christmas is magic, but sad because Gram was not there to share it. Gram and I loved Christmas decorations.

"Hey, Cherry! Keith and I are going to drive around tonight and look at Christmas lights. You want to come?" I do not know why, but my armpits get all wet and my stomach is lumpy like when I eat too many nachos with cheese and peppers or whenever I visit Cherry at Marina Handy Mart. Her black eye is gone and she wears shiny blue glitter on her eyelashes.

"Sure. Yeah. That sounds fun." She looks like she means it. Cherry always looks like she means what she says. That is why I like her. I want to yell yippee and bounce. I wait until I get back to Holsted's to do this.

I tell Keith that Cherry will come, and Manny laughs at me behind the cash register. His hair is so black and thick he looks like a leopard except he does not have spots, paws, or sharp teeth. He is skinny and smells like garlic today.

"Perry's got a girlfriend. Perry's got a girlfriend." Manny sings this real low, so Keith cannot hear.

I tell him to stop. I am embarrassed and I feel my face get hot. Manny is concentrating so hard on teasing me that he does not hear Keith walk up behind him.

"Shut the fuck up, ya little twerp!" Keith always knows the right things to say. He adds, "Merry Christmas, jackass!" and hands him an envelope with one of the bonus checks I helped Gary write.

It made me very happy to give everybody Christmas bonuses. Manny smirks and laughs as he opens his Christmas card from Holsted's. His mouth drops open when he sees the amount of the check inside. He whistles and sings the rest of the day and pats me on the back.

"No hard feelings, Per? No hard feelings? You have yourself a heck of a Christmas, okay?" He does not tease me anymore about a girlfriend.

Christmas is a time for giving things.

The first present I can remember getting was army guys. They were in my stocking. Gram yelled when they got stuck in the vacuum. They were very good soldiers and could sneak everywhere. Keith and I found one inside the heat register when I moved out of our house. That little guy had to be hiding there for years. I was impressed.

Another present I remember was Etch A Sketch. That was the first hard present I got. I would be working on a picture and forget and put it upside down and it would go away. I would cry.

"Quit your bellyaching, Perry!" Gram would always say quit my bellyaching and tell me to try again. Gram said that to me each time I told her I didn't think I could do something.

"Try again, Perry," she said. "Try again! And then keep on trying!"

We would do Christmas stuff the whole month of December. We would write down people's names on a list and decide what to get them. Gram liked lists. I do too. Everything we needed for presents was at Kmart or the Army-Navy store. Keith and I would go back later without her and buy the one thing she especially wanted that year. Three years ago, we got her an electric footbath soaker and two years ago, we got her a back massager that fit on the sofa. Last year it was a giant can of popcorn.

"If a body had that they wouldn't need to make popcorn for a year!"

Gram appreciated anything that saved time.

At Army-Navy, there was always a ton of good stuff.

"Hey how about these?" I found canteens. They were dark green and had US ARMY in black letters on the side. They were totally cool.

We got them for John, David, and Louise. Even though we did not see them very often, we still bought them Christmas presents. They were always too busy to buy us any. That's okay.

Gram would do her witch laugh when we found something really good, and we would buy it for everyone on our list. It saved time. Five years ago it was extra cold and snowed a lot, so we bought everybody long underwear. Keith really liked his and still wears the tops, even though they are stretched, stained, and have lots of holes from cigarette burns. Gram and I had a lot of fun shopping. My eyes get wet when I remember that Gram will not be here this Christmas.

We put more oil in Yo, because he leaks, and drive all the way to Seattle. Pretend snow fluffs down and it is perfect. Gram called snow that didn't stick *pretend snow*.

"All of the advantages of snow, but none of the problems," Gram said. "No getting stuck in the road, no slipping, no messing up bus schedules. Pretend snow is a damn sight better than real snow and it still makes it feel like Christmas."

Cherry squishes me next to the door, which makes me hot, cold, and bouncy. She sits in the middle. Cherry does not seem to bother Keith like I do when I bounce or talk too much or sit too close. He puts an arm around her and takes it off only when he has to shift gears.

"Hey, look! Snow!" Cherry points at the windshield. Only the driver's side wiper clears the snow, the other wiper just shudders. There is always something on Yo that decides not to work. Keith looks unhappy and pushes his lower lip out while he squeezes the wheel.

"Now, when did that happen? I can't see! Shit! I hope this doesn't stick. It'll be a bitch to get back to Everett if it does." He has me open the window and reach around to push the wiper and encourage it to work.

"Come on! You can do it," I say. After a few pushes it works fine and Keith laughs.

I laugh because he does.

"Sometimes all things need is a little encouragement," I tell him.

When we get to the neighborhood with all the decorations, the snow is sticking on the ground and Yo slides as we turn a corner. There are a lot of other people that have the exact same idea of looking at Christmas lights. We end up in the middle of a long line of cars and have to go slowly, which is fun because Keith usually drives too fast.

The houses all have colored lights that flash and move.

"These people go all out decorating!" Gram used to say. My favorite is when there are reindeer and stuff on roofs.

"I love the blue lights. Look at that one!" Cherry points out to the left.

"Look over there!" I point to the other side where someone put a giant plastic Snoopy in a sled on their porch.

Poor Keith has to look back and forth each time one of us gets excited. He eventually just stares straight ahead, bites his lip, and tries not to rear-end the car in front. When we come to the end, Cherry and I are hungry so Keith stops at Dick's Drive-In for milk-shakes and french fries.

"What's your favorite part of Christmas, Keith?" Cherry pokes him with a fry.

"When it's over." Keith looks grumpy. He is picking his teeth with Cherry's straw.

"Why are you so irked? It's Christmas," she says.

I want to tell Cherry to stop asking questions. They are the same kind of questions that Gram used to ask. Keith does the same thing to Cherry that he did to Gram. He pulls out his wallet, opens it up, and flips out a picture.

"See this? Her name's April. She used to be my wife. And the baby? My son, Jason. It was taken more than thirty years ago. She married my ex-best-buddy, Roger. Last time I saw her was the day I shipped out to 'Nam." Keith's eyes squeeze shut and then open again.

"December 24, 1971," he says in a voice that does not sound like Keith. "I signed both divorce and adoption papers at the same time, hiding my ass under a table in the mess tent while Charlie mortared the fucking hell out of my company. I thought I was gonna die any-way. What did it matter? That's what all those fucking lawyers do if you really want to know. Take advantage of a grunt's fear of death. They're all a bunch of moneygrubbing bastards. I even had to pay for the privilege of losing my wife and son to that backstabbing asshole."

"So, no." He puts his picture away and his wallet back in his pocket. "Christmas is a real drag." He spits this out along with the straw in his mouth.

Cherry is quiet and I am sad now. I would like to meet April and Jason. They look nice.

I know tonight Keith will drink. He will start with beer. Afterwards he will look for the bottles he took from John's house. I know that he keeps them in a lower cupboard in the galley of his boat. They are almost empty. The next day he will be hungover and sick and then he will not drink for days and then something will remind him, and he will start all over again.

It is after eleven when we get back to Everett. Keith parks Yo in the handicapped space.

"Hey! You can't park there," Cherry says. She does not know our rules.

I do not want her to make Keith mad. He is already sad.

"It's for disabled trucks too. Yo qualifies. He leaks enough oil to be anemic." Keith glares at her, and then he looks back down at his feet like he is sorry for snapping.

"Hey, Cherry, you coming?" I ask, and start walking up my stairs backwards. Cherry sleeps in my bed and I still sleep on Gram's couch.

She looks down and kicks her foot in the gravel.

"I think I'll hang out on Keith's boat for a while if it's okay with you, Perry. Just leave the door unlocked for me."

Cherry lifts her head, stares at Keith, and smiles.

He stares back and his face completely changes. He smiles back at her real slow. They do not say a word. They just stare at each other.

"You guys okay?" I ask.

They do not answer me.

"Cherry?" I say again.

Keith's eyes get wide like he is just waking up.

"I'll take care of her, Per, don't you worry. You go on up to bed." His voice sounds squeaky, like a mouse in a trap.

"Okay." I am tired. I need to go to bed.

My arm that got hurt at Marina Handy Mart tingles as I walk

up the stairs. It still sometimes bothers me. I have to open and close my fingers to make it un-numb. I take a shower, get into my pajamas, and stand in front of my window looking out at the falling snow. I put Hershey's Kisses into my mouth one by one and stare outside.

The chocolate melts on my tongue, not in my hand. Ha! That is an ad, I think.

The lights at the pier make the dock look like a Christmas card. It is not good to eat a lot of candy before you go to bed, so I put my bag away, go into the bathroom, and brush my teeth.

When I come back to the window, I can see a yellow glow through the portholes on Keith's boat. I see them flicker and flash, then go dark. After a while, I notice *Diamond Girl* moving. She is rocking hard back and forth. Back and forth. Back and forth. Her lines stretch and snap. I watch for an hour until she stops moving and floats gently on the water. It is quiet. I yawn until my jaw cracks and go to bed.

40

≈

Christmas is a time for giving. It was hard to decide what to buy Louise, David, and John. *Fruit baskets.* Gram told me in my head. *Send them big fancy baskets of fruit.*

I appreciated Gram helping me out.

I sent them checks too. I had to send Louise's fruit basket to John's house because I do not have her real address. I have never gone to visit her. She has a PO, which is a sort of a box. You cannot send flowers to a PO. I think it is too small for a fruit basket. It is only a tiny little place. Louise came by Holsted's three days before Christmas to ask for another check. I heard her because I was hiding in the back room. I peeked out through the crack in the door. Her hair is brown with yellow stripes now. She still scares me. I could hear her nails rapping on the counter. Keith told her to wait and went over to where I was hiding.

"What do you want to do? You want me to kick her skinny little ass outside?" he hisses.

"No." I hiss back. We both sound like snakes.

I kneel on the floor and write another check.

"You don't have to give her money each time she comes. This is just shit!"

Keith doesn't understand. I give her money to go away. Not to make her come.

"Is she gone?" I whisper through the door.

"Yeah, she's gone."

"Are you sure?"

"Yeah, I'm sure," Keith says.

We spend Christmas Eve with Gary's family. Gary's wife, Sandy, is funny and blond and his daughters, Kelly and Meagan, know me from when they come into the store. One is five years older than the other. I used to get them mixed up. Kelly is the older one and Meagan is the younger. Their house smells like turkey, pumpkin pie, and other Christmas food. My mouth is wet and I have to swallow my spit. My stomach is grumbling so loud that Kelly looks at me strange.

"I didn't eat any lunch," I tell her.

Keith brings in the presents from Yo and sets them under the tree. It takes him five trips. He is on his best behavior and only says the H-word once and the S-word three times. He pushes open the screen door with his shoulder when he comes into the house and it swings back and smacks his butt.

"FFFshhhoot!" I hear him say. He is trying really hard.

Meagan and Kelly look impressed with all the earrings on Cherry's face and the colors of her hair.

"I took out my silver stud because it's Christmas," she says, and sticks out her tongue to show them the hole. They both stare into her mouth and then she leads them into the bathroom so she can show them the ring in her navel. Cherry has on a red top with sparkles and a long skirt.

She is so beautiful. I am bouncing because I bought her a present that I think she will really like. If she likes it a lot she might be my girlfriend.

There is a real tree in the living room. Gram and I never had a real one. Ours was made out of aluminum and had a color wheel that plugged into the wall. It was lit by a forty-watt bulb that made our tree change colors until the plastic fell off. We lost first the yellow, then the red, and last Christmas the green fell out. I tried to repair it with construction paper, but the light wouldn't show through. Gram said it was okay because it already lasted for over thirty years.

Gary's tree lights have red, green, blue, white, and yellow bulbs. They move and sparkle. I squint my eyes to make them shine. Sandy gives us all special cardboard glasses and when we put them on, they make the lights turn into bells and angels and stars. We all trade to see everybody else's. I keep mine on even when I unwrap my presents. I am like a movie star. I get shirts, a giant box of Hershey's Kisses, a Game Boy, which is cool, but I do not know how to work it, and lots of other stuff.

Cherry unwraps her present from me first. A pair of diamond earrings that I bought her from Zales. She is so happy she screams and runs into the bathroom.

"I think she likes them," Sandy whispers to me. I think so too.

Gram always said the most happiness you can collect is when you give things to other people that you love. I have a lot of happiness in my heart as I sit with my presents in my lap and watch everybody else open presents I bought for them.

On the way home Cherry talks about her mother, I talk about Gram, and Keith talks about how cold it was in eastern Oregon growing up.

"Snow up to our assholes! Shit! It was cold!" Keith cannot help using those words now, because he held them in all night at Gary's.

"When I was little, before my mom and dad started drinking, we had a tree, and my aunts, uncles, and cousins would visit. After they separated, it just wasn't the same." Cherry looks sad as she says this.

"Gram and I had a fake tree. We put it up the day after Thanksgiving and took it down New Year's Day," I say. "She put it in our back room when it broke. It was all silver. Remember, Keith? It was in the first load we took to the dump."

After everyone went to bed, I laid stockings for Cherry and Keith in front of the TV. It is like a pretend fireplace. I am very good at stockings. First, you buy candy and oranges because they last the longest. Then you buy little stuff like key chains, pens, and crossword puzzle books, or maybe tiny flashlights and hand soap samples. I do good stockings.

I sleep on the couch and Keith and Cherry sleep in the bedroom. The thumping noise only keeps me up a little while. I am very tired. The next thing I know, I smell pancakes and Cherry is poking me in the ribs to get up.

"Santa came last night!" she sings.

And oh boy! Did he! Santa, which was most likely both Cherry and Keith, brought me my own laptop computer. Another stocking with my name on it was right next to theirs. I got a hat, new socks with sailboats on them, and a whistle that I blew until Keith yelled, "Shut the fuck up, Per!"

That's okay.

Cherry showed me how to use my computer and I wrote down all the directions. She said she would give me computer lessons every day as part of her present. Christmas is always a good day. But this Christmas was double wonderful. Keith and Cherry went back to *Diamond Girl* after dinner for a smoke. I sat up until late playing with my computer. Before I went to sleep, I heard Gram's voice.

Merry Christmas, Perry, she said.

Merry Christmas, Gram, I said back. *Merry Christmas.*

41

≈

My words today are *pass, passable,* and *passage.* I type them into my new computer. I started my new book in Word. I like that. Word. That pretty much tells you what it is. Word for my words.

Pass. The first definition I read makes me sad. It is right on my computer. Like Gram and Gramp. It means die. To pass on. I had to shut down my Mac, that is what I call my computer. I look for my *Gram Remembers Book* so I can think about her again.

The lottery reminds me of Gram.

When we would buy tickets she would say, "You know, Perry, life's all just one big goddamned lottery. Some of us have brains, some of us don't. Some people draw cancer. Others win car accidents and plane crashes. It's just a lottery. A goddamned lottery."

I like to think that Gram was happy. I did not win the brains lottery, but I won the other kind. Then I start to wonder. Is there a happiness lottery too? A sadness lottery? Does God sit up in heaven drawing numbers for people? Like for Keith? Like for me? It makes me wonder about God. Is everything in life just numbers?

January is cold and wet in Everett. I send more checks to my cousin-brothers. They still want my Power. Soon it will be February. It will still be gray, but that is the heart month.

I wonder what kind of Valentine's Day present Cherry would like. I think she might be my girlfriend now. She wears her diamond earrings all the time. Maybe I should buy her chocolate. Girls like chocolate. I like chocolate. They also like jewelry and books. Cherry is always reading a book. They have large brown men with bare chests and hair on the front. Sometimes one is holding a lady who has her boobs hanging out. Big ones. They are not too hard for me to read and the stories are fun, like shipwrecks and men panting over a girl's crotch, and spies. I learn a lot. When Cherry finishes a story, she lets me read it.

When Keith picks up one of her books, he laughs at us.

"Why do you want to read that crap?" He hands Cherry some of his books. *The Sea Wolf, The Electric Kool-Aid Acid Test,* and *The Illustrated Man.* She reads them all, then gives them to me. They are harder and I don't understand some of them. Except *The Sea Wolf,* which was cool. Cherry is a fast reader and I am very slow.

"You know, Keith, you need to read one of our books before you can judge whether it's crap or not," she says. Next thing we know Keith is reading Cherry's books too.

"Damn these are great!" He wriggles his eyebrows like a letch. I know this because that is what Cherry calls him.

"You're such a letch!" She yells this after he smirks and pinches her bottom. A letch is someone who grabs a lady's bottom. I would never grab a girl's bottom, because I think it is not a very nice thing to do. Cherry just laughs at Keith and makes a face. Cherry's faces are good because she has all those earrings like on her nose and tongue. She makes great faces.

Keith tells me he reads Cherry's books each night before he goes to bed. He will take the book to work when he gets to an especially exciting part and read when it is his turn to do the register. Sometimes he makes customers wait, when he does not want to put his book down.

"Does wonders for me, Per! I didn't know what I was missing!" Keith has to cover his book with brown paper so that Manny and Gary do not see what he reads.

I WATCH THEM from my window at night.

Keith lurches around the cockpit probably pretending he is a pirate coming to ravish Cherry. Ravish sounds like radish and has something to do with sex. Cherry tells me everything. She says she and Keith act out some of the stories. That is like playing games.

"It's really fun, Perry! It's good for the imagination and the sex is great!" My ears turn red when Cherry says that. Imagination is a good kind of lying. Sex is something you are not supposed to talk about.

Keith and Cherry fight sometimes when he watches basketball on my TV and then has a few beers like eight or twelve. I have to count the cans.

"You need to stop drinking this shit!" Cherry screams very loud. She is as feisty as Keith.

Keith yells back. "It's none of your fucking business and I'll fucking drink if I fucking want to!" Then Cherry cries and Keith hugs her and tells her she's his *Diamond Girl*. He whispers in her ear and pets her hair, and they kiss and make up, which is cool.

Sometimes I get embarrassed when they argue in front of me.

"Perry, it's no big deal. It just means we're a family and families fight in front of each other. We're all one family. Families fight, then kiss and make up." Cherry rubs my hand.

Families are cool. I used to have a family with Gram and Gramp and now I have a family with Keith and Cherry. We are also a family with Gary and Sandy.

We have spaghetti nights together on Saturday, just like with Gram. People can be nice when they get to know you. I told Gary about our spaghetti nights when I thanked him for Christmas.

"I really miss those spaghetti nights. Keith, Gram, and I played cribbage, and I used to beat them both," I said.

"Having spaghetti night sounds like a good plan," Gary said. "Maybe you can beat Keith on a regular basis in cribbage, but I don't think you can beat me in Scrabble, and for sure not Sandy," he teased.

Sandy likes the idea of a family game night, now that Kelly is getting older. Gary tells me teenage girls are scary.

"It's horrible! She's going to drive me to an early grave. Kelly just turned thirteen and already she wants to date! And the makeup? She piles it on with a shovel!" Gary talks to anyone who will listen about having a teenager.

Keith calls Kelly a *tween,* which makes her crazy.

"Tween! Tween! Tween!" He sings this in a high and whispery voice. Only Kelly and I can hear, because we know all about teasing. Most people do not know about teasing. There are special voices and things you say. Keith is very clever at this. I am glad he is my friend and does not tease me. Cherry calls him a troublemaker and Kelly calls him a butt-head. She throws sofa pillows and popcorn at him.

Sandy and Gary yell at Kelly.

"Act your age!"

"Give it a rest!"

"You're making a mountain out of a molehill."

This is not fair and it makes Kelly even madder.

Keith sings under his breath. "Molehill! Molehill! She's a little molehill!"

It is fun to watch.

"Mooooooom!" she howls like Gigi. "Daaaaad."

But they just tell her to grow up, which is, I think, what she wants to do most of all. I tell her growing up is not all it's cracked up to be. Like Gram used to say when I would complain about being too young to do something.

"Perry, you grow up, then you grow old, and then you die! Don't be in such a goddamned hurry! Growing up is not all it's cracked up to be!" After she said this, she would rub her hip with Ben-Gay and smoke a cigarette.

Sandy's tomato sauce is almost as good as Gram's. When we do not play cribbage or Scrabble we play crazy eights, or Monopoly. Keith is good at Monopoly and beats us all. I am still best at cribbage, but I am getting pretty good at Scrabble too because of all my words. I did not know there was a game for words. I think I might end up liking Scrabble best. Cherry is not good at games and mostly just watches. She helps Sandy in the kitchen, and reads her book.

"*Echt.*" I get a triple word score and my H is on a double letter square.

"That's not a word!" Kelly likes to complain about games and rules.

"Kelly is a whiner!" Keith sings.

"Yes it is. It means true or genuine," I say.

"I don't believe you. How do you know all those words?" She wrinkles her nose at me and looks like a pig. I would tell her this except it could make her even madder and not be nice. She pinches me when she is mad. I do not like to be pinched.

"I read the dictionary," I say. This is true, or *echt.* "Gram always made me do words." After I say this, I scoot away from her on the sofa so I am not near her pinching fingers.

"Put your money where your mouth is," warns Keith. "Delay of game! You want to challenge?"

"Yeah, sure, I'll challenge him!" Kelly runs into the den and comes out with the biggest dictionary I have ever seen. I would not be able to live long enough to do that one. I would have to do at least twenty pages or even fifty pages a day. I am impressed. It even has foreign words like from France, Germany, and Outer Space.

"Hey, Kelly, you'd have to do twenty pages a day to finish that one if Gram had been the boss of you."

"Gross!" She pages through the E's. I see her face fall. "It's not fair! He tricked me!" Then, "Moooooom! Daaaaad!"

Keith cackles like Gram used to. "Hee! Hee! Hee!" He makes a big line under Kelly's score. "You were the one who picked out the dictionary with foreign phrases! You should have grabbed *Webster's.* Don't ever get in a tangle with Perry over words," he says.

He doubles my points and Kelly loses her turn. She sinks deeper into the corner of the sofa. Her lower lip is practically on her chest.

"You could read pages from the dictionary every day," I suggest. She turns her head to the wall, squeezes her mouth shut until it disappears, and rolls her eyes back so only the whites show.

"That would be soooo totally a waste of time," she says. The next thing I know she has the big book on her lap and is thumbing through it.

"Ha ha ha ha ha!" she taunts. "Here's one I bet you don't know! Tyro!" She points to the page with a very dirty fingernail. Kelly is right. I have not gotten to the T's yet so I do not feel bad. I am still on P's.

I win that game. Keith is second. Gary is third. Meagan is fourth and Kelly is last.

"Dinner's ready!" Sandy calls and Kelly sticks her tongue out at Meagan all the way to the table. Kelly carries the dictionary and sits with it open on her lap while she eats. Meagan kicks her through the chair rungs. I watch them the whole time. It is very entertaining.

"Kids are a joy. Right, Sandy?" Gary smiles kind of funny when he says this. I change my mind and decide maybe that this is why he is losing his hair.

42

≈

Keith and I have a meeting with Gary and then we go to his lawyer's office. Gary's lawyer is Tom Tilton.

"Hey, Mr. Tilton, my cousin-brother's a lawyer," I say.

"Never mind that, Per," Gary says.

"Call me Tom, Perry. Would you prefer to use him?" Tom asks.

"No!" Both Gary and Keith say this at the same time and so loud I have to put my hands over my ears.

They do business talk, but I listen carefully. I am an auditor.

What can we do to protect Perry from his brothers and that conniving bitch Elaine?

How can we protect his future?

I've been thinking of expanding. It's good timing.

How does Perry feel about all this?

He's wanted to be a part of Holsted's for a while.

What kind of partnership do you recommend?

LLC? Sub S?

We're a corporation, but we're family-owned.

I listen closely. Even though I am an auditor, it is hard to understand, but I try.

I write Holsted's Marine Supply a very big check with many zeros. Keith has to help me fit them in. I am now an investor. I have lots of papers to take home and keep. It makes me a businessman. I spent a lot of the money in my checking account. Over half. But it is still more money than I ever had before. I still have my savings account. I do not touch that. It is for my future.

"Save half and spend half." That is what Gram used to say.

"He's protected, right?" Keith looks over my shoulder. "Let me read that, Per, before you sign." Keith is my friend. So is Gary. He says I get a bigger salary now that I am an investor. That is so cool.

I have lots of protection now.

I have Keith.

I have Gary.

And I have Mike Dinelli.

John comes with Mike sometimes. I hear them talk.

We need more time. We can convince him. We just need a bit more time.

Time is something you're running out of. My partners need some guarantees that the money will be replaced. That you can get your brother to cooperate. They are getting impatient.

Very impatient.

He sounds hungry when he talks like that.

Doing business must make people hungry, I decide. Even Gary, Keith, and I are hungry after we do our business. We decide to go to Gary's house and order pizza and eat ice cream.

It is like a party except we do not have balloons or cake.

Kelly sticks her tongue out at me across the table and says she is up to the C's. Gary and Sandy smirk at each other and then at me.

"I wish I had known how easy it was to make her study vocabulary words before this." Sandy leans over and whispers in my ear,

"You're a good influence on her." And she rubs my shoulder and smiles. It feels good to be touched like that. Like we are friends.

Before the lottery, people did not like to touch me. Gram used to say they were afraid, but I could never figure it out. The mailman would not shake my hand and the cashier lady at QFC grocery would always give Gram my change even though I handed her the money.

"Hey!" Gram would say. "Look at him! He won't bite!"

Now when I go with Keith or Cherry to get groceries the clerks call me by my first name and wave me over to their checkout stands. When any of them goes on a trip to Vegas, I have to touch their lucky coin or pet their rabbit's foot. That is sad. I mean, why cut off a poor rabbit's foot for luck? It is not that lucky for the rabbit, I think, losing a foot and all.

Gary holds a glass of wine in his hand and leans against his sofa. "So, Per, I'm curious, what else do you think we need to do at the store?"

I make myself think hard. I am an official businessman now.

Sandy and Cherry are in the kitchen fixing ice cream. They yell at us asking whether we want more chocolate or strawberry in our bowls. It distracts me.

Sandy shouts from the kitchen for Kelly to come help with the dishes.

"Mooooommmm! Nooooooo." Kelly can fit more vowels in a word than anybody I have ever heard. It is fun just to listen to her whine and it distracts me again.

"Well?" Gary asks.

"I am still thinking," I say.

I think better when it is quiet, but this is good practice for me. Businessmen need to be able to think even when they are distracted.

Keith is drinking a beer and watching basketball on ESPN. Every so often he snorts or pounds his feet on the floor and howls, "Shit, why'd they do such a fucking stupid thing!"

When he moans, "Awww, sweet Jesus! No!" I have to start all over with my thinking.

"Keith, your language. Okay?" Gary has to remind him to not say bad words.

I do not tell him both Kelly and Meagan say much worse things when he and Sandy are not in the room. I think about what Gary has asked me, while I shuffle the cribbage cards. When I do something with my hands, it helps me think.

"Sailing books and cards, a place that you can learn to do boat stuff," I say. "Fishing stuff. Magazines. Things with boats on them and people who know a lot about sailing."

Gary nods his head up and down just like the fake dog in the back window of Manny's Dodge. He was always nice to me before, but now he listens. I am not faster, but it is like people think I am. Money has made the slow part of me not so important.

Keith treats me the same. He still yells at me, slaps me on the back, and farts. He still looks worried and gets cranky, like when I bug him about calling April and Jason. He is the same person and so am I.

"Maybe they want to hear from you. Know where you are." I said this to him yesterday.

He just shook his head.

"No they don't, it's too late. You don't know what you're talking about, Per," he said. "Shut the fuck up!"

Being friends means you can say shut the F-word up.

But I do not say the F-word.

43

~~

worry about Keith, especially when he drinks. So does Cherry. I worry like Gram did.

"I worry about Keith," Gram would say, but when I asked her what she meant, she would only say, "I just worry."

There was one time we went to watch the fireworks over the harbor. Keith invited Gram and me to sit in the cockpit of *Diamond Girl* and watch Fourth of July.

"The City of Everett is going all out this year!" Gram complained. "All our goddamned tax money wasted! They're just shooting it up into the sky and burning it to bejesus!" she crowed.

Keith was okay the first ten minutes, and then he looked all sweaty and started clenching his fists. Green and red sparkly aerials scattered and faded across the black sky. I could not take my eyes off the glitter above my head. Loud explosions and bangs. One right after another. *Diamond Girl*'s slip was close to the sandbar where they set off the fireworks. We could feel the vibrations.

Keith started going crazy in a quiet way. Gram noticed it first. I was still looking up. My eyes on the sky. When I finally looked down, Gram was holding Keith. He was sobbing and crying into her chest. I had to look away. I was embarrassed and scared for him.

"They were kids," I heard him cry. "Just tiny babies. Women and babies." He moaned in her arms.

"They blew them up! The bastards just fucking blew them up like they were nothing!"

When the fireworks were finished, Gram and I sat on the rocking boat until Keith fell asleep. We had to take the bus back home.

I asked Gram later what happened.

"Was Keith sick? Was he afraid?" I asked.

Gram shook her head and sighed. "Keith's had too much happen in his life for just one person. There's only so much a body can stand," she said.

"What do you mean?"

She did not answer right away, but shook her head and pressed her lips together until they were gone inside her mouth. "That goddamned war," she finally said. "It destroyed him. Vietnam ruined Keith. It ruined him."

She said this over and over.

I remember being confused whenever she said this.

"Vietnam is a country," I said to Gram. "How did it ruin Keith?"

"That war. That goddamned war," she would answer, then turn away and walk out of the room.

44

~

Boyfriends give girlfriends presents on Valentine's Day. I give
Cherry a card, a box of chocolates, and a gold bracelet with her
name on it in red stones. I went to Zales again. They were nice. They
like me because I spend money.

Cherry has the day off at Marina Handy Mart and comes downstairs to eat lunch with us.

"Ohhhh I *love* it, Per!" She kisses me on the cheek three times
and hands me a card and a box. I unwrap it. It is a giant box of Hershey's Kisses.

She knows exactly what I like. The card says Happy Valentine's
Day, Love, Cherry. She called me Per. She loves me. She wrote it
down. That means it is true.

My mouth is dry and my heart is beating fast. Cherry must be
my girlfriend now.

She gives me a hug and says, "At least someone around here

remembers Valentine's Day." She sticks her tongue out at Keith, but he ignores her.

"I'm taking Sandy out tonight. You guys want to babysit? Per? Cherry?" Gary asks.

"Cherry won't be able to. She'll be busy tonight." Keith says this quickly.

His voice has something in it I have never heard before. I see two red spots form on Cherry's cheeks.

"Yeah, sure." I am disappointed. Cherry will not be babysitting. "I'll do it," I tell Gary.

"It's just so they don't kill each other, Per. We really hate to leave them alone together. I'll bring you home with me and then run you back when we're done," he says. "We shouldn't be too late."

I wish I could talk to Cherry about being my girlfriend before I leave, but she and Keith are in a corner of the store with their heads together. I see Keith take one of Cherry's hands and bring it up to his lips.

Gary talks to me nonstop all the way to his house.

"So what's up with Cherry and Keith?"

He looks at me sideways as he asks me this. I do not know what he means.

"I don't know," I say. "Nothing."

I do not think anything is up.

Sandy has a list taped to the kitchen counter.

"It's a school night, so they have to finish their homework before any computer games or TV. I'm counting on you, Perry." Sandy has a black fuzzy dress on and pink lipstick.

Meagan hugs me around my waist and I hear Kelly before I see her.

"Moooooooom!" Kelly flings herself into a chair. "I don't have any homework."

"Meat loaf, mashed potatoes, and carrot cake for dessert. The number of the club is on the fridge. We really appreciate this, Perry."

Gary comes in with Sandy's coat, grabs her around the shoulders, and sings out of tune, "I'm taking my best girlfriend out dancing for Valentine's Day!" He swings her around the kitchen. She covers her ears.

"I better be your only girlfriend!" Sandy warns as Gary leads her out the door.

It must be really hard to be a parent, I think, as I eat dinner with Kelly and Meagan.

"You guys got homework?" I ask.

"No!" says Kelly.

"No!" says Meagan.

Being a babysitter is easier than being a parent. All you have to remember is kids lie and they tattle on each other.

"Kelly, you have homework. Meagan told me," I say.

Kelly slaps Meagan.

"Hey, I never told!"

"You butt-face!"

"You're the butt-face!"

"Am not!"

"Are too!"

I watch the clock.

Three hours later, I hear a key opening up the front door and I am very glad. Sandy must have seen the relief on my face as she set her purse on the sofa.

"Oh Perry! Were they awful? I'm sorry!"

"It's okay," I say, and go outside to Gary's Jeep.

He drives me home, tells me about their dinner and dance, and asks me again about Keith and Cherry.

"Sandy thinks there's something there." He pulls up in front of the store. "What do you think?"

"We're friends," I say. "We're all friends. We're a family. I do not know what is there." And I tell him good night.

Yo is nowhere in the parking lot and *Diamond Girl* is dark and still. I take a long, hot shower and throw myself down on my couch. I am all TVed out after Kelly and Meagan, and fall asleep on my stomach with my arms under my face.

The night glows. The moon is out. Music wakes me. I think I am dreaming.

"Diamond girl . . . sure do shine . . ."

My eyes open. My clock flashes. One-sixteen. The sound is coming from the parking lot. I get up. My head spins and I sit back down. When I feel better, I tiptoe to the window, and look out. It is dark. The stars are brilliant. They are on fire. All the lights in the world are reflecting in front of me in the water. Yo is in the parking lot and the driver's door is wide open.

Music comes out of the inside of Yo. Keith and Cherry are dancing close together. I see their breath make little ghosts in the air. Keith is wearing a suit. I have never seen him in one and he does not look fat. Cherry's dress is long, sparkly, and drags on the ground. Keith takes one hand and closes it around Cherry's hair. He brings her head close to his and kisses her hard. They kiss for a long, long time. I watch them turn and walk slowly all the way down the dock, weaving to the boat, arm in arm.

Dancing. They look like Sandy and Gary.

"Day or night time. Like a shining star."

Like a couple. The truck door hangs open. Music drifts through the air. And then I get it.

Dancing. Cherry is Keith's girlfriend.

Not mine. And I start to cry.

The next morning Yo's battery is dead.

45

≋

My list is two pages long and I show it to Keith.

"What's this?" he asks.

"The lottery list. See, I marked off TV, trip to Hawaii, and fix *Diamond Girl* and Yo. Remember our game we played with Gram?"

"What's this next thing?" He squints his eyes. Keith needs glasses so he can read.

"The plot at Marysville Memorial Park. That is a cemetery," I say.

"Plot?" He looks confused.

"I want to buy the plot next to Gramp so Gram can be with him."

Keith tells me he thinks this is a good idea and that he will drive me to Marysville in Yo.

"Where is it again?" He asked this three times during breakfast.

"At the cemetery," I remind him.

Cherry says she thinks she knows where it is and comes with us.

She does not.

We have an easy time finding Marysville but a hard time finding Marysville Memorial Park.

I know where it is, but I do not know how to get there. Keith does not know where it is and does not know how to get there. Cherry does not know where it is, but thinks she knows how to get there.

We stop at IHOP to look through their phone book. Then we have to eat pancakes. We also have to stop at the Chevron station in Marysville to ask and at Katy's Bakery to get doughnuts. There is a Shell gas station at a stoplight, so we ask again just to make sure we are on the right road. This time Cherry writes down what they say.

Marysville Memorial Park is green and wet because either it has rained or maybe they just watered the lawn with sprinklers. The office is dark and has lots of wood paneling. I pet the walls and it feels like a metal slide. I can see myself on the surface and I make a face. Cherry sticks her tongue out at me like I am teasing her. We make faces at each other in the shine of the wall until Keith pokes us.

"Can I help you?" A tall white-haired man in a black suit walks out from behind a counter. He must be the cemetery man. He looks just like Gramp except Gramp had a mustache, was shorter, and is dead.

"We want to buy the plot next to George Crandall." Keith knows exactly what to ask. We tell him Gram died last August and I start to cry. Cemetery man looks a little confused until I put Gram's box on the counter. I do that just in case he needs to see her or talk to her or something. Like the evidence on Court TV. I like those kinds of shows. They are very cool.

The cemetery man's name is Leo. That means lion.

It is going to cost more than $2,600, Leo says. I can buy the plot next to Gramp, but I still need a vault for Gram's urn. That is a little marble house for dead people. It was very interesting. There are lots of other charges too.

"Do you want a graveside service?" Leo asks.

I look at Keith. "What do you think, Keith?" I ask.

"We can do our own," Cherry tells Leo. Then to me hard in my ear, "They charge you for that, you know. They charge for everything."

Cherry is very cost-conscious, that is what Keith says. "It's good we have someone with us who watches the bottom line," he says behind his hand.

We need someone to dig the hole for the vault and someone to bury it and then someone to fill the dirt in plus any engraving we want on the headstone. Then it will be eighty dollars for a special brass vase to hold Gram's flowers. After Leo adds it all up, I write out the check and make it out to Marysville Memorial Park. They take Gram and I say good-bye. I am kind of sad because it was nice to have her at home, but I know she will be happier to finally be buried next to Gramp.

"You know you can have a small urn with some of the cremains inside to keep." I do not know what Leo is saying and I jab Keith with my arm.

"What does he mean?" I ask. "What's cremains?"

"You don't want to know," he tells me, and then to Leo, "Per would prefer to keep her all together."

I have to cry again and even Keith looks teary. Cherry has to hug us both—first me, then Keith. We write what we want engraved on the graph paper.

Keith prints in big block letters: DOROTHEA MARIE KESS-LER CRANDALL

"Anything else?" he asks. "How about dates?"

"No."

"Why not? How about at least the years?" Cherry suggests.

"Okay," I say, and write down the years.

"What about a saying?" Leo asks.

This is getting complicated. "What do you mean?" I ask. "I only thought about her name on the stone like Gramp's."

"You know like *Rest in Peace*. That sort of thing," Cherry offers.

I know she is just trying to be helpful. "Gram never rested. She just slept and then was dead," I tell her.

"Was there a poem she liked or a Bible verse you want to put under her name?" Leo asks.

I try to think of something, but Gram was never one for Bible verses.

"What about *She will be missed* or *We loved her dearly?*" When Leo says this all three of us start to cry and he has to open another box of Kleenex.

Then I get an idea, probably my best idea. When I write the words down, Keith laughs and Leo frowns.

"Are you sure?" Leo asks. "Are you very sure?" When we tell him yes, he takes our filled-out paper and says everything will be ready in twenty days.

Three weeks later Keith, Cherry, and I drive back to Marysville Cemetery with two huge bunches of purple irises, yellow daisies, pink roses, and white baby's breath and we have our very own little private service.

Gram and Gramp are together now. The single large red granite headstone reads *George Henry Crandall* on one side and *Dorothea Marie Kessler Crandall* on the other with all the right dates below. And underneath in the middle?

Don't Be Smart.

Gram would like that.

46

We need to talk." John is on the phone. David, Louise, Elaine, John, and Mike call me each week. They ask about a check, about signing papers, about my Power, about selling the lottery payments, about investing. When I think it might be them, I sometimes let the answering machine get it. CeCe is the only one who does not call.

"She's too busy buying shit for that pissy little dog of hers, that's why," Keith tells me.

Today I was expecting a call from Sandy so I picked up the receiver as the machine clicked on. Cherry recorded a greeting on my phone machine. It was in her voice, which sounded like I had my own secretary. That was so cool.

"Perry L. Crandall is not available to take your call. Please leave a message and he will get right back to you. *Beeeep!*" I liked it because it sounded very businesslike, but Keith told me I needed a much cooler one.

He recorded, "Perry L. Crandall is out smoking dope and spending all his money and has no intention of returning any of his calls. *Beeeep!*"

John got upset when he heard it and called Keith rude and irresponsible. David laughed and said it was funny. Louise hung up because she thought she dialed the wrong number and Elaine screamed many bad words that were recorded.

"My family does not like my phone greeting," I tell Keith, Gary, and Cherry.

"That's tough!" Keith says.

"Too bad," says Cherry.

"What greeting?" asks Gary.

Keith and Cherry are now having the answering machine wars and I have nothing to do with it.

Today it says, "Perry L. Crandall is hunting yurts in Mongolia. If he survives he will return your call." Yurts are tents, Keith told me. You do not hunt them and I am not in Mongolia. That's okay.

"Perry! Are you there?" John's words are loud like he thinks I cannot hear. We are being recorded because I picked up the phone too late.

"Yes, I am here."

I do not know what he wants me to say. It is hard to guess what will make them hang up or what will make them happy. I try to figure it out just to get them off the phone. I wish Keith were here, but he is downstairs.

My family makes me uncomfortable when they call. They ask how I am. They ask what I am doing, but before I can answer, they ask about the money.

"How you doing, Perry?" John does not wait for me to talk and asks, "Have you thought any more about cashing in the lottery payments and investing in—" I hear something that sounds like *trust-mutualdividendsandinvestintaxshelterannuities*. It is one long word and does not mean anything to me.

Gram said my cousin-brothers never called after Gramp died
because they were afraid she would ask for money. She never did.
We had everything we needed, although it would have been nice to
have our TV fixed when it broke. Louise is better to deal with because she asks for a check and I can just mail one to her now. I do not
have to see her. I do not have to talk with her. I have no idea what
color her hair is now. Mailing checks is easier than talking.

"What, John? What do you need?" Even though I ask, I know
what it will be about. He wants to talk about the money. He always
wants to talk about the money. Before the lottery, he never called.
Before the lottery, we had nothing to talk about. Now we do. We
talk about the money. We talk about money and checks. David,
John, and Elaine all want to help me with the money.

"Things are coming to a head here. We're running out of time.
Mike and I were discussing your situation the other night. Everybody's worried about you. Do you have a will, Perry?" John speaks
extra slow like he thinks I do not understand American.

"A will? I don't think so. Why?" I know this has something to do
with the money, but I have nothing else to say.

"We think you need one. Mike says you're a real businessman.
He says you need a will to be a businessman."

"Mike is smart. A will sounds cool." I like it when people call me
a businessman.

"Look, Perry, Mom's not doing too well with her investments.
She needs money. I have some pressing financial obligations. David
has money problems of his own. We were all hoping you'd help us
out. After all, we're family. We want you to sell your lottery annuity. Invest in the family trust. Share your winnings. It would be the
fair thing to do. I mean, we would if it were us."

I hear Gram snort in my head. *Likely story.*

I am thinking hard. "What do you want me to do?"

He sounds excited now. "Have you talked about what you want

to do with the money to Mike Dinelli? About signing a Power of Attorney?" John asks. "He's an excellent financial adviser. He works closely with us. Let him know you want to work with him. Want to sign. Take his advice. He wants to help you. Help us. We can set up another meeting. I'll tell him you've agreed to sign the Power of Attorney. We're friends. He's a great guy." John's voice sounds like he is sucking one of those balloons that make you talk funny.

"Yeah," I say. "He's my friend too." There is that word Power again. I feel like the Hulk.

I hear Gram in my head again. *Careful.*

"You should listen to what he has to say. Tell him you'll listen. Tell him you'll sign. Please, Perry, this is important." John will not stop talking.

I want to ask why but I do not. The word *why* makes John the maddest even though he does not shout when he hears it. I can tell he is angry whenever I use it. It is scary to annoy him. Right now, he acts like he is happy. He sounds even more excited.

"Perry, it will be so much better when you finally let all of us help you. There are legal ways of decreasing the tax bite. It's ludicrous that you haven't taken advantage of our expertise before. It's a real waste. For instance, when we create the trust, we can manage it for you. You wouldn't have to do a thing. Just spend your money. We will do all the work. You'll see. I'm setting up a meeting. You won't regret it. You hear me?"

I do not say a word. I do not have to. John does all the talking. He always does. One minute he and David want to help me invest my lottery money, and the next, they want to split it between us. It is very confusing.

When I hang up, it is pouring. I can see wet drops on my window. I used to call rainy days sad days.

"The sky is crying," I would tell Gram. "The sky is crying for Gramp."

It is crying now for both of them. I look down. Keith is in his boat. I see him pulling a plastic tarp. His hatches must leak. Maybe we should order new gaskets from the store. I watch him work. He tucks in the edges carefully and clips them with bungee cords.

I go into the bedroom for Gramp's music. *Ride of the Valkyries* the cover says. There are horses and someone with a beard on the cover. He reminds me of the man at Marina Handy Mart who grabbed me by the arm. He was scary but he is in jail now. I remove the disk, place it on the turntable, click the on switch, and set the needle on the record. I pretend I am in a movie and shut my eyes.

I am in a boat. I hear trumpets and they sound like waves. Like wind. I am sailing. Standing at the bow of *Diamond Girl*. I taste pretend salt on my lips. I feel the lurch and crash of the hull against the water.

I was sixteen when Gramp died. We had taken *El Toro* out for a sail. *El Toro* means the bull in Spanish and was an eight-foot sailboat. A bull is a boy cow. When we picked her up from the dealer, Gramp told me to name her.

"She has a name," I said. "There." And I pointed to the plastic letters on her side.

"That's just the class, Perry. It means the bull. It's a brand name. Like Coke or Pepsi."

"The bull. I like that. I like *El Toro*," I insisted.

We named our boat *El Toro* even though it was a she.

We sailed her every weekend and sometimes during the week.

The last time when we left the dock Gramp looked worried. I could tell because he was sweating. I knew he gave money to someone and had to go to the bank later that day. I knew he always had business stuff to do, but out on the water all his worry lines would go away. We took turns on the tiller—first me, then him. The wind would quit, then come up fast and catch us by surprise. We both laughed as *El Toro* lulled, then jerked forward.

"I love you, Gramp!" I said.

"You're a good boy, Perry. The best." Then he reached across and lifted my hair out of my eyes. When we got to the marina, he stepped off *El Toro*, and sank to his knees onto the dock like he was doing a prayer. Like in church. I wound the line on the cleat, then grabbed for his hand. He always helped me up before. Not this time.

He said my name. *"Perry."* It turned into a whisper. His eyes rolled back.

And he was gone.

Marty was there when it happened. I did not know what to do. Gramp was lying on the dock. People ran to help. Someone, I think it was Gary, called Gram. The ambulance guys came, but there was no siren when they left. Gram heard it from Marty.

"Dropped like a stone," he said. "Dropped like a stone." He held her hand tight.

We lost the boatyard after that. The bank took over. *El Toro* had to be sold. We could not afford to keep her. That is what Gram told me. The boatyard was bought by someone else and Gary Holsted gave me a job. He said it was the best investment he ever made. I am glad. I like working at Holsted's.

I play Gramp's music and walk into the living room to look out my window. The water is a color I do not know. Maybe gray or green. Keith's blue tarp is over his cockpit. I see lights through the ports. They shine like candles inside of a pumpkin. I know Cherry is in there with him and wish they would ask me down for a visit tonight.

Cherry is Keith's girlfriend and Keith is my friend. I know this now.

I miss Gram. I miss Gramp. I want Cherry. My throat is full of sadness. My heart hurts. I listen for Gram's voice, but she is somewhere else. Maybe with Gramp. I wish she were here too. I lean my forehead against my hands onto the cold, cold window and think about what I should do.

47

~~

As spring gets closer, we have more days that Gramp would call sail days. Mild, but breezy. Cherry has never sailed, and now that *Diamond Girl*'s engine has been fixed, Keith says maybe we should all go to Whidbey Island for the weekend.

"Oh yeah!" I am excited. "Yeah, Keith, let's go."

"What do we need to bring?" Cherry is practical. "Let's go to the store."

Keith took us to QFC with a cooler.

"If it doesn't fit in here it doesn't go." Keith knows what we need.

Diamond Girl has only one small propane stove with a single burner.

"Bread, cheese, mayonnaise, cereal bars, cookies, crackers, juice . . . ," she says.

"Hey, Cherry, you're great at provisioning," I tell her. "Are you sure you've never done this before?"

"You're kidding, right? That just means buying food for people to eat on a boat. How hard is that?" She grabs more cans off a shelf. "I can make chili. What else do you guys want?"

I look at Keith and he grins. Beans make him fart. I do not think chili is a good idea but I do not tell Cherry this.

Instead, I ask, "Is your anchor line okay, Keith?" I remember Keith said the chain and rope on his anchor needed replacing.

"All taken care of," he says. He has done more work on *Diamond Girl* in the last three months than he has the last three years.

"When do you plan to be back?" Gary asks. "I can watch out for you." He hands Keith a brand-new VHF handheld radio and adds a package of batteries.

After we used a screwdriver to put in the batteries, Keith let me try it out. I have not used a radio since Gramp. It was so cool.

"Everett Marina. Everett Marina. This is *Diamond Girl* requesting outbound clearance. Over." The radio crackles and pops.

Roger that, Diamond Girl! You're clear outbound. Over and out.

We wanted to leave the slip by eleven, but it is now nearly two in the afternoon. The sun sparkles on the water. *Diamond Girl*'s motor goes PUTT. PUTT. PUTT. Keith steers out toward Whidbey and I wrap and stow the lines.

"How'd you know how to do that, Per?" Cherry watches me from the cockpit. "I'm a tiny bit afraid of being out in the water in a boat. They sink, don't they? Boats do? You guys know I can't swim, right?" she asks.

"That's okay," I say. "I can't swim either, Cherry. Keith tried to teach me in Hawaii, but we didn't have enough time." This does not seem to make her feel any better.

I pull Keith's life jackets out.

"See, we have these. This will keep you from drowning. You can wear one if you want."

"Yeah, I think I will. What if I fall in? What do I do?" She takes one from me and I help her put it on. I have to lengthen the strap that goes around her waist. I accidentally touch her boob, but she does not seem to notice. Touching is okay if it is an accident. I get hard anyway.

"The water is so cold here you'd freeze to death before you'd ever drown," Keith says. He is just trying to be helpful.

"Get her up, Per. Raise the mains'l." Keith sings this to me in his pirate voice, and then to Cherry, "That there's sailor talk. ARHHH!" Then he grabs her boob.

Keith points *Diamond Girl* straight into the brisk breeze and shifts into neutral. I pull hard on the sheet. Sailing is something I know how to do. When the sail is raised, I tie off to the cleat on deck and quickly sit down.

"Watch your head, Cherry!" I yell as the boom shifts. The wind is at our beam and *Diamond Girl* heels to one side. Cherry's eyes get large and she grips the side of the cockpit.

"Are you gonna puke?" I ask. Sometimes people get seasick. She shakes her head no.

"Are you sure? I can get you a sack," I say.

We are flying. We are free. We are sailing. The wind hits my face and I open my mouth to taste the salty air. Cherry watches me and does the same.

We fly for minutes. For hours. I can do this forever. Gramp is with me in my head. So is Gram. I close my eyes and decide if I have to die, I would die right now. I am that happy.

Keith knows a small bay around the corner from the Whidbey Marina. The sun lowers in the sky. We need to anchor before it gets dark. My stomach is growling. I remember I did not eat lunch. We coast along the shoreline, and then tack back and forth. The waves push us along.

"Here," Keith says, and stops the motor. I help him drop and set the anchor. We are not far from the beach. *Diamond Girl* does not draw much water. It is only about twenty feet deep. I cannot see the bottom, but the way the anchor set, I can tell it is rocky and not mud.

It slowly gets dark. Cherry opens cans of chili and heats them on the propane stove. We are all so hungry we eat bread with no butter with chili on flat paper plates. We do not want to wash dishes. We use fake spoons. Cherry mixes hot cocoa and we munch oatmeal cookies and Oreos. *Diamond Girl* floats. The breeze dies down. The water is glassy smooth. Car lights move and flash from shore. We watch them while we talk and doze.

"They wish they were us," Cherry says sleepily and leans against Keith. "They wish they were us."

I think that is true. It is *echt*.

I wrap a blanket around my shoulders and stretch out on the other side of the cockpit. This is where I always sleep on *Diamond Girl*.

I am happy and start to bounce, but Keith says, "Per? No bouncing on the boat, okay?" Keith does not like me bouncing on *Diamond Girl*. He goes below and comes back up with a guitar. I am surprised because I did not know Keith could play any instrument. He strums and sings to us. His voice is clear and deep.

What do you do with a drunken sailor . . .

My grandfather and me . . .

Sailing . . . take me away . . .

Cherry snuggles against him while he plays and I see her look up, take one finger, and brush his beard. He turns and sings into her ear. I can tell he likes Cherry and she likes him.

I wish Cherry liked me better than Keith but I do not think she does. Even though I bought her presents, she likes Keith best. Even though I am rich, she likes Keith best. He is poor, and rude, and crude, like Gram would say. But Cherry still likes him best.

It is hard.

Keith sings to me. To us. I can listen to him forever, but I fall asleep with him singing in my ear. I am asleep. And *Diamond Girl* rocks.

48

≈≈

Gram hardly ever talked about my father.

I thought he was dead.

I wondered about how he might have died. Probably in a car accident. That is how most people die. In a car. Or maybe a heart attack from cholesterol. Maybe that. He could have been murdered. That is not likely, but it is possible. Possible. Like winning the lottery.

Then I heard John and David talking. They came to visit after Mike Dinelli left on Thursday. They always come when Gary and Keith are not at Holsted's.

He agreed to a meeting. We're getting close! I know it!

What did Mike say to that?

He said we'd better be. We don't have much time.

Mike suggested Perry needs a will. He pointed out that Mom would get all the money if Perry died now.

You think he'll die?

Anything can happen.

What exactly do you mean by that?

Don't be naive, David. You probably believe in the Easter Bunny, Santa Claus, and that Dad actually sends Mom money each month from his stash in the Cayman Islands.

My father is alive.

They said he was alive. I had no idea.

David said the Cayman Islands were like Hawaii. All sunny.

I had no idea my father was lying in the sun in the Cayman Islands after stealing a bunch of his client's money. No idea at all. I wondered why he stole money. I wondered why he left and I wondered why I never knew.

I asked Gary and Keith if they knew the answer to all my whys. I wanted to know. I could not stop thinking about it.

Gary sighs and looks up at the ceiling. "I think it's time you knew, Perry." And tells me about my father.

"It went on for years. He sucked them dry. When he got in trouble, your Gramp took a loan out against his business for the bail so your dad wouldn't have to go to jail before the trial. When he skipped town, they lost the money. It was a struggle . . ." Gary looks up at the ceiling again. I look up too, but there is nothing there.

"I think your Gramp still could have made it. He mortgaged everything to buy the hoist for the yard. It was his last chance to turn it all around. When things got tough, he just needed a break, a loan to tide him over. Those bastard grandsons of his never got back to him. Ignored his messages. Wouldn't return his calls. Then it was too late. He lost it all," Gary says. "Everything he worked for his whole life was gone." His voice is low, as if Gram and Gramp would be upset with me knowing.

There was one thing Gary said that was not true. Everything Gramp worked for his whole life was not gone. Gramp worked for me.

I am still here.

That is true. I know this. It is *echt*.

When the people you worked for your whole life are still here, you have everything.

Keith listened to the story without interrupting, which is hard for him to do. All of us are thinking at the same time and no one is speaking until Keith clears his throat and says, "I wouldn't be surprised if they tried the same crap on Perry."

"No," I say. "They just want my Power."

"Shit!" Gary leaps to his feet. He does not say the S-word very often. Keith says enough bad words for everybody.

Power of Attorney? Could they be that stupid? That underhanded? Perry did you sign anything? Anything at all?

Gary dials the phone. "Tom? I need to talk with you now!"

Something is going on, but I do not know what it is.

Gary and Keith say things I do not understand, but I listen. I am an auditor.

What did your lawyer say?

He said it's not easy to declare someone incompetent, but that's not the real danger.

How much did that cost?

Nothing. Don't be so cynical, Keith. All lawyers aren't like that. Tom said there are other ways.

Other ways?

Better ways of getting his money.

Like what?

With a Power of Attorney, they could sell his lottery annuity. Embezzle all his money legally. Shit! What are we going to do?

We have to watch out. Make sure they don't get him to sign anything.

"Aren't you upset about all this?" Keith asks me. "Aren't you worried about what your brothers are doing? About what your father did?"

I can tell he wants to help.

"Cousin-brothers. They are my cousin-brothers, and no I'm not upset," I say. "I am sad. I am sad for Gram and Gramp. I am sad for everybody. I wonder why Gram didn't want me to know. It was only money."

And I walk back upstairs.

It was only money, I think, as I lay on my couch.

I wonder about things like this in the morning before I get up. Morning is a time for wondering. Gram and I used to wonder all the time in the morning. We would have wonder competitions.

"I wonder how they get the cream inside a Twinkie." That would be me.

"I wonder how you can eat so much." That would be Gram.

"I wonder how they know twelve makes a dozen." That would be me.

"I wonder how all those assholes in Congress got elected." That would be Gram again.

It is important to wonder. You find out things when you wonder. That is how I found out Louise was my mother and how David and John were my brothers and my cousins. I was ten. I know this because I wrote it all down in my third book. I called them cousin-brothers.

"Sometimes people don't live with their families," Gram said. "Like when a baby is adopted it means someone else can take better care of them. Will love them more."

I was crying because Kenny down the street said my parents didn't want me and that was why I didn't live at home with my mother and father.

"Your parents gave you away. I know who your brothers are. They're both creeps and you're retarded. Your dad's a scumbag and your mom's a slut!" Kenny pushed me all the way across my yard. Gram was in the back weeding the garden.

"You're only with her because you're retarded!"

"I am not!"

"Are too! She's the only one who wanted you. Retard!" Then he pushed me down, hit me hard in the face, and gave me a bloody nose.

I yelled for Gram. *"Gram!"* I cried. *"Gram!"*

"Get the hell out of my yard!" Gram ran fast, but Kenny was faster.

I did not know what scumbag or slut was. When I asked Gram, she got mad and called Kenny's mother on the phone.

"You keep your boy away from Perry," she said. "You keep your boy away."

Kenny and I used to be friends. I remember. We used to play together before either of us went to school. He was five and I was four. We played in my yard because I had a sandbox made out of an old dinghy that Gramp used to have at the marina. A boat filled with sand. We covered it every night with a tarp to keep the cats out. All the kids loved to play at my house. When Kenny's mom went to work, Gram would watch us both.

Then Kenny went to kindergarten and I could not because I had a late birthday and too many toilet accidents. Kenny would bring friends home to play after that.

"Why do you play with that retard?" they would say. My feelings would be hurt.

Look! He crapped his pants!

He smells!

Retard! Retard! Retard!

Even his parents don't want him!

They gave him away!

Retard!

Gram tried to explain why I was not allowed to play with Kenny anymore.

"People are cruel. They tell you to do things. They have to think they are better. They like to tease and torment anything they think is weaker than them."

That was news to me. I was weak? I did not think of myself as weak. Only slow. This was something else I started to wonder about. Why do people tease? I started watching people and tried to figure it out. I worked hard at being an auditor.

Manny used to tease me in a bad way, especially when he first started working at Holsted's. He only did it when Keith and Gary were not around. He does not tease me anymore. Now he says, "How you doing, Per?" And "What we having for lunch?" and stuff like that.

Now Gary looks right into my eyes when he asks me about ordering.

"What do *you* think?" he asks. "What do *you* think?"

Everybody looks right into my eyes. That feels good. They never used to look into my eyes before. They used to look away or up in the air or in their wallets. Never into my eyes.

Keith is the same as always. He still farts next to me. He does not fart next to Cherry. He tried to once, or maybe he did by accident, and she slapped him hard.

Farting next to a girl is rude.

49

John has been calling all week about a will. My will.

He says he has someone who will help me. It is important, he says. Mike Dinelli can help too. He can help us both. I need to sign some papers for protection.

Keith is at the Veterans' Hospital for an AA meeting. He is trying not to drink, which I think is a good thing. He goes to AA now every Saturday morning at nine. Cherry went to Marina Handy Mart to buy powdered-sugar doughnuts. We have to eat them quickly before Keith gets back because he is trying to lose weight and we are not.

My phone rings. It is always ringing.

"Is your friend Keith around?" John asks.

"No." I do not have time to say he will be back later.

"I got you a present. A case of Hershey's Kisses. They're at my office. You ever see a case of Kisses?"

"Yeah!" I say. "That's so cool. A case is a lot. We get cases of stuff at Holsted's. I have never seen a case of Kisses before."

"Well, I'm leaving now to pick you up and take you to my office. It's very important you have a will. You're a businessman, Perry. You can make your will and pick up the Kisses at the same time. It will be a surprise for your friends. You like surprises, right?"

I did not mean to forget he was coming. It was just that when I put on my jacket and walked downstairs to find Cherry, Gary asked me if we could babysit Kelly and Meagan.

"It's Sandy's birthday. I got tickets to a matinee at the Rep. I've got it all planned. If you two could watch the girls until six, it would be great." Gary knows it is easier if both of us watch them.

I forget all about John. I love to play computer games with Meagan and Kelly.

Cherry gets back with doughnuts and hands me one.

"Yeah, I'll babysit with Per. Can I take a bath?" She likes to go over to Gary and Sandy's because there is only a shower at my place. Anytime we go over there to babysit, Cherry takes a bath. She uses bubbles and everything. We spend so much time talking to Gary that Keith gets back. He pulls into the parking lot right in front in the only handicapped space.

"Is Yo leaking oil again?" I ask. I have to wipe powdered sugar off my mouth before he notices.

"Yo's bleeding to death!" Keith takes off his leather jacket and crawls underneath to spread cat litter on the ground. Gary hates oil drips in front of the store.

"You want to come babysit with us, Keith?" I ask.

"Like a dozen needles in my eyeball," Keith says, and puts his jacket back on.

"Gross! Keith!" Cherry doesn't appreciate his way of saying no thank you. I can tell by the way she rolls her eyes and sighs. He gives her a hug and a big sloppy kiss on the mouth.

"I'm going to patch some blisters, sand some bottoms, and make a few bucks." When he says this, he slaps Cherry's butt. "You guys have a good time and I'll see you later." Keith waves good-bye.

Gary gives us a ride so Yo can bleed to death in peace in the parking lot.

Sandy meets us at the door. "Thanks a lot, you guys, I really appreciate it. If we leave them alone, they fight the whole time. Last week, they broke a mirror in the bathroom."

Gary does not even turn off the engine. He pulls out as soon as Sandy hops in.

We open a giant bag of potato chips, Kelly pours us all Cokes, and we sit in the kitchen. Cherry excuses herself and runs to the bathroom. She is in there a long time.

When she comes out, she looks green.

"Hey, Cherry, are you all right?" I follow her into the living room. Kelly and Meagan are right behind.

"Yeah." It is hard to understand her. She is mumbling and holding her stomach.

"You going to take a bath?"

She shakes her head. "Not today. I don't think so." She scrunches herself down into the sofa.

"You okay?" Kelly is nosy. "Are you sick? Are you? Are you? Are you?"

Meagan slaps Kelly and then hides behind me. In a few minutes, both of them are fighting and I am stuck in the middle. Cherry ignores us all and goes to sleep on the couch. I have to separate Kelly and Meagan five times, so they do not murder each other.

I wish I had rope to tie them up, but that would not be nice. I still wish I had rope. With Cherry asleep, it is very hard to keep those girls separated. It would have been easier with two of us. I am tired and want to take a nap myself. It has been a long day. I am glad when Sandy and Gary get home.

It is dusk and all the outside lights are bright in the marina when Gary drops us off. Holsted's windows are black. Today it was Manny's turn to close the store.

"You want to order a pizza or something?" I ask Cherry. I am hungry and need some real food.

"Sure. Let's see where Keith is." Cherry looks more awake. She is still a little green. We walk along the dock. Keith is lying down in his cockpit with a wet washcloth covering his face.

"What's the matter, Keith? Are you sick, hon? You got a headache?" Cherry lifts a corner of the cloth. Keith's eye is purple.

"Wow, that's almost as good as Cherry's was," I say.

"Per?" Keith sounds like he just might be mad at me.

"Yeah?" I wonder what I have done.

"Do you think it might be possible that you could let me know when one of those brothers of yours is supposed to show up?"

"Oh no! Oh jeez! I was supposed to meet John! I forgot. I'm sorry. I was supposed to go somewhere with him instead of over to Gary's. I forgot!" This is all my fault.

"What happened? Did you get in a fight?" Cherry is rubbing Keith's forehead and he is rubbing her butt. I have to look away because I am embarrassed.

"That asshole John came with his fucking Mafia buddy looking for Perry. They accused me of hiding him. Shit! I have better things to do than hide Perry. I told them, but they didn't believe me!" Keith grumbles. "That friend of his is a thug. Are you sure you know everything that brother of yours is up to?"

"That's it?" Cherry is now kissing the tips of Keith's fingers. "That's all that happened?"

"Well, maybe a few more things. I threw a hammer. He threw a rock. I threw a screwdriver, and then his scumbag friend threw a very lucky punch."

Cherry moves his washcloth to peek underneath again.

"Oww! Careful. That hurts!"

"In the movies they put a steak on a black eye. I saw that in *Rocky* one, two, or three. Or maybe you have to eat raw eggs." I am trying to be helpful, but Cherry looks sick again.

"Shut up, Per!" Keith sounds grumpy.

That's okay.

Cherry helps him to his feet, gives him four aspirin, and we go up to the apartment. We call in our order to Pizza Bob's. They come by so often and I am so famous that we do not even have to give them directions, or even our names. They recognize all our voices.

We watch a DVD while we wait for our food. I like to watch movies with boats, sailing in storms, and guys yelling. This one is great and many people die. Keith and Cherry are cuddling on the sofa. I try to watch the movie instead of staring at them. Keith has his hand on Cherry's boob. I would like to put my hand there, but I do not dare. She is not my girlfriend and that makes me sad. My privates get hard and I have to excuse myself and go to the bathroom.

If Gram knew what I was doing, she would wash my mouth out with soap or something.

I don't know why, but it feels good.

50

≈

The warehouse on the other side of Carroll's Boatyard is for sale. Gary wants to buy it and I want to be a businessman. It is a good idea, so I decide to spend the rest of my checking account money on investing in Holsted's. I do not touch my savings. We meet with Gary's lawyer Tom Tilton again. Keith comes with me. He helps me with my business. He tells me the same thing that Gram said. About advantage, only he calls it up-and-up.

"Make sure this is on the up-and-up," he says, and looks like a guard dog except he doesn't bark and has no collar or fur.

Up-and-up means fair. It means right. It means no one will take advantage. Keith's shirt is tucked in and his hair is clean and combed. His ponytail is tied neatly in back. His beard and mustache are short and trimmed. I notice he has new pants and shoes.

"You look nice, Keith," I say. He does. He looks real good.

"Are you wearing Old Spice? Gramp used to wear Old Spice. You look like you lost weight." His smell reminds me of Gramp.

Everyone starts to talk at once. I listen. I am an auditor.

Is there a way we can protect Perry?

It's a lot of money for him to handle.

He's doing great so far.

Power of Attorney? LLC? Incorporate?

But what can we do? Those brothers of his are up to something.
I know it.

This is boring. I start to think up ideas.

"Hey!" I say. "I need a will! Can I do a will?"

"You want a will?" Tom looks surprised. He wears a shiny blue tie that sparkles and long hair like a rock star, but he does not have a guitar.

"What kind of tie is that? I want one." It is smooth and soft.

"It's silk," the lawyer says.

"He has expensive tastes now," Keith explains, but he is wrong. I just like the shiny blue color and how it feels. The lawyer takes out papers and helps me make a will.

"I can help you make a will. Who would you like for your beneficiary?"

"My what?"

"Who do you want to leave your money to when you die?"

"When I die? Am I going to die?" I look at Keith after I say this. I am worried. "Do you die right after you make a will?"

"No, Per. A will is when you get to decide what happens to your money, just in case you die." Keith speaks calmly. He knows I do not want to die.

Gary says, "It's just a precaution really, but as a businessman, it's important to take care of these things. It's a pretty good idea. What made you decide to make a will?"

"John did," I say. "Mike did too. They wanted me to come to his office and make one. Do I have to go there or can I do one here? He has Hershey's Kisses for me. A whole case."

Keith and Gary look at each other.

Why in the world would they suggest a will?

What could they hope to gain?

They're the closest relatives.

No, there's Louise.

His mother would get all the money, not the brothers, unless Per specified otherwise.

But he'd have to die before they'd get it.

Holy shit, do you think they'd risk it?

Instead of thirty pieces of silver—bags of Hershey's Kisses?

"I'll tell you what," Keith says. "We'll both make wills."

"So who do you want to have all your money after you die? You're in business now. You have assets. It shows financial responsibility when you make sure things are taken care of after you die." Tom talks fast like a machine gun in a movie.

"But I'll be dead," I tell him.

"What about your loved ones?"

I have to think. Then I get a good idea. "I want to leave all my money to Keith, Cherry, and you, Gary."

"What about your family?" the lawyer asks.

"They already have lots of money. That's what Gram always told me. That's why she gave everything of hers to me. She even gave me the house."

"She left the house to you? I thought it went to your brothers." Gary has wrinkles on his forehead.

"No, I gave John my Power and he signed thirty-two times. It was escrow. That's how I got five hundred dollars."

Tom writes on a yellow pad. "How do you know your brothers have lots of money, Perry?"

"Gram would grumble each time she paid the electricity bill or the phone." I used my Gram voice to say, *"Those brothers of yours have plenty of money,* she would say. *They don't need any of mine.*

The house goes to you, Perry, free and clear. She said it was mine but John needed my Power. Just like the Hulk," I tell them.

Keith starts fuming. I almost see smoke out of his ears. "Gary, what did I tell you?"

Keith! Sit down! You're like a bull in a china shop!

Gary, I fucking told you that you were naive and you said not to worry! Those were your exact words! Don't worry, they wouldn't dare! They've already done this before! They know exactly what they're doing!

Stop. Just stop.

Tom?

We have a saying at our firm that successful small swindles always precede big ones. I can't say there was anything illegal. That any laws were broken. It certainly sounds immoral, but being immoral is not against the law.

They want Per to make a will. That's what worries me.

You're not the only one.

"What about my will?" I ask. They are boring when they talk to each other and not to me. It is rude to ignore your friends.

"I tell you what, Perry. It's not a good idea to exclude relatives like that. You should leave them something or it's possible your will could be contested." The lawyer looks at Gary as if he is waiting for an answer. I think he should be looking at me. It is my decision. He should be looking at me. He tells me contested means they wouldn't have to do what I wanted.

"I've got an idea," Keith says, and starts laughing. "How about this?" and he tells us his plan.

I think it is a good idea. The lawyer asks me if I am sure.

"Yes, I am sure!" I say this in my shouting voice.

Keith has a very good idea. If I die, my mother gets $5,000 and Gramp's record player, David gets $5,000 and my twenty-seven-inch flat screen TV, and John gets $5,000 and the best thing of all. Gram's couch.

Gary laughs and says, "If anything will guarantee Per's safety, that will."

"What about their wives?" Keith asks. "You can't forget them."

"I know!" I say. "Elaine can have my bike and CeCe can have my green jacket with the hood." It only has a little paint on it. It is a good, warm jacket.

When we finish, Keith and I get copies of our wills. I feel like a good businessman because I will have many papers to take back to my apartment.

While Gary finishes talking to the lawyer, Keith goes to the bathroom to take a leak, and I take out my calculator and do my adding. My bank statement for this month is folded in my pocket. I will have my next lottery check in October. I get interest from my savings account, plus I get my regular check from Holsted's. I will get an even bigger salary now because I am partner. I told Gary that I do not need as much as him because I am not married and I do not have two children, a wife, and a mortgage, but he said we are partners and partners have to share. He said Holsted's is doing well. That is so cool.

I still do not talk about my savings account. Gram said not to. My checking account does not have as many zeros now, after my last investment in Holsted's, but it is still a lot of money. That's okay. I am a businessman.

At Holsted's Gary tells everyone I am a new partner. He announces that we will be expanding. He promotes Keith to manager. Manny looks grouchy until Gary promotes him to assistant manager. Keith's first job is to hire more employees. He brings in Charles from Pacific Marine Supply and tells me he already hired another employee.

The next day I see who it is. Manny stands at the computer register with Cherry. Instead of Manny showing her how to use it, she is showing him all the things that he did not know before.

"This is the same machine I worked with at Marina Handy Mart," she tells him.

Cherry only has earrings in her ears, and her long-sleeved shirt covers her tattoos.

"See? You can make extra copies of the receipt right here." She looks very pretty and professional. "You can access inventory by going into this program."

Manny watches Cherry for a while then says to me, "That girl knows her stuff!"

I can tell he is impressed. I see him try to peek down the front of Cherry's shirt when she bends over to get more register tape.

Cherry only throws up in the morning before she gets ready for work. I let her use my bathroom because she is my roommate too, not just Keith's. *Diamond Girl* only has a small head. Cherry could throw up in my kitchen sink or use a paper sack, but she says she prefers the toilet. That is okay.

Cherry is wonderful with the customers, especially the ones who do not know what they want. Instead of making them feel stupid, the way Keith and Gary do, she helps them figure out what they need. Usually that means they buy more than they actually want because they are so grateful to her.

Soon she will not let Keith or Gary help customers.

"Only Perry, Manuel, and I should work the register. You and Keith do not have good people skills," she lectures.

Cherry has been reading the management column in the newspaper and she is the one who takes my picture and sends it into the *Everett Herald* business column "People on the Move."

"Holsted's Marine Supply Adds a Partner," it says above my photo. It has my name underneath, how long I have worked at Holsted's, and says that I won the Washington State Lottery.

Cherry is very smart.

It is good advertising.

51

≈

We are doing business for our new warehouse. It is big enough to store boats during the winter and we get the keys today. It is called closing. I think that is funny. I mean, we get the keys. Shouldn't they call it opening?

Gary's lawyer is talking. I do not understand what he is saying.

"What language is he speaking?" I whisper to Keith.

"Bullshit!" he whispers back. "He's talking Bullshit with a capital B. All lawyers learn it at school."

Keith does not usually say the B-word. He says the F-word, the S-word, and sweet Jesus. I can say sweet Jesus. That is not a bad word. Gary says jeez and crap because he has kids. John says the Ch-word, and David says the H-word. I do not say any of those things.

Keith has on a blue tie that looks just like mine only mine is green. I like green. I am bored. I kick my feet against the chair until Keith looks at me and puts a finger to his lips. That means I have to be quiet. I look around the room and listen. I am an auditor.

I sent copies of Perry's will to John, David, and Louise as you suggested. I told them I thought it was in Perry's best interest that they had this information. Just in case something happened to Perry. They were rather surprised, as you predicted.

Jeez! Did they say anything?

Not to me.

When I get home, I do my words. They are *rice, rich, riches, Richter scale, rick,* and *rickets.* I thought rick was a guy's name, but it is a stack of hay. I think that is interesting. Words sometimes mean different things. Rice is a food. I do not like rice because it is little pieces and gets in my teeth. Rich. That is me. I am rich. That is so cool. Richter scale is about earthquakes. I think I was in an earthquake once. The ground shook. Or maybe somebody was mad. Rickets is a disease.

I did not hear from my cousin-brothers for two days. David called first.

"Perry, we heard about your will. We just wanted you to guard your assets. That's all. Hell! I was only trying to protect you. Make sure you made the right decisions."

I can make my own decisions, I think, but I sent him a check. I have to make each check amount smaller so I do not run out of money in my account and make the bank mad at me.

John called next.

"Don't worry, Perry, we'll always be there for you. Christ! We were all just concerned." He breathes hard through the phone.

I mailed him and CeCe each a check.

Elaine calls. She asks if David came by. He was supposed to come by, not just call, she says. She sounds mad.

Careful, I hear Gram say.

I send her a check too.

When people are concerned, they want checks.

Everybody wants checks.

52

≈

bug Keith again and make him mad. I do not mean to, I just can't understand why he doesn't want to meet his son, Jason. See what he looks like. He could take a vacation and go. I would if I found out I had a son.

"Cherry and I can watch *Diamond Girl*," I say. "Friends do jobs for each other like watch their stuff while they are gone. Don't you want to see him?"

Cherry looks worried when I ask about Keith's son. I can tell because she has wrinkles in her forehead. We sit in the cockpit. It is sprinkling. It always rains in Everett.

"Don't be so freaking stupid! How many fucking times do I have to tell you? No. I. Do. Not. Want. To. See. Him. I was stupid. I was an ass. I signed my rights away. She married my best friend, Roger. Jason is *his* son now. So leave it the fuck alone!"

"Don't talk to him like that!" Cherry speaks loud when she is mad. Her face is all red and not from her makeup. She puts a hand on Keith's chest, but he pulls it off and leaps to his feet.

"Don't you start with me, woman!" Keith jumps out of the cockpit and marches down the dock. We can hear his feet pound all the way to Yo.

Diamond Girl rocks with the force of his leaving, like she wants to follow. We hear the roar of Yo's engine and the spatter of gravel in the parking lot. Cherry is shaking and her eyes are wet. She touches my hand.

"Don't worry, Per, he doesn't mean it. Really." Then she starts to cry and I hold her.

"I know," I say as I pat her back. "I know." My feelings are hurt and my throat is thick.

Keith is my friend. I am unhappy. I hope he comes back.

"He's trying to stop drinking you know," Cherry says. "He is trying to stop."

I tell Cherry I understand.

"Alcohol is the devil. The very devil himself. It's a demon, Perry," Gram said. "I wish I could help Keith see that. But he'll have to see for himself. It's the very devil."

"Why?" I would ask Gram. "Why does he drink?"

"Demons and regrets," she would say. "Demons and regrets. The two worst things in the world."

"He's trying to stop." Cherry has stopped crying. She wipes her eyes on her shirt and sniffs.

"That's good," I tell her. "Gram always wanted him to stop. Keith always said he didn't have a reason to."

"He'll have a reason to now. He'll stop now, because he'll have a reason." Cherry sounds sure of herself and smiles while she rubs her belly.

My stomach flips. She is so pretty. I pat her hand. I am relieved. It worries me when Keith gets upset and mad. I do not like it.

We sit together in the cockpit. It feels like spring and the weather is warm.

"Perry?" Cherry says my name in a question. She licks her lips like she is nervous. "Ummm. Do you like working at Holsted's?" she asks. It does not sound like that is what she really wanted to ask me.

"I love it. It's the best job in the world," I say. That is true.

"How long have you worked there?" She looks over at the parking lot like she is willing Keith to come back.

I have to count. "Almost sixteen years. A long time." I try to think of something else to say. "How about you, Cherry? Do you like Holsted's?"

Cherry pulls her sweatshirt down over the edge of her sweatpants.

"No one has ever asked me what I think about my job," she says, "but yeah, I like it a lot. I love it actually. It's the best job I ever had."

It is quiet and the water laps against *Diamond Girl.* I wonder how long Keith will be gone.

"What's that?" Cherry points to a bird.

"A baby gull. They are brown instead of white. You want to feed it? Where's some bread?"

Keith never used to have much on his boat. Cherry goes below and brings up a package of crackers. We spend an hour breaking them up into pieces and tossing them into the air for the birds, and the water for the fish. We laugh and talk about birds, fish, and boats.

Keith is gone a long, long time. It is dusk. We hear Yo's engine whine in the parking lot and then go silent. When he climbs into the cockpit, his shirt is wet. He is breathing hard like he has been running and not just driving Yo.

"I'm sorry, Per." He grips my shoulder. "I'm so sorry." He hugs me hard.

"I'm sorry, hon. Forgive me?" He wraps Cherry in his arms and kisses her so long, I have to look away. Cherry whispers something in his ear and he whispers back. They hold each other tight and turn into one giant person. I do not see where Keith starts and Cherry ends. They do not notice me leave.

When I look down out of my window later on, they are leaning against each other sitting in *Diamond Girl*'s cockpit. I stand there and watch the sun go behind the mountains.

I am an auditor, but there is nothing to hear except the beating of my heart. Now I am a watcher, I think, as I stand and stare out. Half of the sun shines, half is behind the jagged peaks. It sinks until just an edge is left.

I wondered where it went when I was young. It was one of my wonders.

"I wonder where the sun goes," I would tell Gram.

"China," she would say. "It goes to China and Australia."

I think it would be wonderful to know so much. To be so smart that if someone asked you any question you could say the answer. Gram was like that. So smart. Keith is like that too. So is Cherry. I watch Keith and Cherry hold each other on *Diamond Girl*. I watch the sunset. I watch all the colors and try to say their names.

"Red, pink, orange, gray . . ." I say this softly, like I used to talk when I did not want to wake Gram up. "Purple, lilac, yellow . . ."

What's the matter, Perry? I hear her voice. She is here with me. Like when I would come home crying from school. Like when I would have a tough day at work before I knew what to do. Like when I missed sailing with Gramp.

What's the matter, Perry? I hear her voice. And I talk to Gram.

I tell her how much I love Cherry and I cry.

I cry.

53

≈

There's been an accident."

Gary's face is serious. His voice is flat. "There has been a terrible accident." He talks quietly into my ear. "I have to go. There may be some mistake. I have to go."

"Who?" I ask. "Who is it?"

When a person dies in an accident, they have to be identified. They have to be identified, just in case it's not them. In case it is someone else.

"Who?" I ask.

Gary looks down at the floor and says nothing. I see the tiny muscle in his jaw move and jump. I know. I think I know.

I ask Gram in my heart to please make it someone else. Please not make it Keith.

"Please, Gram?" I whisper. *Please?*

"Officer Mallory thinks it might be Keith," Gary whispers softly. And he turns and walks out the door.

I put away boxes while I wait. Box after box. They are brown. I peel the tape carefully. I do not want it to rip. To tear.

Please, Gram.

Cherry is in the employee bathroom. She has to pee again.

"You gonna be in there all morning?" Manny bangs on the restroom door.

"Now, don't you start!" she shouts at him as she comes out.

"Quiet! *Be quiet!*" My voice hits the ceiling it is so loud.

They both stare at me with their mouths open but I look away and hide my face.

Keith teased Cherry this morning, right before he left for his AA meeting.

"Woman, you spend a lot of time in that bathroom. Are you ever coming out?" Keith rattled the knob. "I'm leaving now. Give me a kiss good-bye."

"I'll kiss you when you get back!" Cherry yelled through the door.

I cannot say anything. Gary told me not to until he was sure. Until he returns. I do not say a thing. I open box after box. Carefully. I do not tear the tape. I wish on the tape. If it does not rip, if it does not tear, then Keith is fine. Keith is okay.

Please, Gram.

Manny and Cherry both know something is wrong. They walk wide around me and do not talk.

I hear Gary's Jeep before I see him. He walks through the door. His face has no color. No color at all. His voice is low and scratchy like when you walk on gravel. Low like a bulldozer far, far away. Low like an airplane so high you cannot see it.

Please, Gram.

When he tells us what happened Cherry's mouth falls open, but nothing comes out. She gets smaller and smaller until she is gone. I am crying so hard my eyes are shut tight, but I make no sound. I hear nothing. Just a roar. A roar of sad.

Manny just says, "Jesus God. Jesus God. Jesus God." Over and over.

Hitting a tree at fifty miles an hour is not a good thing. Keith was not even drinking. He came around a corner. There was a lady and two kids in the road. Their car was stopped and the hood was up. He had to hit them or a tree. He and Yo hit the tree hard. That is what the lady told Officer Mallory. That is what Officer Mallory told Gary on the phone. And that is what Gary told us when he got back from the morgue.

A morgue is a cold place they keep dead people.

"I want to see him! I didn't kiss him good-bye. I want to kiss him good-bye!" Cherry wails.

"God, no, Cherry, please," Gary says, and holds her shoulders.

"I have to, Gary. Please? Take me? Please?" Her voice is a piece of wind. I feel it in my chest. "Please?"

Gary takes us both to see Keith. We have to sit on a hard brown bench. The walls are green. We wait. The man asks us if we are sure.

"Are you sure? Are you sure you want to do this?" He is kind. I see that in his eyes. I want to say no.

No, I am not sure, but Cherry says yes. She says yes so hard I feel her breath on my neck. The man unzips the bag that Keith is in. He looks like he is asleep. We can only see part of his face. The rest is covered by a sheet. His beard has small bits of glass in it that glitter. They sparkle under the light. They are pieces from Yo's shattered windshield. That is what the man says. I asked him at first if they were little jewels but he said no, and told me what they were. There is a small purple bruise above Keith's brow and his skin looks empty like there is no one inside.

I hear a shudder. I feel it vibrate through me as Cherry bends down to kiss Keith's cheek. I hold Cherry tight with my arm and with my other hand brush Keith's hair off his forehead like he used to do to me.

"Your fucking hair's in your eyes, Per." That is what he used to say. "You look goofy. You look goofy, Per."

"You don't look goofy, Keith," I say. "You don't." And my voice cracks.

I have never heard a sound like the one that Cherry is making. It is like her soul flying out. I shut my eyes tight because they are wet again.

It is harder than Gramp. Harder than Gram. Harder than anything. When I open my eyes, Cherry is being sick on the floor. She cannot stand and Gary helps me carry her back to the car.

We go to Everett General Hospital emergency room. The same place I got my arm fixed after I got beat up.

"Can we do something for her?" Gary asks the clerk at the counter.

"Please? Can't you do anything? Give her something?" he asks the doctor.

They give Cherry a shot and a bottle of sadness pills.

I did not know you could get pills for sadness. It was something I did not know.

When we get back to the apartment, we lay Cherry down on the bed. Gary takes off her shoes, and covers her with Gram's blanket. I stand and watch her lying there. My heart is breaking. I feel it breaking like Yo's windshield. My heart has disappeared. It is gone. I want it back, but it has left with Keith.

"Stay with her, okay? I'll get Sandy." Gary hugs me and goes downstairs. I hear the engine of his Jeep rumble as he drives away. I am alone with Cherry.

Gary or Sandy would know what to do. What to say. I do not know what to do or say.

I drop to my knees next to the bed. There are black streaks of mascara over Cherry's cheeks. Her eyes are open but her breathing is deep and slow.

I hold her head in my hands. I pat it like Keith did, over and over. Her eyes turn to me. They ask a question with no words. They ask a question that I am unable to answer.

I can only say, "I'm sorry."

"I'm sorry, Cherry," I cry.

But her eyes just stare into space. They just stare.

I'm sorry, I hear Gram say.

"We're all so sorry," the fishermen say.

"So sorry," our suppliers say.

"We're so very, very sorry," everyone says.

54

≋

Diamond Girl's engine starts on the first try. BROOM! BROOM! I feel it shaking under my feet. I watched Keith take her out so often I knew I could do it myself.

I can do it myself, I think. I have no trouble casting off the lines. Gary's family stands by helplessly and I tell them what to do. Where to sit. Cherry is beside me.

I hear Keith's voice.

I could do it blindfolded.

I could do it with my head up my ass.

I could do it with one arm behind my back and jerk off at the same time.

Keith was crude and rude, Gram always said. She would laugh. "That boy is crude and rude!" She loved Keith and I loved Keith too.

Six people on *Diamond Girl* are as much as she can handle. Gary brought three brand-new life jackets still wrapped in plastic from the store so we would have enough. The Coast Guard says you need one PFD, personal flotation device, for each person. My head says this over and over. PFD. PFD. PFD. In time with the engine as it throbs.

We head out towards Whidbey Island. The sky is so blue it looks fake. It looks like it is painted on. Like a picture. Like Cherry's eyeshadow. There is one big cloud shaped like a flower. I like that. A flower for Keith. Puget Sound is green and shiny.

Diamond Girl cuts through the water.

THROB. THROB. THROB. Her engine goes.

Meagan and Kelly are quiet. They sit close to each other. Meagan's eyes run with tears. She liked Keith a lot, even though he called her a twerp. The one I worry about is Kelly. She has a mask face like Halloween and her eyes are dry. She is younger than I was when Gramp died.

I think I know how she feels.

I think I know what she must be thinking.

She and Keith argued. He teased her all the time. I know she feels guilty. I can see it in her eyes. I felt guilty for years about Gramp. I thought I killed him by going out for a sail. Kelly probably feels the same way. She and Keith fought just last week.

"Are those *boobs* I see, Tween?" he asked.

Sandy made the mistake of telling Keith that Kelly got her first bra.

"Drop dead, you fart-face! Drop dead!" Kelly shrieked.

He just laughed at her. We all did.

Drop dead.

Drop dead, Keith.

I know her words cannot be unsaid. They float behind her eyes. I know this. I hold her hand while I work the tiller.

"I didn't mean it," she whispers to me. "I swear I never meant it."

"I know," I tell her. "We all know. It's okay. It will be okay."

I am doing Keith's job. It is up to me.

Steering. That is what he used to do. When I think of this, my tears come and I cannot see clearly. I let go of Kelly's hand and Cherry puts her arms around me. I give the tiller to Gary, and he guides Keith's boat.

We go out into the strait, and head into the current, until we feel it is the right place. The perfect place. A place Keith would want to be.

Spread my ashes out in the Sound, he told me. *I want to travel the world for free.*

I said that I would.

"I promise," I told him.

And I keep my promise.

When we toss Keith's ashes out into the water, the seagulls swoop and flap overhead. They think we are giving them food, but it is only Keith.

We have to laugh because Keith would have roared and yelled, "Fuck you! Fuck you, birds!"

He never liked seagulls. Not one bit.

"Fuck you, birds!" We all call out.

It is the first time I have ever said that word.

I will not say it ever again.

Keith's ashes fall with a clump onto the water like little pieces of gravel. Some of his dust flies back into my eyes and makes me tear up. Cherry cannot look at all and hides her face until we tell her he is all gone. He is gone.

A seal pops up next to *Diamond Girl.* He swims around and around and follows us all the way back to the slip. I think it is Keith telling us he is okay. I think this is true. This is *echt.* The seal hangs around *Diamond Girl* for hours. We feed it fish that we steal from Marty's bait pail and sit on *Diamond Girl* until it is dark and talk. We do not want to leave. It is like the last time we are with Keith.

Cherry asks Gary about the first time he met Keith. The first time he saw him.

"He just walked up from the docks into the store. Said he just sailed in from Portland. His rigging was in pieces. His jenny tattered. Said he was on his way to Canada. That he needed a job for a few weeks. It seems now like I knew him forever," and Gary chokes up.

Gary's family leaves together and we watch them from *Diamond Girl*'s cockpit as they drive away. When they are gone, Cherry gives me a sadness pill and tells me about her dad. I swallow it dry and it sticks in my throat. It tastes like that finger stuff Gram used to paint on me when I bit my nails.

Cherry leans against me. Her head is on my chest. I stroke her hair with my fingers.

"I just turned eighteen. He can't touch me now," she says. "Nobody can."

"You look a lot older. I thought you were twenty." I wish I knew she had a birthday. I would have given her a present.

"Thank you, Per," she says, and looks pleased even though she is still crying.

We both take another pill, and wait for our sadness to go away.

It is hard to tell how old people are. For example, Gary seems older than he really is and Keith always seemed younger. He will never get older now. He will stay the same age as he was. I think about this as I hold Cherry.

"My dad is such an asshole." She talks about her family and about Keith.

"He beat him up for me. Keith beat the crap out of him for me," she says, and starts to cry harder. Her tears drip down my arm. "We were gonna be married. He wanted to marry me. I loved him, Perry. I really did," she sobs.

We do not want to leave the cockpit. We do not want to stop talking about Keith.

"I will never stop loving him," she tells me. She says that she wants to die.

"He was the best thing that ever happened to me and he loved me back. He loved me back. I know he did," she cries.

"*You* were the best," I tell her. "*You* were the best thing that ever happened to him. That is the truth. It is *echt*," I say. It is *true*, I think, and hold her close.

We take another pill each.

Sadness pills.

It is such a crock.

A gyp.

They do not work.

And we cry.

55

$\approx$

After we run out of the sadness pills, I wake up at the same time each night. The clock flashes two-zero-one. My heart hurts when I breathe and my eyes are wet. Whenever I wake up, I remember Keith is dead. He is gone like our pills.

I cannot think and my pillow is wet. I need to use Kleenex. I see a shadow in the room. Cherry is standing by the window staring. I get up and grab her hands. They are like ice. Her face is dry. Her breath comes in sharp pants like a dog. Like a running dog. I lead her back to bed. She lies on her back, but her eyes are open. When I know she will stay put, I go back to Gram's couch, wrap Gram's afghan around myself, and shiver like I have a fever.

When the alarm goes off in the morning, Cherry is still in bed.

She is not dressed and her privates are showing.

"Get up, Cherry. You need to get up," I tell her. I cannot look at her body. Her eyes are wide. They do not blink.

"We've got to go to work. You have to get up." I look in the dresser drawer and find a pair of her clean panties. They are blue and have stars on them.

"Get up, Cherry. Please?" I ask, and cover her privates with her panties.

She does not move.

I thought we were getting better. I thought our sadness was leaving us. On Wednesday, we even cleaned the apartment together. Cherry scrubbed the kitchen and I scoured the bathroom shower. After we finished, I started the washing machine while Cherry went into the bedroom to gather up all our dirty clothes.

She did not come back.

I found her sitting on the floor with Keith's stained jeans held to her breast.

"We have to keep these, Perry. Don't wash these, okay?" I could hardly understand her words she was sobbing so hard. I heard her gulping.

She spent the rest of the day in bed covered with Keith's dirty clothes. His socks. His underwear. She would not let me wash them. Instead, she took a flannel shirt, covered her face, and breathed deeply through it. She looked like a ghost except she had clothes on her face.

She sleeps later and later each morning.

Today she is not even talking.

When I walk back into the bedroom, she still has no clothes on. I pull her up and slide her panties up one leg. Her thighs flop and I have a hard time lifting her bottom. Her boobs are rolling around. I cannot find a bra so I pull a sweatshirt over her head. I grab her pink sweatpants out of the middle drawer.

She is like a big stuffed doll from the Evergreen State Fair. Like one of those you can win by throwing a ball into a hole. I always tried, but I never did win one. Gram would ask me what I would do with a doll that big anyway.

Now I know. It would be really hard to dress.

"Come on, Cherry. You are hard to dress." She makes no sound.

She wakes up a little when I push her upright. I pull her to make her stand and lead her over to the kitchen table. She stumbles once and I catch her. I have to press her shoulders down to make her sit.

She has not eaten in two days.

I fix oatmeal, set a bowl in front of her, and give her a spoon.

"Come on, Cherry, you have to eat," I tell her, "or you will get sick."

She lifts the spoon and slides the cereal into her mouth. I am glad because I did not want to feed her. That would be spooky. As if she were a big baby.

By the time we get downstairs to the store, we are an hour late. Charles, the newest guy, is at the register, so I decide to have Cherry help me unpack boxes.

Boxes are good. You do not have to think to unpack them. First you slice them with the cutter, second you pry open the cardboard, and third you lift the stuff out. Popcorn filler drops to the floor. I get a broom and sweep it up. I do not think. It feels good not to think.

Gary brings Sandy and the girls in to help.

We need a lot of help at the store without Keith.

I have to set the alarm extra early each morning so there is time to help Cherry get dressed. I cannot sleep because I need to be ready to put her back to bed when she gets up in the middle of the night to stare at *Diamond Girl* through the window. I am so tired, and so sad, there is an ocean of hurt in my heart.

My eyes open. It is late.

There is a voice. Keith's voice.

Take care of her, Per. Take care . . .

I hear Gram.

Careful . . .

I see the moon shining over the floor.

Cherry is not at the window, but I hear a noise.

It is coming from the kitchen.

Drawers open. One. Two. I hear them slide.

I get up. It might be a burglar. The bedroom door is open and I look inside. Cherry's bed is empty. I walk into the kitchen.

When I see what she is doing, I feel fear at first. But I am like the Hulk. I become strong.

"No!" I shout. "Don't," I tell her. "Please?"

She holds a knife. She is holding a knife to her wrist. It presses into the skin and starts to make a cut. I move to her side, grab her arm, and pry the handle from her fingers. There is one small drip of blood that trickles down her arm. It is bright red. I lead her into the bathroom and put a Band-Aid over her wound. My hands shake as I smooth it over her skin.

"Don't do this, Cherry. Keith would not want you to," I say, and brush the hair off her neck. I smooth the tears off her cheek.

"I don't want you to," I tell her.

I do not know what else to say.

I lead her back into the bedroom, lie down next to her, and hold her in my arms until her eyes close and she falls asleep.

56

$\approx\approx$

We get less sad even without the pills. We get less sad because *life goes on*, as Keith always said. As Gram said.

Cherry gets up on her own now without my help. She fixes us both oatmeal for breakfast and talks to me. She tells me she is pregnant. That she is having a baby.

"I'm having Keith's baby," she says.

She needs my help.

It is not too late for Keith. It is not too late for him to be a father. I want to be a father for Keith. I never even imagined that I would help Keith be a father.

Cherry wants me to know that she does not want to take advantage of me.

"I don't know if I'll ever love anybody again, Per. I'm sorry, but I don't know what to do or where to go," she says.

Cherry also wants me to know that she still loves Keith best even though he is dead. I say I understand, because I do. I love Keith best too. Sometimes friends have to take care of friend stuff. This is one of those times. I still hurt. I still feel guilty for liking Cherry. But I can do this one thing for Keith. This last thing for Keith.

I know he would be excited to be a father, but I am excited too. It is like a job I can do for him. A big favor. The biggest favor.

Cherry said she never had a boyfriend before Keith.

"I'm fat and ugly, Perry, really I am," she says.

I definitely do not think she is fat or ugly. It is mean what people say. We talk about how mean people can be and how we are okay.

"People would stare at me when I ate. My aunt would tell me to lose weight. My cousins would call me fatty."

"Kids at school would call me retard." I do not like to tell anybody this, especially Cherry. I am afraid she will think it is true.

"I am not fat and you are not retarded. We are us!" she says, and gives me a kiss and a hug. That is so cool.

Cherry quit smoking, won't watch horror movies anymore because she says it may bother the baby, and only eats vegetarian pizza. We order half Meat Eaters for me and half vegetarian for her. That's what she calls me now, a Meat Eater.

We talk about names.

"We will call him Baby Keith," I say. It will be another Keith.

"What if it's a girl?" she asks.

"It won't. I am positive. It will be Baby Keith."

"Perry, it might not be."

"Yes it will." I am sure of this.

It will be Baby Keith, I hear Gram say.

Gary helps us fix up the apartment. Cherry chooses the colors.

"Yellow," she decides. "Like the sun, and blue like the sky."

I am happy. I was afraid she would want the colors in her hair. I like her hair, but not on our walls. While Gary and I paint, Cherry stays on *Diamond Girl* so the smells will not make her sick and hurt the baby. We make the nursery in a corner of the bedroom. We order a crib from Sears, and when it comes, Sandy and Gary help us put it together.

"Starting over," Gary says. "A new beginning. A new life."

Our apartment looks cool. We have Gram's couch, my TV, a coffee table from Kmart, and my TV trays. We bought a brand-new bed. I found sailboat bedspreads in the catalogue and ordered them for the store. I got an extra one for us.

We sold all the spreads that I ordered in one week. Gary just laughs. He tells me to order anything I want for Holsted's.

Cherry is smart. She has us study the business news every night and shows me how to go online and find message groups from sailors.

"See here, Per? Sailors from all over the world go online and talk. They tell people smart enough to listen what they need. Those smart people are us." She has me take notes. "We gotta read them all, Perry. We have to keep up. It's a way to find out what new stuff boaters want. We have to be proactive." *Proactive* is another word Cherry learned from the business news. *Proactive* means taking charge. She tells Gary that she is taking charge and making us a website so boaters can order from us anywhere direct.

We always stand at the window each night and watch. It is a habit now. We look out at the water, at the reflection of the lights and at *Diamond Girl*. I hold Cherry close. My arms fit around her stomach. It is getting bigger because of the baby.

Cherry will talk about Keith at these times and cry.

"I wish I had told him about the baby." She says this over and over.

I do not say anything and the voices come.

He knew, Gram says. *Tell her he knew.*

I knew, Keith says. *Tell her.*

Tell her.

"Cherry, what do you mean?" I say, and take a deep slow breath.

Truth is many things. Sometimes truth is what we want or maybe what we have. It may be what we choose to believe. Sometimes it is something real. Something *echt*. Something genuine. Sometimes you know the truth when you speak it. I am slow, but I know this.

"He knew, Cherry. He knew you were having his baby," I say.

I feel her sink. I feel her sag. It may be the truth or it may be a very good lie that turns into the truth. I do not know.

"How do you know this?" she asks. "How do you know?" she breathes into my chest.

The answer comes out of my heart and I know exactly what to say.

"He told me. He told me he could tell. He told me." When I say this, I know it is true, and I believe it myself.

It is true. It is *echt*. It is genuine.

Cherry cries. Big gulping sobs. She cannot stand and I hold her up.

It is a good truth.

The best one.

I reach my arms around her tight and I do not let her go.

57

≋

I|t is late at night. Our lights are off. We are ready to go to sleep. Me
on the couch and Cherry in the bed. The rain plops against the door
like tiny knocks. I sniff because I need to use a Kleenex. We are both
blurring our eyes watching *Diamond Girl* outside. Pretending Keith
is there, tying her up in the rain.

"When will Keith be back?" Cherry will ask.

"Soon. He's putting on another line. The wind's blowing hard. If
he doesn't tighten her up, she may pull loose. See him there?"

"Where?" she will ask.

"Right there. See?" I will point. "He's waving." And we will
wave back.

It is a game we play.

Tonight Cherry is silent. She does not wave at the pretend Keith.
Instead her arm crawls around my waist, and she pulls me tight. I
pat her hand and she hugs me even closer. Her other hand rubs my

belly and moves down. My stomach clenches and drops like I am on a roller coaster ride.

My head is all mixed up with thinking. I am happy Cherry is with me, but I am sad Keith is not. My privates are getting hard and my nose is running. Cherry takes my hand and puts it on her boob. My head gets dizzy and I am spinning.

She takes both my hands and leads me walking backwards into the bedroom. Her steps are sure and even, mine are not. I jerk forward and she catches me. Her bare hand touches my privates. I am shaking and sweating. My feet stumble again and I am scared, but I am not so scared that I want her to stop.

I do not want her to stop. I cannot catch my breath. I hear it in my ears. I do not know exactly what will happen, but I can guess.

Keith and I talked about man things. He told me about privates and what they do. We sat in his cockpit while he drank beer and I drank Coke. He told me all about the hot Mexican babes he knew in San Antonio. When he got back from 'Nam.

"Hot, Per. Hot! Beautiful and smart. I should have married one while I was there. Whoa, Momma!" he said.

Gram would have washed both our mouths out with naphtha soap if she had heard us. I asked Keith questions.

"You put it where? But how do you know when to do it and what to do?" I asked him.

He told me all about it and then said, "All you have to do is let nature take its course."

"Does nature feel good?" I asked.

"Yeah, Per," he said, and closed his eyes. "Nature feels real good."

I wish I had paid more attention. I wish I could remember everything he said, but there is nothing in my head but wind and waves.

She takes off my shirt.

She unbuttons my pants.

She pulls me down on top of her. Cherry is soft and moves against me. When she does this I find out it is true. Every bit of it.

All you have to do is let nature take its course.

And nature feels real good.

Just like Keith said. He was right.

It is fireworks. I am flying. It is better than flying.

I laugh. "Ha!" And then I cannot talk at all. I cannot breathe. I cannot think. I just am.

My thinking turns into black and I fall asleep.

When I wake up again the clock is flashing three-three-zero. Three-thirty in the morning. I have no clothes on and Cherry is naked. I watch her breathe. In and out. She is so beautiful. I do not say a word, but it is as if she hears me watch.

Her eyes open. She smiles.

And I know exactly what to do.

58

≋

have been rich for almost a year.

When my cousin-brothers found out about Keith they started calling even more, but I did not talk. I did not answer. I had to think by myself. And then I knew.

I knew what to do.

My words today are *share, shareholder, sharer,* and *shark*. Share means you give part of your things to other people and a shark has teeth and bites.

I dial David's number first, then I dial John's. "People should get what they want," I tell them on the phone. I say it is time for another Family Meeting. I call the Family Meeting this time. It is my decision. I am like the Hulk. I have Power.

Both my cousin-brothers come to the apartment to pick me up. John's hand is on my shoulder pushing me a little, as I walk down the stairs. One of his ragged nails catches on my jacket. I stretch up and push back.

Cherry is behind the counter at the register. I can see her through the plate glass window as we walk by. David gets into the front seat of a long black car and I sit in back with John.

Mike Dinelli is at the wheel and revs his engine.

It's about time, he says. *It's about time.*

It's almost too late for you, John. My associates have been discussing the increasing likelihood of some unfortunate accident befalling you.

BROOM! BROOM! The engine of the car sounds like *Diamond Girl.*

We drive away in short spurts. I can hear gravel hit the side of the building. I see Gary running out of Holsted's, but Mike goes fast out of the parking lot. I crane my neck around to see Gary through the back window. He is waving and yelling.

"Stop! Come back! *Stop!*"

Don't worry, Gary, I think. I know what I am doing.

We drive to John's office. It is in a tall building that stretches to the sky. It stretches to heaven. I look up to the top. I look up for Gram and Gramp. I look for Keith.

I have never seen John's office. There are pictures on the wall with scribbles.

"What are those?" I ask. It looks like when I was little and could not color in the lines.

"Abstract art, Perry. They're valuable. John is a collector," David whispers.

I laugh. "Ha! I think they look like mistakes."

We step into a room with a big brown table. When John sits down in one of the chairs, the leather makes a sound like a fart and I think of Keith. I think he would understand what I am doing.

I know he would.

I will give my family the lottery money. I do not need to wait. I do not need the next lottery check. I am a businessman. I have my salary from Holsted's. I have my savings account.

I will sign papers so my family gets the rest of the money. I will not give them my Power. I do not need to. I am the Hulk and the Hulk is not fooled.

And another thing.

I will not tell them about my savings account. It is not their business.

I see John spread his hands on the table then curl the ends of his fingers under. I think he does this so no one will see that he bites his nails. That is what I used to do until Gram made me stop.

It is important for me to sign papers, Louise says. Important, John says. Very important, Mike says. Crucial, Elaine says. It is crucial. That means bigger than important. I sit at the table. My family surrounds me. They look like jackals. I know what jackals are because I watch Animal Planet. They all have pointy teeth. Just like the sharks, I think. Pointy teeth. You see this when they smile.

Louise's head is covered. I cannot tell what color her hair is today.

It is for the family.

It is only fair.

David owes money to creditors.

Elaine wants a bigger house.

John owes money to Mike's company.

Louise needs to be maintained. She is very expensive.

Everybody owes something to somebody.

They are the ones confused. I am not.

Mike Dinelli is a good friend.

He has to clean some money for his firm.

It is business, only business.

I do not need to do Power, I tell them. I will sell the lottery payments to Mike. He does not have Hershey's Kisses today. John does not either. That is okay.

Families are important. Even Gram said that. If you can help your family, then you do it. I sign my name fifteen times. *Perry L.*

Crandall. Mike hands me each paper to sign. The pen is heavy and silver. The ink is black like at the police station.

"What's the L stand for Perry?" Mike asks.

"Lucky," I say. "The L stands for Lucky."

He does not laugh. He does not even smile.

Palmer Financial Planning Services is Mike Dinelli's company. They buy the rest of my lottery payments. I tell them the money can go into the family trust. Managed by the trustee.

They cannot agree on a trustee.

Not you, John! Not on your life! Do you think we're idiots? You drained your client's accounts. How can we be sure you won't do the same with us?

Well, not you, Elaine! I won't go for that!

Who, then?

Not Mom. She doesn't have a clue.

David.

Yes. David. He can be the trustee. He's too stupid to try anything.

Such a nice sentiment for a wife, Elaine.

At least he's an MBA, but Christ, don't take any of his advice about investments. You'll lose your shirt.

Trust.

That is another word for David now. He is the trustee. It is for the family. Not me.

I do not tell them about my savings account and they do not ask.

I hear John and Elaine still arguing in the background as I sign more papers and talk to Mike. They talk about putting money in the trust. Taking money from a laundry. Mike is using all the money from the lottery and giving them other, different, dirty money. I do not care about that.

I don't believe it! We didn't even need the Power of Attorney.

He signed. He just signed it away.

We went to all the trouble.

He wouldn't have done it if we hadn't worked on him. He trusts us now.

Are you sure?

Are you sure about that?

Keith and Gram are quiet in my head. They know I can make this decision. It is mine to make. This is my good idea. My family tells me they are handling things so I do not have to, but I know there is nothing to handle. I am calm. I am very calm. My hands are not shaking and I hold them out in front of me. They are good hands I think. I have good hands.

The trust is set up. For our benefit.

A trust. I remember. Gram said my father set up a trust once. She said this to me: "A trust is something you don't, Perry. You remember that."

He just signed the money away. He just signed it away. I can't believe it.

My troubles are over. I'll get a check to you tomorrow or the next day, Mike, after this cash is deposited. Everything will be back to normal.

Make sure it stays that way, John. Or I can't promise what will happen.

Are you okay with this, Perry? Are you okay?

Shut up, David.

It isn't right. We need to give him something. We should have had him wait until he got the next payment.

David, give it a rest! It's over! If you feel guilty, give him part of your share. If Elaine will let you. Ha! Ha! You need the money just as much as we do, just ask your wife.

Isn't that right, Elaine?

After all the papers are signed, the money is gone and I am free. They do not need me anymore. Louise and John are arguing with Mike. Elaine is sitting at the table with a calculator, smiling.

David is the only one who hugs me good-bye. He holds the trust papers in his hand.

"You take care of yourself, Per," he says, and pats me on the back. "It will be okay." Then winks.

It is the first time he has ever called me Per. That is so cool. He walks me downstairs and calls me a cab.

The taxi takes me back to my apartment. The driver's name is Gary.

"Hey, I know a Gary!" I say.

The bill is twenty-eight dollars. He waits in his cab with the engine running while I go upstairs. I did not bring enough cash. I find two twenty-dollar bills in a bowl on the dresser. Gary takes the money and starts to drive away.

"I need my change," I say. He stops and hands me twelve dollars and I give him five back as a tip.

"Thank you," I say.

He did a good job. You should always give people tips and thank them when they do a good job.

I walk back upstairs to my apartment.

What goes around comes around, I hear.

Life goes on. It is Keith's voice. Like the song, I think. It is Keith. It is what he used to say.

And now I hear Gram. *You're a lucky boy, Perry L. Crandall,* I hear her say. *That L stands for Lucky!* I know she is right. And I know two other things. Two true things. Two *echt* things.

I am not retarded.

And if you can give people what they want, you should. It is good to give people what they want. This is a great day. No one in my family will bother me anymore. They have what they want. And so do I.

I have Cherry.

I stand by my window and watch *Diamond Girl* bounce against the dock. She looks lonely. She looks like she wants to go look for

Keith out into the Sound where he is floating. I wonder where his ashes have gone.

I hear footsteps on the stairs. Cherry comes through the door.

I open my arms wide and she walks right into them. I can still see *Diamond Girl* over her head.

"Are you okay?" I hear her ask. She has wrinkles on her forehead and I kiss them away.

I say nothing.

I am so okay, I cannot speak.

Our door swings open again and it is Gary.

"Are you all right?" he asks. "What did they want?"

"The money," I finally say. "They just wanted the money."

He has wrinkles on his forehead too, but he does not need to worry. There is no reason for wrinkles. He did not knock on our door before he walked in, which is rude, but he is my friend, so I do not tell him this.

"It's okay now," I say. This is true. This is *echt*. It is okay. It is.

59

~~

have an interview on TV. That means they ask you questions. After Gary found out about what happened, he called Marleen. He suggested she might do a special story on lottery winners. Her bosses, the television guys, thought it was a good idea.

Before the program starts, Marleen gives me a hug.

"I'm sorry about your friend Keith," she says.

"I am too," I say. "He would have really liked to be on TV. He always wanted to be famous."

A man named Roy clips a microphone to my neck. It scratches.

"When that green light comes on, there'll be over a million people watching you," he says.

That is so cool. I squint my eyes and try to see them through the big shiny camera lens. There are six of us sitting onstage with Marleen. She has the biggest chair and talks to me first.

"So your father is G. J. Crandall?" Marleen wears a blue suit, high heels, and dark red lipstick. She looks totally different. TV is so cool. She reads words off a card. That is such a gyp. I always thought they had to memorize the stuff they say, but they do not. It is all written down for them. If I had known it was all written down, I would have tried to be a TV guy.

"I guess," I tell her. "I did not know my father, but he is famous too. We are both famous. He is famous for stealing money and I am famous for winning money."

Marleen looks into the camera. "Investors want to buy the annuities from the lottery winners. Organized crime uses lottery winnings to launder money."

She sounds like she has just figured this all out, but I know it is written on a card in front of her.

She turns to me. "So, Perry. Is all of your lottery money gone? Is there anything left after you sold your lottery annuity?" She has very white teeth. Her makeup has rubbed off onto her shirt collar. I did not let them put makeup on me. That would be gross.

"Did your family take it all?" she asks.

"Yeah, I guess. It was a trust. They said it was a trust for investments." I tried to remember all the words they used, but I cannot.

I do not tell her about my savings account.

Marleen moves to the lady sitting next to me. Her name is Lucille. She won twenty million dollars. Her money is all gone. She tried to invest and her friends and family helped her.

"I said I was going to share it with my family. I didn't realize they could sue me for it if I said that. I sold my annuity and divided it up, but that wasn't enough. They came back for more. I still owe taxes." She starts crying. Marleen hands her a Kleenex and she blows her nose hard. I hope she does not have a cold. You can catch someone's cold if they blow their nose right next to you. I turn my face away from her.

Other people lost their money even faster than Lucille did. Five months. Eight months. A year.

All the people are sad. They won money and they are sad.

We lost everything, they say.

We had it all, they say, *and we lost it.*

We could have had millions.

We had millions.

"So you're worse off. You're all worse off now, after the lottery," Marleen says.

"No," I say. "No. I'm not." But nobody listens.

Nobody hears what I have to say.

I am a partner in Holsted's. And I have Cherry.

I do not tell them about my savings account.

I do not have Keith, Gram, or Gramp. That is the hard part, but like Gram always said, life is tough. It is full of surprises. It is full of obstacles to overcome, like when the people you love die.

Sometimes misfortune just smashes you upside the head. It is difficult. Most things in life are difficult, Gram says in my head.

Marleen asks again about my family.

Gary told me it was important to tell the truth on TV. But I have no reason to lie. The reporter says that my family took all my money. I tell him that they did not take it. I gave it to them.

"You gave it to them? Why?" Her mouth is open. She does not look like she believes me.

"Because they asked, because it was fair, and because they were my family," I say. "Because people should get what they want." Those were the reasons.

Then I say something that she does not understand. Not one bit. Nobody does.

I have to say it twice.

"Because I didn't need it," I say.

"Because I didn't need it, and they did," I tell her.

"What? Why?" Marleen's eyes are all squinty. That distracts me. It is hard to explain to someone who will not understand.

Gram used to say I was suggestible. I may have been. Maybe I still am. But letting my family have the rest of the money was fair because they seemed to need it and I did not.

When I get back to the apartment, Cherry says I looked real good on TV.

That is so cool.

60

≈

How about the name Holsted and Crandall Marine Supply, Perry? How does that sound?" Gary asks me.

"I think it sounds fine. I think it sounds pretty good," I say.

We are partners, Gary said. We are a family. We are Holsted and Crandall Marine Supply. He says I have good ideas, like the time I told him to have a coffee place. People like to drink coffee when they shop. We make a lot of money from people buying cookies, brownies, and coffee. We sell fancy takeout picnic lunches for boat people.

We have a fishing corner in the store that is bigger now. I tell Gary about a retired friend of Marty's, named Rick, who sits on the dock every day. He knows a lot about fishing. He talks to people in our store about how to catch fish. He teaches fishing the same way big hardware stores show people how to lay tile. I know this because Gram and I watched at Home Depot one weekend when we wanted to fix our bathroom. I tell Gary this is what we need to do.

"So, what? We need to have workshops each weekend?"

Gary wanted to call them workshops.

"No," I say. "People like to play. They work all week. We need to be different. We need to call them playshops."

"You're fucking brilliant, Per. You know that?" Gary hardly ever says the F-word. When he does, I think that he hears Keith's voice. I think that Keith is in there with him.

"You make a good partner," Gary says. "A really good partner."

It is still not nice to say the F-word. I will never let anybody say that word in front of the baby when it is born.

We have playshops on caulking teak decks and filling in bung-holes. We have them on patching fiberglass and sail repair. We have them on anything that a person might need to do on a boat. We have people who sail around the world come in and sign their books.

Cherry organizes the playshops and schedules them. She is a good people person. She is the best people person. Our playshops are a success. Success is doing well when everyone thought that you would not.

I am a success.

EVERETT CHAMBER OF COMMERCE TO HOLD
BANQUET HONORING LOCAL BUSINESSES

Holsted's is getting an award for having big ideas. That is what Mr. Jordan from my bank says. Cherry will wear her new dress. It is long and red. Her stomach is huge. She will have Keith's baby any day now. She likes red. You can only see one small tattoo when she puts it on. That is okay. Her hair is brown now and very short. I get mine cut and buy a new suit. Gary helps pick it out.

"Navy blue, Per. That's your color."

The person looking back at me in the mirror is someone I know.

It is me. I look like a policeman or a doctor. I look like a businessman. I look like Perry L. Crandall.

I do not look retarded.

A banquet is a big dinner. They give you fancy hot food and real
napkins. My collar is tight around my neck and makes it hard to
swallow my dinner. I am not used to suits. They make me walk
funny. Gary has to make a speech, and Mr. Jordan from Everett
Federal introduces him.

"I'd like to present this year's Business Vision Award to Holsted
and Crandall Marine Supply."

When Gary stands up, he grabs me by the elbow and drags me
up to the front of the room with him. White faces stare up at me. It
is quiet. I cannot even hear our feet on the carpet and I have two
good ears. I am still an auditor.

"I'd like to thank you all. Winning this award is a great honor.
The person responsible is standing right next to me," Gary says.
"My partner, Perry L. Crandall."

He pushes me in front of the microphone and whispers, "It's
okay, Per. Just talk to them like you talk to me. Go ahead."

I have to say some words to a lot of people I do not know through
a microphone that squeaks. I am so scared, I think I might wet my
pants. I do not know what to say. All I see are faces. Then I hear
them. I hear Gram. I hear Keith. They are saying words. Telling me
what to do. But they are words I already know. And I am not scared
anymore. I do not need them to tell me what to say.

"My name is Perry L. Crandall and I am not retarded." I say this
and take a deep breath. "My Gram always said the L in my name
stands for Lucky. It does. I am lucky." Some faces laugh because they
know about the lottery, but that is not the luck I am talking about.

"I am lucky to be a businessman and I am lucky to have a family.
I am lucky because I am a good worker. Being a good worker is very
important. I learned how to work hard from my Gramp. I learned

how to try hard and do words from my Gram, and I learned all about love from my friend Keith." Some of the faces are smiling. Some of these faces knew Keith, some knew Gram, and some knew my Gramp.

"They would be happy that people get to know me now. They would be happy that after people get to know me, they decide maybe they like me, or maybe they don't. But that's okay. They get to know me. I am a businessman. That is so cool. Thank you."

The people stand up and clap. They clap for a long, long time. Mr. Jordan hands Gary a wood thing to hang on our wall. It has both our names on it.

My PICTURE IS in the business section of the Sunday paper. I think I look goofy. Cherry tells me no.

"It's a great picture, Perry. I'm cutting it out. We'll put it in your book."

The headline was at the top of the page.

EVERETT CHAMBER OF COMMERCE NEWS:
HOLSTED AND CRANDALL MARINE SUPPLY
WINS VISION AWARD

The Chamber of Commerce is a bunch of businesspeople that give each other awards. That is what Gary says. He tells me I am a true businessman because I have won an award.

61

~

The money is all gone.

That is what the newspaper said when they printed the interview story. That is also what Louise said in the letter she wrote to ask me for more money.

They still do not know about my savings account.

"I think the publicity will help protect you from them taking advantage again. People like your brothers don't like everybody knowing their business," Gary said.

But they did not take advantage. He does not understand. I know the money is all gone. I knew it would be. Louise wrote me saying she saw my picture in the paper and asked me to sell my share of Holsted's. I said no.

No.

It is what I decided.

Gram said no in my head. Keith is there with her. He said no.

And Cherry is beside me and helped me write the letter answering Louise.

"NO WAY!" she wrote in giant letters on the outside of the envelope.

"No fucking way, Per!" Cherry yelled. She sounded exactly like Keith.

And then she went into labor.

Labor is when you work really hard to have a baby. I am glad he did not hear all the bad language she used, because he wasn't here yet. He was still inside.

It took him fourteen hours to decide to come out.

He is a thinker. Like me.

Baby Keith was born the next day at noon. I was the second person to hold him besides the nurse. Her name was Carol. She was dressed all in blue.

Keith Perry George Crandall. Eight pounds and seven ounces.

He was huge. Keith would have been proud that he had the biggest baby in the hospital that week. I was hoping they gave a prize but they did not. That is such a gyp.

A WEEK LATER, we are reading the paper and looking for Baby Keith's name. He is listed in the paper on the back page under birth announcements. The front page has a photo of my cousin-brother John. Cherry is the one who found it.

"Perry, look at this! It's your brother John. It says he's in protective custody. He's turning state's evidence for some money-laundering scam. Holy crap!"

Cherry can say crap. That is not a bad word.

Cherry says protective custody means John is in jail. She says it means there are bad people out there that want to hurt him. The newspaper says that his brother David is gone. He has disappeared.

I do not feel bad for John, but I am a little sorry for David.

"What happened, Cherry?" I ask her. "Read me the rest."

"It says here that David Crandall is wanted for questioning. He hasn't been located. They think he's left the country with the proceeds of the trust." She laughs. "Like his father! He ran off. Va-moosed! He ditched that bitch of a wife of his, dumped John, and ripped off Louise. Grabbed all the money and dug out. Elaine, John, and Louise are left holding the bag. David took it all! Ha! Good for him, Per. Good for him!"

Holding the bag means somebody took what was inside and you have nothing.

Except for a bag.

"I wonder where he is," I say.

"The Caymans. South America. He's probably with your father spending all the money." And she laughs again.

Baby Keith sucks on her boob. That is so cool. I did not know boobs gave out baby food.

Two months later, a postcard comes in the mail addressed to me. There is a beautiful picture of a white beach with palm trees. The postmark is from the country named after a nut. It is not signed but I think it is from David.

"It's just like you said on TV, Per. Everybody should get what they want. Take care and God bless."

"I don't think you have to worry about any of them anymore, Perry," Gary says again.

But I do not worry.

Gary says Holsted and Crandall is our future and we cannot sell it.

"If someone ever asks you to sell, they are trying to take advantage of you, because they think you're retarded. They're making a big mistake when they think that. A very big mistake." He laughs. "You're definitely not retarded, but you know what, Perry? It wouldn't make a damn bit of difference. You're still one hell of a businessman."

We are going to open another store in Anacortes next fall. It is another place with lots of boats and people who need boat stuff, just like Everett.

Gary asked my advice and I told him. It was my idea.

"Lots of other boats stop in Anacortes on their way to the San Juan Islands. Those boaters always forget something. We should have a store there," I say.

"That's what I mean, Per, one hell of a businessman," Gary says.

Epilogue

Wolfgang Amadeus Mozart said, "Neither a lofty degree of intelligence nor imagination nor both together go to the making of genius. Love, love, love, that is the soul of genius."

This was written inside the card Cherry got me for my birthday. It was tied to the collar of a brown puppy.

"He's chocolate Lab and something else. The lady didn't know what," Cherry told me.

That was so cool. I was so excited I bounced, and my puppy did too. Just like me.

"Everybody should get what they want," Cherry said, and kissed my bouncing chin. "Especially you."

A dog! He licks my face and follows me around. I named him Bounce because that is what we both do when we are happy. He knows his name and I already taught him to sit. He is very smart. He comes when I whistle and asks to go outside when he has to poop and pee. I take him for walks and do not even need a leash. That is so cool. Even Gary likes that we have Bounce. He says dogs are good for security and can bite robbers in the ankle and chase cats.

When I look deep into Bounce's eyes, when I pet his soft head, I see Gramp there. I see Gram. I see Keith. I see them all in his eyes.

The card Cherry gave me sits on my desk at work. I read it every day. I do not understand the first part, but I understand the second. *Love*. It is something that cannot be taken. I think that is true. I keep the card to remind me that I have what I want. I have always had what I wanted. Love. I have always had love. When I was young, I had Gramp and Gram. When I got older, I had Gary and a job. Older still, I had Keith. And now I have Cherry and Baby Keith. And Bounce. I finally have my dog.

Baby Keith will be one year old next week.

I play with him every morning when I help change and feed him. He started eating real food like us. He only has four teeth. Cherry says he will get more soon, but I am not sure. I never saw a baby grow up before.

We do the same games that Gramp and I did. Hide the nose. Peek-under-the-blanket. Bouncy-bouncy. We do the last part with Bounce. Whenever Baby Keith cries, he stops right away when I pick him up. That is so cool. He started walking at nine months. That is fast for a baby, Cherry says. If he falls down or is hungry, he will stop crying just for me.

"He loves you, Per." Cherry will watch us and smile. "Like me," she says.

I know this.

Baby Keith says, "Da. Da. Da." He grabs my hand and puts it into his mouth.

"He's beautiful," I say, and my fingers brush his cheek the same way Gram's brushed mine. Cherry kisses me hard and says I am the beautiful one.

Baby Keith comes into Holsted and Crandall's every day. He is quiet and looks around with wide brown eyes. I know what he is doing. He is studying what he needs to do when he grows up. He is practicing for the time he will work at our store. I help him walk around and give him boxes to push and cardboard to tear.

Cherry and I are married now. I thought about this for many months.

First, I heard Gram's voice. *Are you going to marry her, Perry? Are you?*

Then Keith's voice. *Marry her, Per.*

"Should we get married?" I ask. I want to, but I do not know if it is something she wants or needs.

"Why?" she asks me. "What difference would it make?" Then she kisses me and says, "But I will if you want to."

That is a good answer, I think. *If you want to* is a very good answer. People should get what they want.

"I want to, Cherry," I say. "Baby Keith needs a mother and father with the same last name so when he goes to school nobody will tease." This is very important for Baby Keith, I tell her.

She takes my hand and says, "You're right, Per. You're absolutely right."

Absolutely means very sure. It is like *echt*. It is true.

We get married on *Diamond Girl* and have something called a honeymoon. It is a tiny trip that you take after you get married.

We do not go far. We sleep on *Diamond Girl*. She stays tied to the dock. The water laps against the hull and Baby Keith sleeps between us. Bounce stays up in the cockpit. He is too big for down below now. He grew fast because his paws were too big for his body.

Cherry and I talk about Keith. She still loves him best and so do I. That's okay.

Life goes on, Keith says in my head.

Life always goes on. Gram agrees with him.

Their voices stay with me always.

Diamond Girl is mine. Keith left her to me. I scrub her gelcoat and wax and polish her sides like I always wanted to do for Keith. I do it for us now, for Cherry and me. She shines now like a real diamond, both her and Cherry.

A lawyer told me I was Keith's beneficiary. A beneficiary means your best friend died. I would rather have Keith alive, but a sailboat is cool. I also got seventy-five thousand dollars from Keith's life insurance policy from Holsted's. It will be for Baby Keith's education. He will go to college. He is smart and not at all slow.

Cherry and I invest together.

"Almost a quarter of a million dollars in the savings account now." That is what Cherry says. "A quarter of a million. That's a lot of money." Then she looks at me and smiles. "But it's only money, isn't it? It doesn't really matter. It is us that matter. It's us. That's just for our future." She says that just like Gram.

"For our future," we both say.

She knows it is not just for mine alone. It is for hers too, and Baby Keith's.

We are a family.

I am teaching Cherry how to sail. Out on Puget Sound the waves are green. The sky is blue with gray clouds over Whidbey Island. It is warm and there is just enough wind. Baby Keith is asleep, wrapped in his life jacket and harness. He lies sideways on the floor of the cockpit. Bounce sits next to me looking for seagulls. He is a good seagull finder.

"No, Bounce," I tell him. "Quiet," I whisper. "You will wake Baby Keith." And he looks at me and does what I say. That is so cool.

I am very careful with Cherry and Baby Keith. Sometimes I worry.

"Am I too slow?" I ask Cherry. "Am I too slow for people?"

But she only smiles. "You are fast enough for me," she says.

We watch seals dive and swim and think of Keith. Cherry puts her hand in the water and we talk about him. And remember. Then she blows me a kiss and laughs. It is good to hear her laugh.

I turn *Diamond Girl* around and teach Cherry how to work the tiller.

"Push! The other way!" I say. "You can do it!"

She pushes.

"It's the opposite of what you think," Cherry says. "Not like a car. It's the opposite."

She tries again. "Like a lot of things," she tells me. "Like money. Like love. The opposite of what you think."

I still do my words every day. I am up to the U's because sometimes I have time only for two words. I am very busy. I have lots to do, like work at Holsted and Crandall's, play with Baby Keith, and walk Bounce every day. I buy blank books for Baby Keith, just like the ones Gram got for me. I am taping pictures on each page and writing things down just like Gram. I still get imitation crab sandwiches at Gilly's and I buy Slurpees at Marina Handy Mart. My family has Saturday spaghetti nights with Gary's family. *My family*.

My name is Perry L. Crandall and I am not retarded.

I am a businessman. I have Bounce. I have Baby Keith. And I have Cherry.

Gram was right about my name. The L does stand for Lucky.

This is *echt*.

This is true.

Acknowledgments

It takes many people, places, and experiences to make any book possible. My thanks to the good people of Everett, Washington. Forgive me for taking liberties with the location of the waterfront commercial area and the anchorages off Whidbey Island. I was born and raised in the Pacific Northwest and it is very dear to me, but this is fiction after all.

My sincere appreciation to:

Orion, who rocks and nurtures my soul as I write; my muses, Girl Kitty and Touloose; and Gordon, my husband. You all make it possible for me to pursue my dream. To my son, Andrew, for being so supportive and answering my computer questions, no matter how ridiculous. You are always good-natured about my constant demands. To my late mother, Bernice, who taught me a good book is a way to dream and instilled in me a lifelong love of reading. To my father, Ragnar—you were an enormous resource and gave me much insight into how it actually feels to win the lottery. Thank you for sending me all the junk mail that you still receive after this many years. You can stop now.

To Canadian author Holly Kennedy, who got me started on the path to publishing and has been there for me to lean on and to listen to my agony and diatribes. To Paul Theroux and his wife, Sheila Donnelly Theroux, who provided wise words while I tortured them both during their horseback-riding lessons. To my good friend Nodie Namba-Hadar. She was the one who told me about the good fortune of dragonflies and allowed one to land on my manuscript. Thanks also to her husband, Lulik (Sam) Hadar, who was always so patient with me.

I could not have made my books better without my trusty beta readers. I thank them all from the bottom of my heart.

To Bob Miller of *Wandering Star*, my first beta reader, plot analyzer, and general all-around story adviser, and his wife, Renee. A heartfelt thanks to Pizza Bob's in Haleiwa for all the pizza we consumed. To Pat Stuart—you had no doubt I would be published one day, and told me so continually. To Peggy Kaahanui, my full-service friend: sailor, canvas maker, horsewoman, and reader; and to her husband, Ken, who provided invaluable website assistance. To Rebecca Marks, my dear friend, who always comes back into my life at exactly the right time. To Kevin Keys, who read my book and offered advice, while I cut his hair. To Dee Vadnais, who first read my book while on a passage across the Pacific Ocean. To Mary Gullickson-Gray and Cheryl "Work It, Work It" Conway for amateur photo-shoot help, along with their beta-reader duties.

A big thanks to Dr. Steven Brown, who taught me the danger of the word "that" and who aggressively forced me to write with correct grammar. He is responsible for introducing me to the disability rights movement and disability culture, and my life is richer for it. Thanks also to the Center on Disability Studies at the University of Hawaii, Manoa. Your program serves such a vital need in our society.

Thank you to Brett Uprichard and Big Bamboo Stock, for professional photography. Thanks to my legal eagles, John Fetta of California and Ken Christianson of Washington. Thank you to everybody at New Tech Imaging, especially Cindy Joy Manago, most excellent copyreader. Thank you to all my friends and neighbors at Ko Olina Marina, who provided a cheery word and made me come out of my boat to eat at least one healthy meal a day. Thank you to my other full-service friend, Francie Boland, attorney, who not only believed in me but also has read every word I have written, and provided sound legal advice, which I have consistently ignored at my own peril. And much thanks to Miss Snark's blog and for her sage advice.

Thanks to my Arizona beta reader, Steve Draper, my favorite cousin. Your ability to look at story structure and characterization was beyond helpful. Thank you to my aunt Myrtle Strom, who provided much encouragement throughout my writing journey. Thanks to my sisters, Kay Broten, Kris Francis, and Andrea Dahl, for saying, "I told you so." Thank you to Shannon and John Tullius of the Maui Writers Retreat and Conference. They provide so many resources and have been instrumental in giving a jump start to the careers of many emerging authors. Thanks, also, to Renee in the office, whom I drove completely crazy!

Thank you to Jacquelyn Mitchard, my teacher and friend. You have always given selflessly of your knowledge and time. Your encouragement means so much. Thank you to all the writers I met and worked with in the Vanda Room at the Maui Writers Retreat (you know who you are). Your constructive criticism was instrumental in my development as a writer. Thank you to Lea, Russ, and Zachary Wells, who have shown me that Gram had it right all along, and there are many Perrys out there in the world.

A huge thank-you to my amazing editor at Putnam, Peternelle Van Arsdale. I knew right away that we shared the same vision for

Lottery, and I adore working with her. I deeply appreciate all the other wonderful people at Putnam: Neil Nyren, who, when I met him at the Maui Writers Conference, talked about *when* my book would sell, not *if,* and Dan Conaway, who was so encouraging. To Peternelle's assistant, Rachel Holtzman, who is so patient with my continuous convoluted e-mail messages, phone calls, and forgotten attachments. All of you deserve mass quantities of chocolate from Hawaii every single day.

A giant thank-you and virtual hug to my fabulous agent extraordinaire, Dorian Karchmar from the William Morris Agency. Thanks also to her assistant, Adam Schear, and to Georgia Jelatis-Hoke, and Mac Hawkins. You all now know exactly how many hours' difference it is between New York and Hawaii.

I am so blessed to have obtained an agent such as Dorian. She loves *Lottery* as much as I do, and called at five-fifteen in the morning, July 20, 2006, to tell me so. (I was awake, honest.)

And finally.

To Jeri Kesling.

Your life has been an inspiration.

Readers Guide

for

Lottery

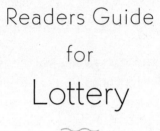

DISCUSSION QUESTIONS

• Discuss the author's use of language. What techniques does she employ to take the reader inside a mentally challenged mind?

• At several points in the novel, various characters use the word *retarded*. How do you feel about this word and other words that are used to describe the mentally and physically challenged?

• Gram tells Perry that his brother David is weak, and that "the weak are more dangerous in the end." Discuss the character of David and his interactions with Perry. Is Gram's warning justified?

• Perry calls Gram "a good teacher. She didn't mind that I was slow, but lots of people do." How do Gram's lessons prepare him for the challenges he faces throughout the novel?

• Keith and Cherry, Perry's closest friends, have both lived traumatic lives—Keith served in Vietnam, Cherry has been abused by her father.

Why do these characters form such a close bond with Perry? In what ways do their life experiences inform their relationships with him?

• Which character are you most drawn to? Why?

• Perry views things in highly literal terms, as illustrated when he refuses to spread part of Gram's ashes in Hawaii because "she needs to be kept together." In what ways does this literalism prove to be an asset? In what ways is it a deficit?

• Perry says that Gary "was always nice to me before, but now he listens. . . . Money has made the slow part of me not so important." Discuss the relationship between Gary and Perry. In what ways does it change after Perry wins the lottery?

• Perry's vocabulary words are a motif throughout the novel. Discuss these words in terms of the chapters in which they appear and the story as a whole. What symbolic or metaphoric insights do they offer?

• What do you think of Perry's decision at the end of the novel? What would you have advised him to do?

• Does money buy happiness? Does it buy love? What do you think Perry's life would have been like without it?

ABOUT THE AUTHOR

Patricia Wood was born and raised in Seattle. She has served in the U.S. Army, worked as a medical technologist, been a horseback-riding instructor, and most recently taught marine science to high-risk students at a public high school in Honolulu. An avid scuba diver, she has assisted with shark research, won the Hawaii State Jumper Championship with her horse, Airborne, and crewed on a thirty-nine-foot boat sailing Honolulu to San Francisco. She is currently a Ph.D. student at the University of Hawaii. Her work has focused on education and the study of disability and diversity. Wood lives with her husband, Gordon, aboard *Orion,* a forty-eight-foot sailboat moored in Ko `Olina, Hawaii. She has one son, Andrew, who lives in Everett, Washington, where *Lottery* is set.